A STRANGER'S PROTECTION

"Don't you have any sense, flaunting yourself like you did? You only got what you deserved."

"What do you mean?" Regaining her breath, Johanna shrugged herself free of the stranger's grip and said unsteadily, "Riggs attacked me!"

Ignoring her reply, the stranger said coldly, "So you know him. Who is he?"

Uncertain why she responded to his question, Johanna said shakily, "He's the man who's driving my wagon."

"Your driver?" The stranger glanced again at the unconscious man, and then demanded, "Where's your husband...your father...somebody who's watching out for you?"

"I don't need anybody to watch out for me." Johanna took a deep breath, her senses gradually returning. Reaching into her skirt pocket, she withdrew her derringer and said, "I have my own protection."

Other books by Elaine Barbieri:

SIGN OF THE WOLF
HAWK'S PRIZE (Hawk Crest Saga)
HAWK'S PASSION (Hawk Crest Saga)
TEXAS TRIUMPH
TEXAS GLORY
TEXAS STAR
HALF-MOON RANCH: RENEGADE MOON
TO MEET AGAIN
THE WILD ONE (Secret Fires)
LOVE'S FIERY JEWEL
NIGHT RAVEN
AMBER TREASURE
HAWK
WISHES ON THE WIND
WINGS OF A DOVE
EAGLE
AMBER FIRE
TARNISHED ANGEL
CAPTIVE ECSTASY
DANCE OF THE FLAME

The Dangerous Virtues series:
HONESTY
PURITY
CHASTITY

ELAINE BARBIERI

NIGHT OF THE WOLF

LEISURE BOOKS NEW YORK CITY

A LEISURE BOOK®

October 2007

Published by

Dorchester Publishing Co., Inc.
200 Madison Avenue
New York, NY 10016

ISBN 10: 0-8439-5852-9
ISBN 13: 978-0-8439-5852-2

Visit us on the web at www.dorchesterpub.com.

PROLOGUE

Marry me, Letty. I love you. I may not have much to offer you now, but I'm going to strike it rich, and I'll make you wealthy someday. I promise you that. In the meantime, I'll take care of you and Meredith. I'll give you both a good home. And you can believe me when I say that I will love you both for the rest of my life.

It was not John's fault that his promise was so short-lived.

Letty stood at the open window of her luxurious bedroom. Her diaphanous negligee fluttered in the night breeze as she looked down into the shadows of New York City's Park Avenue. Dark, unbound hair untouched by gray rested against her narrow shoulders, classic features that defied age were tightly composed, and fathomless dark eyes touched by anxiety devoured the moonlit scene below. All was silent except for the warning howl of a wolf trailing into the stillness. The sound was foreign to city streets, but it was frighteningly familiar to her. It had awakened her with a start, although she knew by now that only she could hear it. The howling had continued, growing louder until it echoed against the vaulted ceiling of her bedroom—until she could no longer remain abed due to the sense of foreboding it raised.

Letty recalled again John Higgins' heartfelt entreaties. He had been so sincere, so earnest. Blond, pale-eyed, and slight, he did not compare with the bigger-than-life image of her first husband, Wes. With a sadness that was inescapable, she had known that no man ever could. Yet the look in both men's eyes was the same. It was loving and protective—and she had been so alone.

A chill moved down Letty's spine at the memory of the howlings that had haunted her throughout the night before Wes was killed, leaving her a pregnant widow at seventeen. The same howlings had sounded again the night before John was also killed when she was expecting his child.

Left with two young daughters to support, she had tried vigorously to deny the howlings that had forecasted every momentous event in her life—the howlings that had kept alive the shadows of a Kiowa heritage she had been taught to refute.

She had been desperate and alone when she took the opportunity to escape by leaving her daughters at a Texas orphanage and embracing a new life as maid to a traveling couple: Archibald and Elizabeth Fitzsimmons. She returned with the elderly couple to New York City and grew to love them both. When Elizabeth died, her sincere grief established a bond between Letty and Archibald that fostered the birth of her third daughter, Justine.

Letty recalled with a bitter smile that after Justine was born, she'd sent for the two daughters she had left behind. Yet they had all barely had time to become a family before the howling sounded again. The union between Letty and Archibald Fitzsimmons had not yet been formally legalized when his death left her with three fatherless daughters to support.

Letty remembered the decision she'd made in the middle of a lonely night following Archibald's death. She determined then that she would never become a victim again—that if she were to be alone, it would be by her own choosing.

With the help of her extravagant beauty and the contacts she had developed as Archibald's "fiancée," she had established a social club that became the unexpected rage of the city. She capitalized on her image as a mysterious, sensual woman. She realized too late, however, that ignoring her daughters while she enjoyed her new life was a mistake.

Her daughters grew up each as extravagantly beautiful and as strong-minded as she, while bearing no physical resemblance to her. They had also declared themselves independent of her as soon as her youngest daughter came of age. She had not seen them since.

Letty raised her chin, uncertain exactly when visions of *Grandfather* began accompanying the persistent howlings during the night. She was uncertain how or when she came to use that name for him. The slight, wizened old man with long gray hair and sun-darkened skin was unlike anyone she was able to remember; yet he was familiar to her in so many ways. It was Grandfather's advice, an expanding sense of loss, her own guilt, and the persistent howlings that prompted her to attempt to bring her daughters home.

She had hired Pinkertons to find her daughters, but the eldest had already refused to come home. The knowledge that Meredith was safe with a man who loved her, however, had almost struck Letty's concern from her mind.

The whereabouts of Justine were still a mystery, but Letty's attorney had recently advised her that the Pinkerton assigned to Johanna's case had finally found her, and that Johanna—an inexperienced city girl traveling alone—had decided to head West.

The howling had redoubled since that revelation. Shuddering at the thought of what it portended, Letty wondered—did the danger that Meredith had barely managed to escape also stalk Johanna?

That question haunted Letty as the howlings reverberated around her. Terrified at what the answer might be, she shuddered as she walked back to her lonely bed.

CHAPTER ONE

The trail was deeply rutted and dusty. It bounced Johanna's recently purchased covered wagon from side to side with a seesawing motion that was almost nauseating. The wagons ahead of her kicked up a dust that settled inevitably on every-thing, coating her skin, the plain cotton dress she wore, and the simple coil of her hair with an itchy layer of grit.

Yet another difficult lesson she was learning.

Johanna gazed at the terrain through which they were passing. Rolling plains surrounded the long line of forty-odd wagons strung out evenly under the noon sun. The brilliant color of wild-flowers spotted waving grasses, and the blue sky overhead was unmarred by a single cloud. The flat Texas landscape stretched out as far as the eye could see, as beautiful as it had been described in the articles that had whetted her appetite for this journey. Those descriptions had not prepared her, however, for the reality of insects that buzzed relentlessly around her sweat-dotted forehead, for the lack of bathing facilities, for the tedious pace of the wagons as they moved slowly forward, for the merciless heat that baked her skin. Reality was far different from the highly romanticized description of the "last wagon train heading west."

The journey will give you an opportunity to really see the country as you travel toward your appointment with destiny.

That statement, spoken by a fast-talking salesman, had convinced her to buy into the dream. A naïve Yankee city girl recalling every book she had ever read about the West, she remembered considering herself fortunate to have arrived in Texas in time to become a part of this "historical experience."

Her first mistake.

Johanna suppressed a frown as she glanced at the swarthy fellow driving her wagon. Thomas Riggs was shaggy-haired, bearded, and unwashed. His eyes were bloodshot, his skin was oily, and he stank; but he had not looked or smelled like that when she'd hired him to drive her wagon a week earlier. He had been reasonably well dressed then, and he had been sober, too. She had purchased a wagon and team of horses infinitely more difficult to manage than the docile horse and lightweight buggy she had occasionally driven, and she had realized her only recourse was to find a person who could handle that job for her. Since she had already invested the majority of her savings in the venture and the wagon train was leaving the following day, she had hired Riggs on the spot.

Another mistake.

Johanna looked again at the swaying, slobbering drunk who held her team's reins so precariously. They had been on the trail for only a day when Riggs appeared less than sober. Within two days, he was drinking openly in her presence. A week later, he had revealed his true colors by becoming argumentative and uncooperative about every aspect of the journey. Actually, he embarrassed her in so many ways that—

"Get that wagon in line, Riggs!"

Johanna turned toward the source of the booming command that snapped Riggs' attention to the wagon master who rode up beside their wagon. Openly agitated, Gerald McMullen was gray-haired, bearded, of medium height, and tightly muscled despite his years. He was also obviously experienced in a job he took seriously, and was angry enough to spit. Johanna didn't blame him. McMullen was responsible for the safety of this "last wagon train heading West," and he had warned Riggs countless times to keep the wagon in line . . . not to allow it to drift . . . not to let it fall behind, but his warnings were ignored. McMullen was getting tired of it, and so was she.

Watching as McMullen rode away with a deadly warning glance, Johanna poked Riggs in the ribs and ordered sharply, "You heard the wagon master. Get this team in line, and catch up to the rest of the wagons."

"Don't go giving me orders, lady!" His expression ugly, Riggs said through yellowed, tightly clenched teeth, "That wagon master is picking on me and you know it!"

"Picking on you? McMullen has warned you countless times not to lag behind the others."

"So that's the way it is. You're taking his side against me."

"Taking his side? McMullen is responsible for everyone's safety and you're making things difficult." Her temper flaring, Johanna stared into Riggs' eyes and said more softly, "Do what he says, and do it now!"

"You're turning out to be a feisty little runt, aren't you?" Riggs' sickening smile flashed as he looked at her more closely. "Maybe I should let this wagon fall back even farther so we can settle things between us once and for all."

"Keep up with the train, Riggs!"

Riggs drew back slowly on the reins and said, "Maybe I don't want to."

His implication unmistakable, Johanna reached under the seat in desperation and gripped the handle of the derringer she had placed there. She drew it up into sight and pointed it at him with an expression that gave no quarter as she said flatly, "You don't have to believe I'm a good shot, Riggs, considering all the errors in judgment I've made so far, but at this distance, it won't make much difference. So I suggest that you keep this wagon in line just like Mr. McMullen says."

Uncertainty flickered briefly across his expression as Riggs said, "You wouldn't shoot me. You wouldn't have nobody to handle your wagon for you then."

"Maybe I wouldn't, but then again, maybe I'd be better off without you."

"You can't keep that gun on me forever."

"No, but I can keep it on you until you sober up."

"I ain't drunk!"

The sound of approaching hoofbeats turned Johanna briefly toward McMullen as he approached again. He stopped beside the wagon to question tightly, "Is this fella back-talking you, ma'am?"

Johanna hedged, "He's drunk and he's feeling his oats."

"Maybe he should sleep it off, then."

Riggs laughed at McMullen's response. "This wagon won't drive itself, so you'd better come up with another answer, boss man."

His wiry brows locking, McMullen replied solemnly, "Maybe I will, but in the meantime, I'm warning you to behave yourself. Keep that wagon in line and don't force the lady to use that little gun she has pointed at you ... because if she misses, I won't."

Staring at him a moment longer, the wagon master rode off as Riggs sneered, "Maybe he's the one who should sleep it off. There ain't nobody else on this wagon train who's going to take over the reins of this wagon, and he knows it."

"You think so?" Her expression stiffening, Johanna said warningly, "Just remember one thing: This wagon train may have been a mistake for me, but I'll do what I have to do to get by. I always have, and I always will. That's why I've got a gun pointed at you right now, and that's why I'm not afraid to use it."

Silent for long moments, Riggs grunted and then slapped the reins on the lead horse's back. Inwardly quaking, Johanna breathed a sigh of relief when the team surged forward and swung into line.

She had been saved—but she was sure of one thing: She would have pulled the trigger on Riggs if she had needed to, because she had meant what she said. She had made her full quota of mistakes already. She would not allow herself to make another.

What was that sound?

Pausing to draw back cautiously on the reins of his heavily lathered horse, Wade Bartlett scrutinized the flat, sunlit plain surrounding him with eyes that were darkly ringed with exhaustion. There was no one in sight for miles on the flat terrain, and he made a gruff, disgusted sound. He had been riding with only short breaks for days. His mount was fatigued and he was getting jumpy from lack of sleep. That was to be expected, he supposed, when a man was fleeing from a persistent posse, but he didn't like it. He didn't want to start hearing or imagining things that would dull his reactions if and when a threat finally appeared.

The hand that had gone automatically to his gun relaxed, and Wade nudged his mount into motion. Murder—a deliberate, single shot that had ended the life of an innocent young woman—had infuriated the small town of Millborn, Texas. He couldn't blame anybody for that. The only problem was that the posse was after the wrong man.

It was true that he had been a stranger in Millborn, and that with dark hair and eyes, an intense, unsmiling expression, and an intimidating stature—not to mention the gun that was never far from his side—his appearance was naturally threatening. The fact that he knew how to use his gun was also apparent. And it was true that he had gotten friendly with Mary Malone, but he hadn't used his gun on her. Mary had been sweet and sincere. Their friendship might eventually have turned into something more, but he'd had no reason to kill her. He had simply arrived for dinner at the ranch she shared with her father and had found her lying in a pool of blood. He had tried to revive her and had been found with her blood on his hands.

He had been arrested on the spot when his gun was checked and found to have one bullet recently fired. No one gave him a chance to explain that he had killed a rattlesnake that was coiled and ready to strike as he had ridden toward the Lazy M that day. The sheriff had done his best to protect him, but Wade's unwarranted reputation as a gunslinger had fueled the anger of the community. He had seen the mob gathering outside the jail.

He had also seen the rope knotted into a noose meant for him.

Wade lifted his hat from his head and ran his fingers through the heavy dark hair matted to his scalp. He took a deep breath and squared broad shoulders covered with a faded, sweat-stained shirt. He was starting to become too tired to think. He hadn't shaved, bathed, or even slept in a week. He needed to rest.

Taking another deep breath in the hot breeze, Wade wiped his arm across his sweat-beaded forehead and put his hat back on his head. Then he pushed his weary mount on, truly uncertain when and how he had earned his reputation as a gunslinger.

Granted, he had become a drifter after his pa died when he was seventeen, leaving him alone. During the eight years that had passed since then, he'd had no desire to put down roots. He had worked as hard as any man when his funds ran low, and he had used his gun only when necessary; yet somewhere along the way, his accuracy and quick reflexes had earned him a reputation that others sought to challenge. He had met those challenges when pressed, but despite the drawback of an unfounded reputation, his expertise had never before become a personal threat.

Suddenly aware that his mind was beginning to wander, Wade frowned more darkly. He needed to get out of the sun for a while—somewhere safe. He was too easy to follow on the flat, naked plain, and the posse tracking him was relentless.

Wade drew back on the reins as a familiar dark line moved slowly into view.

Could it be . . . a wagon train?

It was either a wagon train or a mirage.

Hesitating only a moment, Wade kicked his mount into motion, determined to find out.

Gerald McMullen drew his horse to a halt and squinted at the fellow riding toward him. He had spent the greater part of his youth leading wagon trains west, and he had jumped at the opportunity to repeat those glory days for the last time. The pay was good, but he was older now, and he was fast becoming wiser. The responsibility for guiding people who had sold off most of their possessions in order to follow a dream was heavier than he remembered. He needed to do right by them.

Aware that the stranger approaching the train was another potential problem, he scrutinized the surrounding plain with a quick glance. There had been attacks on deserted ranches in the area in recent months. An innocent-looking rider had been used as a decoy to find out more about the potential prey each time while the rest of the gang moved into position. He was well aware of the vulnerability of his train.

McMullen straightened up in the saddle as the rider came closer. He frowned when the man drew his horse back so he could ride alongside him.

"There hasn't been a wagon train in these parts in a dog's age," the rider said. "Where's this one heading?"

McMullen studied the fellow with a wary eye. The stranger was a big man with dark, shaggy hair. He had dark brows and eyes ringed with exhaustion. He was sporting a week's worth of beard, his clothes were sweat-stained, and both man and beast had the look of a pair badly in need of water and rest.

In spite of it all, the stranger looked dangerous.

McMullen studied him a moment longer, silently reasoning that no one with a lick of sense would expect this fellow to lull anyone into a false sense of security.

McMullen responded cautiously, "We're heading west . . . to Oregon territory. Most of the folks in these wagons are traveling in answer to a promotion that offers them an opportunity for free land and a new life if they participate in this 'historic journey.'"

"Oregon territory, huh? That sounds good to me." The man offered offhandedly, "My name is Wade . . . uh . . . Mitchell. Do you mind if I ride along for a few days?"

McMullen replied, "Nobody rides along on this wagon train without working his way. I could use an extra hand if you're at loose ends, though, so if you're willing to pull your weight while you're with us, you're welcome."

"I suppose that's fair."

"Damned right it is."

McMullen noted that a trace of a smile flashed across the stranger's face as he replied, "It's a deal, then."

Frowning, McMullen added, "I suppose you can call it that." He paused, adding, "And I suppose you'll be wanting some water for your horse and you."

"That would be right fine."

"You'll be wanting someplace to rest, too, no doubt." At the stranger's uncertain glance, he commented, "Truth is, I can't remember when I last saw a fella looking as worn out as you do."

"There's some truth to that, too."

Making a snap judgment, McMullen said, "My wagon is the first one in line. Tell Bruce I said you could tie up your horse in back and snooze inside for a while."

Noting the stranger's wariness at his offer, McMullen said, "You ain't doing me no favors, you know. I figure you're no good to anybody as tired as you look, and I got plenty for you to do when we stop for the night."

The stranger did not reply.

"Besides, if you don't water and rest that mare soon, she's going to fall down under you."

That last comment seeming to make up his mind, the stranger said abruptly, "You said your wagon is the first one in line?"

McMullen nodded.

The newcomer headed toward the front of the train without responding.

Johanna looked at the long line of wagons ahead of them. She glanced at her driver's furrowed brow. The sun was beginning to set and the train would soon stop for the night. Then everyone would start the ritual of preparing the hot meal of the day, which meant a primitive dinner of salt pork and beans for her, considering her culinary talents. Accustomed to finer fare, she inwardly groaned.

As for Riggs, she had kept her derringer trained on him all afternoon. When he had picked up the whiskey bottle at his side in an attempt to refortify himself, she had knocked it out of his hand. The contents had spilled out onto the ground when it fell, and Johanna was sure that if she hadn't held her derringer steady, Riggs would have vented his frustration on her with a heavy hand.

No, the excursion that she had dreamed about most of her life was not working out exactly as planned.

Johanna blinked back unexpected tears at the thought that a month had already passed since she had last seen her sisters. She had left them with high hopes for carrying out the dream she cherished. The decision to separate had been difficult for her sisters and her, but after years of the restricted lifestyle their mother had forced on them, each was determined to accomplish her own dream.

Meredith, the eldest, had spent most of her life in New York City, but she was born in Texas. Because her mother refused to discuss the past, Meredith had become driven to discover her roots. She had left for Texas as soon as the time came for them to strike out on their own. Johanna could not fault her sister for wanting to fill in some of the empty spaces in her life, but that had not been her goal.

As for her younger sister, Justine had always been a dreamer. Justine was determined to make the most of the beautiful singing voice she had inherited from her father, Archibald Fitzsimmons. As impractical as her dream seemed, Johanna wished her luck. She knew that if anyone could find success on the stage, Justine could.

With unanticipated incidents happening ever since she had started out, Johanna was beginning to suspect that her own dream was just as impractical.

Johanna's mouth twisted wryly. Her sisters and she had agreed to meet after a year spent following their dreams, but the funds she had saved to finance her venture were quickly dissipating. Unlike her elder sister, she had not taken a direct route to Texas. Determined to see what she could of the country along the way, she had traveled down the Mississippi on a riverboat, and had then made her way to Texas by train. It was there that she had impulsively joined the wagon train. Most of her fellow travelers were settlers with dreams of starting a new life for their families in the verdant, bountiful valleys of Oregon, but she'd had no intention of traveling that far with the wagon train.

Determined to learn to handle the wagon and team by herself, she was resolved to strike out for Quijotoa, where gold had recently been found, or for Tip Top or Dos Cabezas when they reached Arizona. Whatever mining camp was nearest would do. She had read about the trials and tribulations that one could expect when prospecting, but she had convinced herself that the covered wagon would provide shelter as well as transportation.

Johanna prided herself that she had not come totally unprepared for her journey to the Wild West. She had made sure that she was well versed in the use of firearms. She could handle her derringer, a revolver, a rifle, and a shotgun. She was a fairly good shot, too, due to instructions from a retired army colonel who worked at the school.

Johanna had not fooled herself that a woman traveling alone would not be suspect. She had not believed, however, that other women on the wagon train would ostracize her simply because they thought they knew what her real occupation would be when she reached the Arizona mining camps. Without a trace of conceit, she accepted that she was beautiful—a fact that had proved a drawback most of her life. With hair a shiny silver-gold, with darkly fringed, luminous gray eyes, delicate features, and a petite frame, she appeared deceivingly fragile and helpless. She also had few domestic skills, which seemed to confirm the suspicions of the other women. But the truth was far different. Her beauty was a family trait—or curse—and her ignorance of womanly skills was a result of the way she had been raised. Unlike her mother, however, she had no intention of relying on her beauty to fulfill her dreams.

Her mother had mentioned Johanna's father only briefly when Johanna was a child. She had shown her a picture of John Higgins just once, but Johanna had never forgotten it. Her father's hair was blond. He was light-eyed, of medium height, and slight. His features were even and sensitive in a way that did not detract from his manliness, and his broad, optimistic smile as he looked into the camera had touched her heart. She remembered that her mother had put the picture away as if regretting their discussion, but when Johanna looked into the mirror afterward, she had reveled in the resemblance between herself and her father.

Tight-lipped, her mother had said that her father had not fulfilled his promise to strike it rich in Arizona. Instead, he had died before she was born, leaving her mother destitute and alone. Deeply resenting her mother's attitude toward her father's memory, Johanna became determined that *she* would fulfill her father's dream. She had sensed that his quest would have turned out differently if he had not met a premature, accidental death, and she was somehow certain that—*unlike her mother*—her father would have loved her dearly.

Unfortunately, however, she was beginning to discover that fulfilling her father's dream wasn't going to be as easy as she had thought.

Johanna looked back at her heavily loaded wagon. Purchasing it might have been a mistake, but she had learned from the experience and intended to make the best of it.

"It looks like the boss man is signaling us to circle the wagons for the night." Riggs looked at her darkly. "You can put that gun away now, you know. I ain't had a drink for hours and I ain't drunk no more."

Johanna warily slid her derringer into the pocket of her skirt as she replied, "I'm glad. I'm starting to get hungry."

"What are we going to eat? Salt pork and beans again?" Riggs winced. "Maybe I can get that pretty little Blocker girl to give me a plate of her mama's good cooking for a change."

"You're welcome to do that, of course." Johanna shrugged, inwardly salivating at the thought of Mrs. Blocker's hearty trail stew. "That'll make my supplies last that much longer."

Johanna's positive attitude did not persist, however, as the night grew darker and the fragrance of Mrs. Blocker's stew permeated the area. Her stomach protesting after she had eaten her own meager fare, Johanna turned toward the stream that flowed through the area with a gentle, gurgling sound. She carried her plate and cooking utensils toward it and cleaned them fastidiously. Other women in the train were performing similar chores there, but they only nodded in her direction without responding to her attempts at conversation.

Johanna raised her chin, silently offended. Well, that was all right with her. She wouldn't be with the train very long, anyway. When she struck it rich she was sure to have no lack of conversationalists bidding for her attention.

Johanna walked back to the wagon, found the necessary implements for an abbreviated toilette, and returned to the stream. She stopped short when she heard an unexpected wolf's howl. Her heart jumping a beat, she turned to a passing woman and asked, "Did you hear that?"

"Did I hear what?" The middle-aged woman looked tired and irritable.

"That wolf's howl," Johanna responded.

"I didn't hear no wolf."

"You didn't?"

"That's what I said, and I don't appreciate your trying to stir up some excitement, if that's what you're doing."

"I just thought I heard—"

Shooting her an annoyed glance, the woman did not wait for Johanna to finish speaking before she turned away and walked laboriously back toward her wagon.

Confused but determined, Johanna moved to an isolated spot in the shadows, where she would have some privacy. She looked around cautiously, and then chided herself for her uneasiness as she sat on a rock and washed her face free of the grime of the trail. No wild animal would dare come so near an area where so many people were walking around. It appeared her sleepless nights were getting the best of her.

Unable to suppress a contented sigh as she refreshed herself, Johanna unbuttoned the neckline of her sober cotton dress to run a cool cloth over her neck and chest. She pushed up her sleeves and scrubbed her arms. Then, succumbing to impulse, she lifted her skirt above her knees, pulled off her shoes and stockings, and slid her feet into the stream.

Ah, the luxury of it!

Determined to use the situation to greatest advantage, Johanna pulled the pins from her hair and allowed her brilliant silver-gold curls to tumble down onto her shoulders as she picked up her brush.

Sighing again, she brushed her hair—unaware of the dark, heated male gaze watching her just out of sight.

Riggs cursed under his breath as he watched Johanna bathe. She'd had the nerve to knock a half-full bottle of red-eye out of his hand. Then she had held her derringer pointed at him for the remainder of the afternoon while he had longed for a drink other than the water she had supplied in its place.

Riggs made a small, grunting sound. He didn't doubt that she would have used that derringer on him if necessary. He'd seen the look in her eye. She was done with backing down, but that didn't make any difference to him because he had the upper hand now.

Riggs glanced around him. Satisfied that the area Johanna had chosen for her toilette was isolated and lit only by the silver moonlight flickering through the sparse foliage, he inched closer. Her smooth, white skin seemed to glow in the moonlight. He remembered the long length of her legs as she raised her skirt, and her incredibly small feet as she stripped off her shoes and stockings. He had panted at the thought of running his hand up those long legs to meet the juncture of her crotch. He had almost felt her wet heat, and he had determined then and there to extract his own payment for the miserable day she had caused him.

Riggs scrutinized the area again. He circled around her to approach from the rear so Johanna would not be aware of his presence until the last moment. No one was going to stop him from getting what was coming to him. She wouldn't dare drive him off afterward, either, even if she had a mind to, because she didn't have nobody else to drive her wagon.

Riggs snickered to himself. If she was good enough, he might even make his attentions a nightly event.

Approaching Johanna silently from behind, Riggs was almost within touching distance when she turned around unexpectedly. Jumping to her feet, she gasped. "What are you doing here, Riggs?"

Riggs delivered a stinging blow to Johanna's cheek that sent her staggering backward into the stream. Catching her before she fell, he whispered, "I'll show you what I'm doing here, sweetheart . . . and I'll make you beg for more."

His mouth seeking hers, Riggs dragged Johanna back onto the bank. As soon as her feet touched down on firm soil she startled him by beginning to struggle wildly. Aware that she was about to scream, he hit her again on the jaw, and she fell backward onto the bank. He did not wait to see if she was totally conscious before he threw himself down on top of her and began tearing at her clothes.

Startled by the hand that suddenly gripped his shirt from behind and pulled him off her, Riggs did not have a chance to protest before a powerful blow to the jaw delivered abrupt darkness.

"Come on—get up on your feet! You're all right."

Still disoriented, her dress clinging wetly to her slender figure, Johanna felt herself being jerked abruptly to her feet. Strong hands supported her as she regained her balance and sought to focus. Her jaw ached, but she remembered. That *bastard* Riggs had attacked her! He had hit her and knocked her down. But Riggs was lying unconscious a few feet away. Who was this fellow holding her upright and staring at her so intently?

Uncertain, Johanna blinked. The stranger was as unkempt as Riggs, with ragged hair hanging over his shirt collar, a scruffy beard, and clothes that smelled as if he had worn them for an uncommon length of time. But he was taller and broader in the shoulders than Riggs, and even in the semidarkness the anger in his gaze was apparent.

"Don't you have any sense, flaunting yourself like you did? You only got what you deserved."

"What do you mean?" Regaining her breath, Johanna shrugged herself free of the stranger's grip and said unsteadily, "Riggs attacked me!"

Ignoring her reply, the stranger said coldly, "So you know him. Who is he?"

Uncertain why she responded to his question, Johanna said shakily, "He's the man who's driving my wagon."

"Your driver?" The stranger glanced again at the unconscious man, and then demanded, "Where's your husband . . . your father . . . somebody who's watching out for you?"

"I don't need anybody to watch out for me." Johanna took a breath, her senses gradually returning. Reaching into her skirt pocket, she withdrew her derringer and said, "I have my own protection."

"A lot of good that little gun did you when this fella sneaked up behind you. Where are your menfolk?"

Johanna dropped the derringer back into her pocket and raised her chin higher. "I don't have any menfolk. Neither do I need them. I'm here on my own. I'm traveling west just like the rest of the people on this train, and I have my own wagon."

"On your own . . . with your own wagon and driver, too, huh?" Not waiting for her response, the stranger said disgustedly, "You don't have the sense you were born with. Just fix your clothes and get back to your wagon. I'll take care of things here."

"What makes you think you have the right to give me orders? I want to talk to Mr. McMullen."

"If you're talking about the wagon master, he isn't here right now, so you'd better do what I say."

A wave of dizziness suddenly assailing her, Johanna swayed. The stranger gripped her arm again and said, "I'll take you back to the train, damn it! Where's your wagon?"

"I don't need your help. I can—"

"You can take care of yourself . . . I know." The stranger steered her toward the circle of campfires and said, "Just tell me where your wagon is."

Johanna insisted shakily, "I don't need your help."

"I suppose you could've taken care of that fella back there if I hadn't stepped in."

"That's right."

Silent for a moment, the stranger stared at her. Then he growled, "You're welcome."

"W . . . what?"

Johanna saw the intensity in his dark eyes as the stranger drew her into the light of the campfires and repeated, "You're welcome."

"What are you talking about?"

" 'Thank you' demands the response, 'You're welcome.' "

"I didn't thank you!"

"I know."

As McMullen approached with brows knitted, the stranger almost shoved her into his arms, saying, "She should go back to her wagon. A fella tried to attack her, and he hit her a few times. She needs to change out of those wet clothes and lie down. I'll go back and get him for you."

"What fella are you talking about?"

"She said he's her driver."

"Oh." His expression hard, McMullen responded, "Do you need some help getting him?"

"I can take care of it."

The sound of hoofbeats beating a quick retreat in the darkness behind them caused the stranger to say, "If I don't miss my guess, that fella just ran off, but I'll go back and make sure. I'll need to pick up the shoes and stockings the lady removed, anyway."

McMullen glanced down at Johanna's bare feet, but he did not comment. Instead, he nodded at the stranger and turned her back toward her wagon. Addressing her softly, he said, "I'm sorry this happened, ma'am, but I'll take care of it. I'll get somebody to look at your jaw, too, if you want me to."

"No, I'm fine. I . . . I just need to rest."

In her wagon minutes later, Johanna pulled the blanket up over herself as she settled into the bed. Weary, her jaw throbbing, she closed her eyes. She did not question that the wagon master would take care of things, but other uncertainties drifted across her mind. Who was that stranger and why did he think he had needed to rescue her? She didn't like his attitude. She could have handled Riggs on her own.

Her jaw throbbed more painfully and Johanna muttered thickly, "Well . . . I could have."

"Is he gone?"

Wade stepped back into the light of the campfires with the young woman's shoes and stockings in his hand. He looked up at McMullen's gruff question. He frowned as he tossed the woman's discarded apparel to the wagon master and replied, "Yes, he's gone—for good, I hope."

Wade frowned more darkly, aware of McMullen's intense scrutiny. The posse seemed to have temporarily lost his trail, but it looked as if he had stepped into another testy situation, and he didn't like it.

Annoying him even more was his realization that he'd been enraged at discovering that he wasn't the only man watching the young woman bathe in the stream.

Wade remembered the sound of the nameless young woman's sigh as she ran the cloth across her face and chest. He recalled her unconsciously graceful movements as she had bathed her arms, then raised her skirt to remove her shoes and stockings. He didn't like the way he had felt when she had bared those long, shapely legs in the flickering moonlight. Nor did he like the desire that had flushed hotly inside him when she had dangled her feet in the stream with such delight.

His emotions had been running high—so high that he had barely controlled his fury when the shadows moved and he realized that another man had been watching her, too. He had snapped into spontaneous motion when the fellow slipped up behind her, hoping to strike her into submission. In retrospect, he was certain that if his first blow had not knocked her attacker unconscious, he would have beaten the other man within an inch of his life.

Wade also recalled the powerful emotions he had experienced when the young woman first looked up at him with those incredible light eyes. He had not realized how beautiful she was.

It was not until she spoke, however, that he also realized she was arrogant beyond belief.

Brought back to sharp reality by that thought, Wade spoke only a few more necessary words of explanation to McMullen before leaving to check on his mare. After taking care of the weary animal, he went directly to his bedroll, but sleep eluded him. Lying on the fragrant grass a distance from the glowing embers of the campfires, he faced the realization that he would not be able to spend more than a day or so with the wagon train before the posse again picked up his trail. He'd be on the run again then, until the posse finally gave up, or until he was caught.

The young woman returned unexpectedly to mind, and Wade frowned. She should have had more sense than to choose such an isolated spot in which to bathe if she didn't have male protection. She pretended to be totally self-sufficient, but he had seen the result of her self-sufficiency. It had not impressed him.

Wade turned restlessly in his bedroll, reminding himself that that was her problem. He had problems of his own.

CHAPTER TWO

Larry Worth walked through the train station with a slow, easy stride. A big man with shaggy brows and a full mustache, he was an accomplished investigator for the Pinkerton Agency. He had handled countless cases for Robert Pinkerton, and he knew the man considered him one of his best agents, which was the reason he had been given this particular high-profile case.

But then, Letty Wolf was high profile to most men who knew her.

Larry remembered that he had seen Letty Wolf on one occasion and had been stunned by her ageless beauty. He remembered thinking that if her daughters were only half as beautiful as their mother, they would be sights to behold.

He had opened the exceedingly slim file on Johanna Higgins that Robert had given him with great expectation; yet the only picture enclosed was that of a sober ten-year-old with surprisingly light hair and eyes that were the exact opposite of her mother's. Nothing in the file had prepared him for Johanna's abrupt, unexpected disappearance after the sisters parted company to strike out on their own. He had finally tracked her down the Mississippi on a riverboat; from there she'd taken a train to Texas. Presently walking across the Texas train station where Johanna had arrived weeks earlier, however, he was keenly aware that he had no idea where she had headed next.

Larry scrutinized the immediate area, his full mustache twitching with uncertainty. His assignment had seemed so simple when Robert had explained it to him. All he needed to do was to locate Johanna Higgins and inform her of the new stipulation that her mother had included in her will—a prerequisite stating that if Johanna wanted to be reinstated in her mother's will, she must return to see her mother before Letty's fortieth birthday, almost a year away. If Johanna refused the terms, Larry was to inform her that her portion of the inheritance would be turned over to Mason Little, a nephew of Justine's father.

Larry recalled that he had smiled when Robert turned Johanna's file over to him, certain that he would make quick work of the job.

Wrong.

His keen-eyed gaze continuing to scrutinize the travelers rushing through the station, Larry glanced at the ticket agents seated in their cages. Strangely enough, they looked almost identical with their wire-rimmed glasses and narrow, clean-shaven faces underneath green eyeshades. Their neat white shirts and ties would have marked them employees of the terminal even if they were not seated in their cramped booths. Larry unconsciously shook his head, wondering how any man could settle for an uneventful, limited life that did not allow him to breathe the crisp, clean air of the outdoors.

He would make the necessary inquiries to see if any of those men remembered Johanna purchasing a ticket from him. If Johanna was as lovely as described to him by others, she would not be easily forgotten—but he did not believe it would be that easy. Johanna Higgins was a mystery that he had not yet solved. Despite the fact that her sisters and she seemed to have met to plan their future travel carefully, she appeared to be conducting her journey almost haphazardly—as if she wanted to do everything she had ever hoped to do in one fell swoop.

That didn't make his job any easier.

Larry adjusted the dark, well-used Stetson he wore so casually. He shared that trademark with another of Robert's agents, Trace Stringer, who had been given the assignment of tracking Johanna's elder sister. Like Trace, he had been born in the West, and like Trace, he had started traveling when his life changed dramatically, in his case upon the death of his wife. With his children married and on their own, he had simply lost interest in his ranch and moved on. He had found a comfortable spot with the Agency, and had worked for Robert over the last ten years.

Larry wondered how Trace was faring, and if he, too, was facing unexpected complications in his case. He would not be surprised if he were.

Whatever—he needed to keep his mind on finding Johanna Higgins.

Larry approached the first ticket agent's cage with his questions prepared. He needed to put this case to rest.

"Larry Worth hasn't found Johanna yet, Mason."

Letty looked at the well-groomed young man sitting opposite her. Of medium height and weight, with fashionable clothes and thinning brown hair that was expertly cut to hide that deficiency, Mason had a muscular physique that he obviously took great pains to maintain. He was intelligent and accomplished and his appearance was faultless, but that had little to do with the reason she had summoned him to her elegant Park Avenue apartment so early in the morning.

Not an actual relative, Mason was a highly respected lawyer and a dear young man who considered her relationship with his uncle as binding as if it had been legitimized. He cared about her daughters, too. He considered them family, and she treasured his concern as well as his advice. Aside from her daughters, who had done their best to dissociate themselves from her, Mason was the only family she had.

And Mason was always *so understanding*.

"You say Larry Worth has found Johanna's trail but hasn't located her yet? Worth is the Pinkerton who was hired to find Johanna and bring her back, isn't he?"

Letty nodded, adding, "He was hired to bring her back only if she agrees to return, but that isn't my only concern now."

Shrugging narrow shoulders covered by the pale yellow silk of a morning gown designed by one of New York City's most famous modistes, Letty was unmindful of the luxury she indulged in daily. Accustomed to the privileges that she had once so ardently sought, she continued, "I suppose I can't really blame my daughters for resenting me. I haven't endeared myself to them."

"I've told you before that you were a good mother to them, Aunt Letty. Nannies, private boarding schools, everything that money could buy—your daughters just never appreciated what you did for them."

"I was very generous with everything but myself, but I didn't realize that at the time." That thought almost more than she could bear, Letty continued more softly, "At least I know where Meredith is. I don't know the whereabouts of my other two daughters."

"What did your lawyer have to report about Johanna, other than that Worth is on her trail?"

"He said that Larry Worth followed Johanna's trail down the Mississippi on a steamboat. A steamboat . . . probably full of gamblers and opportunistic men!" Letty shook her head. "Mr.

Worth said Johanna bought a train ticket to Texas when she arrived in New Orleans. He did the same, but now that he's in Texas, he has lost her again."

"He'll find her again, too, Aunt Letty."

Letty said hopefully, "Mr. Worth said that no one who saw Johanna had forgotten her. She is quite beautiful, you know."

"Yes, I know. Just as you are, Aunt Letty."

"I suppose I am still beautiful." Letty shrugged again. "I've depended on that gift of heredity very heavily in the past, but I think my daughters are grateful they don't resemble me. I think that would be intolerable for them."

Tears filled Letty's eyes despite herself, and Mason said encouragingly, "New York City is full of women who wish they resembled you, even a little."

"I suppose that's true, too." Suddenly unable to carry their conversation any further, Letty rose. Despising the quivering in her voice, she extended her hand to Mason when he stood up beside her. "I wanted to inform you about Alexander Pittman's latest report because I know you care. I appreciate your concern, Mason. I know it's sincere. You were always so kind to my daughters."

"They are my cousins, after all, Aunt Letty."

"Mason . . ." Touched by his words, Letty kissed his cheek lightly. "Thank you. You don't know how much I appreciate that response, but I don't want to keep you. Your office staff is waiting for you to arrive this morning, and I don't want to make you tardy because of my selfishness."

"Selfishness? You're anything but selfish, and I do depend on you to keep me informed about my cousins. But they'll be fine, Aunt Letty. They're resilient, like their mother."

"Resilient? Is that what I am? I think my daughters might describe me differently."

"Aunt Letty . . ."

Wearied, Letty mumbled a few words in response before bidding Mason adieu. She waited only until he had cleared the sitting room doorway before she turned back to her bedroom. Her surprisingly successful salon parties had supplied the acceptance and stability she had sought over the years; yet despite her former eagerness for the adulation they also afforded her, her attendance had become a true chore of late.

Letty closed her eyes as a wolf's howl echoed again in her mind. She knew what that howling meant.

Danger.

Fear throbbed anew.

Mason stepped out onto the bright, sunlit New York City street and strode forward, inwardly fuming.

Johanna is quite beautiful, you know.

He knew, all right.

I suppose I'm still beautiful.

Mason's lips twitched with suppressed anger. His dear *Aunt* Letty knew she was beautiful. She

had played on that beauty after his elderly Aunt
Elizabeth died and his equally elderly uncle became susceptible to her machinations. She had
borne him a child . . . a daughter . . . *his cousin*,
and his uncle had all but forgotten he existed. But
the cunning witch hadn't won out there. Uncle
Archibald hadn't had time to write either Aunt
Letty or the illegitimate child she had borne him
into the will before he was killed, and the bulk of
his money had gone to charity.

To charity!

It hadn't mattered to his dear uncle that *he* had
needed that money to settle his gambling debts.
As a matter of fact, he doubted that his dear uncle
had given him the slightest thought.

Mason recalled that he had written off his uncle's paramour when the old man was killed, but
when the social club Letty had so boldly formed
became an unexpected success among the elite of
the city, he had reconsidered. Her connections
through the club became too valuable to ignore.
Despite his abhorrence of her and her mongrel
children, he had maintained their association diligently, thinking it might prove useful in the future. His effort had appeared worthwhile when
Letty's daughters came of age and declared their
independence from her.

Letty had been furious when she realized they
were gone. In her anger, she had rewritten her will
and made him her sole heir. He had been exhila-
rated! He had been totally nonplussed when she
called him to her apartment sometime afterward

to inform him with tears in her eyes that she regretted her hastiness, that she hoped to coax her daughters to return to her with the offer of reinstating them into her will. She had added that, of course, she intended to leave him *a sizable sum.*

How kind of her! How *condescendingly* generous!

He had smiled through it all. He had pretended to agree with Letty's decision, but her belated offer was too little, too late. Word had already reached certain sources that Letty had changed her mind about making him her sole heir. He had been gambling recklessly, using his potential inheritance to keep his credit good. He was well aware that gambling debts with no foreseeable means of payment would not be tolerated for long.

The realization that his aunt's menopausal vagaries had put his life in danger had infuriated him.

Forcing himself to assess the situation when he was calmer, Mason had realized that the answer to his problems was simple: If Letty's daughters did not return according to her stipulations, the inheritance would be his again.

And so his plan had been born.

It hadn't been difficult to follow through. He had simply hired Humphrey Dobbs, directly connected to the feared Mr. Charles, to whom he owed the most money. Dobbs had been ordered to make sure that Letty's daughters would *not* return to claim their inheritance.

Mason's mouth twitched again. Of course, neither he nor Dobbs had appreciated the news that the thug dispatched to handle Meredith's situation was killed before he could be sure that Meredith would not return. He had turned down Dobbs' offer to "fix things" because Meredith had demonstrated no desire to accede to the stipulations in her mother's will. He had then turned his attention to Letty's other two daughters.

Were he of a different temperament, Mason would almost be amused by how well Letty cooperated with his plan by keeping him informed of every movement the Pinkertons made to find her daughters. As for the information that Letty had supplied that morning, he would simply pass it along to Dobbs, and Dobbs would pass it on to his man in turn. He would see to it, however, that Dobbs did not allow his man to fail this time.

Of course, once everything was settled and he was his dear Aunt Letty's sole heir again, he would need to act quickly. He had already established with Dobbs that Letty's accidental demise was a prerequisite to the success of his plan. He knew that Letty would be deeply mourned in some sectors of the city—but *he* wouldn't mourn her. He had always despised the conniving, opportunistic witch.

With that thought in mind, Mason abruptly hailed a passing carriage. He needed to see Dobbs, and there was no time like the present.

Johanna looked at McMullen as the wagon master stood beside her wagon, awaiting her reply. Breakfast had been eaten and the chaos of the wagon train's morning startup had begun around her. Riggs—*the bastard*—appeared to be gone for good. Her team was still tied up where Riggs had left the animals to graze at the end of the previous day's journey, and her wagon had not yet been prepared for the daily trek ahead.

Earlier, Johanna had glanced at the complicated harnesses and equipment needed to hook the team up to the wagon. Riggs had refused to teach her how to handle that chore. He had not allowed her to observe, either, claiming that he didn't like her watching him. As a result, her present situation was dire. Not only did she not know how to hook up the team, how to handle the wagon, or how to feed or care for the animals, the truth was that the actual size of the horses intimidated her. She realized dispiritedly that only a week into a journey that she had embarked upon with great enthusiasm, she was virtually stranded on the Texas plains in the middle of nowhere.

Johanna glanced again at McMullen. Standing beside him was Wade Mitchell, who had rescued her from Riggs' advances the previous evening— and who looked even worse in daylight! Like Riggs, Wade Mitchell was long-haired, bearded, and as unkempt as Riggs had ever been, but he seemed taller, more powerful-looking, and more menacing in appearance than Riggs had ever been. Yet, despite those physical detractions, the fellow had the nerve to look back at her with what appeared to be contempt in his dark, piercing eyes.

Johanna's gaze narrowed. She hadn't liked the

man's attitude the previous night and she liked it even less now. As a matter of fact, she didn't like *him*.

Johanna's reply to McMullen's question was succinct.

"No."

She decided not to add that she wasn't *that* desperate.

"I don't think you have any choice, ma'am." McMullen's expression was solemn.

"What do you mean, I don't have a choice? I don't want this man to drive my wagon. I might as well be hiring Riggs all over again."

"Like I said, ma'am, I don't think you have any choice. And you're forgetting one thing: No matter how this fella looks to you, he isn't Riggs. Wade's the fella who saved you from Riggs when he attacked you last night, remember?"

Johanna smarted at the look the stranger shot her.

"Isn't that right?"

"Yes."

"Then I figure he proved himself trustworthy enough to be your driver."

Not bothering to hide his impatience when Johanna began to protest again, McMullen said, "The fact is, ma'am, either Wade drives your wagon or you drive it yourself. Nobody else on the train is willing to take on the job. I'd ask Bruce to help you, but I need him as my second in command. Actually, Wade don't plan on staying with the train long, so I figure you'd better pick up some pointers about them horses real fast or you'll be right back where you started."

No response.

McMullen's face reddened as he said flatly, "Yes or no? I need an answer."

Johanna raised her chin. Her lips tightened. She could feel the stranger's eyes boring into her, but she did not look back at him. Aware that Mc-Mullen would not wait much longer for her to respond, Johanna replied with obvious reluctance, "All right. He's hired."

The sun was dropping toward the horizon, signaling the end of another day as the wagon train plodded steadily forward. Keeping a firm hand on the reins, Wade glanced back at his own mount, which was tied to the rear of Johanna Higgins' wagon. McMullen had been correct—his mare had been ready to drop underneath him the previous day. The slow pace of the wagon train was exactly what the animal needed in order to recuperate from the ordeal they had both faced. He had complete faith in the resolute mare. Once it was rested up fully, the animal would be back on the trail without a problem.

Wade glanced out the corner of his eye at the young woman who sat beside him. The contact of her thigh pressing tightly against his on the narrow seat was an intimacy that he knew she resented. What he resented, however, were the memories that sweet pressure evoked of those long, white legs bared in the moonlight. The fact that Johanna Higgins was even more beautiful in daylight than she had appeared at night had not missed his notice. She was dainty in size, but her breasts were ample, her waist was narrow, and those elegantly long legs . . .

Wade halted his thoughts cold, but Johanna did not appear to notice his discomfort. At that moment, her eyes were trained on a point in the distance, exposing her face in profile for his silent scrutiny. He could not help noticing that her dark lashes were a shade deeper than the graceful line of her eyebrows, and that her lashes curled gracefully upward as they shielded her luminous eyes. Her nose was straight, with as delicate a turn at the bottom as he had ever seen before, and her lips were full, enticing, and slightly parted—more than appealing despite the slight swelling of her jaw that had been Riggs' parting gift to her. Considering her arrogance, he was surprised that she seemed to disregard her physical allure and the interest she stirred in the male members of the wagon train. He supposed he might have admired that facet of her character if it wasn't negated the moment she opened her mouth.

Haughty . . . judgmental . . . arrogant . . . *bossy* . . .

Wade made an effort to maintain his patience. The only words the little witch had spoken to him throughout the day were stiff questions about managing the team. She watched everything he did, despite the fact that she had taken a fearful backward step when he had led the horses toward the wagon that morning.

Wade suppressed a smile. Whether Johanna was

ready to admit it or not, the huge, snorting animals unsettled her. He reckoned that his boss was probably accustomed to carefully bred, well-behaved horses, and not the large, weighty animals that pulled her wagon. That thought raised a familiar question. How had she come to be traveling all alone on the wild Texas plains with a covered wagon and a team of horses that were obviously as foreign to her as the plains they traveled through? Although she was simply dressed, she was just as obviously a city woman of privilege. It was apparent in the way she carried herself and in the way she walked in those god-awful laced-up boots that somebody had probably told her were suited to the trail.

Johanna glanced at him. Her expression confirmed that she didn't like him. Well, that was all right, because despite the sensual heat she stirred in him, he didn't like her, either.

"McMullen is signaling." Johanna turned toward him as she said, "He's calling for the wagons to circle for the night."

"I see him."

"You'd better start turning the wagon so you can move into the circle."

"I know when to start turning the wagon."

"Start now."

"Who's driving this wagon, you or me?"

Johanna responded to his curt reply. "You may be driving, but this wagon belongs to me and I'm telling you to start turning into the circle."

"Look, *ma'am*, you hired me to drive. If you

knew how, you'd be driving yourself, so that means I'm the expert here."

"Riggs always started turning the wagon at this point."

"Riggs isn't driving this wagon now."

Obviously exasperated, Johanna said, "I may not have liked Riggs, but I didn't doubt his ability to drive the wagon."

"You don't like me, either, and I can tell you without any hesitation that I know a lot more about what I'm doing than he did."

"What makes you so sure?"

"Defending him, are you?"

Johanna raised her chin, her eyes sparking fire as she replied, "I'm not defending Riggs, but I don't intend to make the same mistake twice. I depended on him, and look where that got me."

"You didn't do so bad. It got you me, and you're damned lucky to have me right now."

"That's your opinion!"

Wade could not resist. "You could be handling this wagon and team yourself, you know."

Johanna did not reply.

"What's the matter? Cat got your tongue?"

Turning toward him, trembling with fury, Johanna hissed, "You're despicable!"

"And you're—" Suddenly aware that a revealing moisture had sprung into Johanna's eyes, Wade concluded their discussion abruptly by saying, "Look, arguing isn't going to get us anywhere. If you don't feel you can depend on me to do my job, depend on McMullen. He's been watching me all day, and he's not going to let anything get past him."

Johanna's gaze snapped toward McMullen. Noting that the wagon master was eyeing them warily, she said stiffly, "All right. If McMullen is satisfied with the job you're doing, I guess that's good enough."

Wade did not bother to reply.

Ignoring his silence, Johanna turned forward, again exposing Wade to the perfection of her profile. His stomach did a spontaneous flip-flop, and he flicked the reins, signaling the team to a faster pace. It did not miss his notice that Johanna climbed down from the wagon as soon as he pulled into the circle, moving away from him as quickly as she dared.

Wade inwardly steeled himself against his rioting emotions. He was uncertain how long he would stay with the wagon train—but he was sure it would seem like a lifetime.

Johanna inwardly steeled herself against her disturbing emotions as she prepared for bed in the cramped wagon. The day had stretched on endlessly as she sat beside the new driver forced on her by the well-meaning wagon master.

Wade had saved her from Riggs' attack, had he? Not as far as she was concerned. He had merely butted in.

Wade knew more about caring for her team and driving her wagon than she did, did he? Well, that was true, but only temporarily.

Wade Mitchell was arrogant . . . condescending . . . a know-it-all . . . *a bully* . . . but she was his boss, whether he wanted to admit it or not. And she would learn to harness the horses and drive the wagon herself if it was the last thing she ever did!

Johanna punched down her lumpy pillow as she twisted and turned uncomfortably. She had seen the look on Wade's face when she served him the meal she had cooked. His reaction was less than appreciative. Well, if he thought he could do better, he was welcome to try. She would tell him that, too. Then let him see what he could do with the simple supplies she had been talked into buying. Admittedly, she was inexperienced in cooking, but she was learning fast, and she'd be damned if she'd let that Wade Mitchell get to her!

Johanna went abruptly still. But . . . what was that?

She heard it again—a wolf's howl—just like the previous night!

Jumping to her feet, Johanna searched frantically through the boxes behind her and finally withdrew the shotgun she had purchased before leaving Texas. She continued her anxious search and had found the box of shotgun shells she was looking for when her wagon flap snapped upward unexpectedly and a male voice demanded, "What do you think you're doing?"

Startled, Johanna turned angrily toward Wade Mitchell and replied, "I should be the one asking that question."

"You were making so much noise in here that I thought something was wrong."

"So you came to my rescue again. How nice." Johanna continued tartly, "I don't mean to disappoint you, but I don't need rescuing. I'm a fairly good shot and I can take care of that wolf by myself."

"What wolf?"

"The wolf that was howling just now."

"I didn't hear a wolf."

"Then you must be deaf."

"There's nothing wrong with my hearing."

"Are you insinuating that I'm imagining things?"

"I'm just saying that I didn't hear a wolf howling, and since you were probably dreaming, you should go back to sleep. The drive starts early tomorrow morning."

A hot flush rose to Johanna's face when Wade attempted to drop the wagon flap, and she responded tightly, "I know what I heard, and I wasn't dreaming."

A step sounded beside the wagon. McMullen appeared behind Wade and asked, "Is something wrong here?"

"No." Wade's response was immediate.

Annoyed that Wade had responded in her stead, Johanna contradicted, "Yes, there is something wrong. Mr. Mitchell stuck his nose into my business when I was simply preparing to protect myself against the wolf that's prowling out there somewhere."

"What wolf?" McMullen glanced around.

"The one that was howling."

"I didn't hear anything."

Wade looked knowingly at Johanna.

Johanna asked McMullen directly, "Are you saying you didn't hear a wolf howling?"

"That's what I'm saying." McMullen paused to add more gently, "Ma'am, I suggest you get back to sleep. We're going to have a long day tomorrow. I think you should put that shotgun away, too. You might hurt somebody."

Dismissing the situation with a tip of his hat and a simple, "Good night, ma'am," McMullen left.

Stunned, Johanna stared at McMullen's back as he walked away.

"You heard him," Wade said. "You'd better put that shotgun away before you hurt somebody."

Too furious to respond, Johanna slapped the wagon flap down in her protector's face, and then lay back on her bed with barely controlled anger. She mumbled under her breath, slid the shotgun under a pile of blankets, and closed her eyes. But she snapped her eyes open again when a wolf's howl echoed once more in the stillness.

Johanna raised the wagon flap and scrutinized the star-studded horizon.

"Did you hear a wolf howling again, *ma'am*?"

Johanna looked at Wade with a narrowed gaze. "I suppose you didn't hear that howl either."

"It's been as quiet as the grave out here."

Bastard . . .

Johanna ordered gruffly, "Sleep somewhere else. I don't need you so close to my wagon that you respond to every sound I make."

"Anything you say, *ma'am*."

Johanna watched as Wade picked up his bedroll

and walked closer to the campfire. Irritated, she dropped the wagon flap, lay down, and closed her eyes, forcing herself to ignore the howling that resounded with increasing frequency.

In the darkness, memory stirred. She remembered hearing similar howls that night long ago before their mother announced to her and her sisters that she was going to send them to different boarding schools. Justine and she had begged their mother not to separate them, but Letty had remained unaffected. Only Meredith was coldly silent. Their nannies packed their belongings the following morning, and by afternoon they were ready to leave. Her only consolation had been Meredith's whispered promise that she would find a way for them to be together again.

Johanna recalled the first night spent alone in her boarding school. Miserable and afraid, she had cried—until she had a dream so vivid that she had almost believed it was real. In that dream, a short, slender, wizened old man approached her in a desolate desert terrain. The setting sun was at his naked back, but she could see that his face was weathered and his hair was long and streaked with gray. His small, dark eyes pinned her with their intensity as the unbound, ragged strands of his hair brushed his bony shoulders in the breeze. When he spoke to her at last, it was in a foreign, guttural tongue that—strangely—she had no trouble understanding.

I will protect you.

His whispered words had reassured her.

I will bring your sisters and you together again.

She had believed him.

Do not fear.

She had instinctively obeyed his exhortation.

The wolf's howl sounded again, and a chill ran down Johanna's spine.

Do not fear. I will protect you.

Johanna turned resolutely into her pillow.

Uncertain how many hours had passed, Johanna awakened to the darkness of night with the rough pressure of a hand across her mouth. Startled, she felt a fetid breath in her face as a shadow crouched over her. "Hello again, boss lady. You didn't think you was going to get away from me so easy, did you?"

Johanna's heart began a rapid pounding. She was not dreaming this time.

"Yeah, it's me . . . Riggs. You didn't expect to see me again, did you?"

Struggling, Johanna felt the pressure of a knife at her ribs.

Riggs warned, "Stay still! I don't know what you said to that fella to make him move his bedroll away from this wagon, but I thank you. I didn't have a chance to get in here while he was sleeping so close by."

"Wh . . . what do you want?"

"Scared, are you?" Riggs sneered. "That's good, because I figure we've got some unfinished business, you and me. You owe me a week's pay, too. I guess you figured you wouldn't have to pay it when I ran off, but that ain't going to happen."

"The money's in the tin can near those boxes." Pointing to the corner of the wagon, Johanna said, "Take what you have coming and go."

"Still giving orders." Riggs' expression grew grim. "You won't be so feisty when I'm finished with you. You'll be begging me to—"

"She won't be begging you for anything, Riggs."

Startled by the deep voice, Johanna looked up to see Wade's gun glinting in the semidarkness.

"Use that knife and you're a dead man," he warned.

Riggs responded hotly, "This lady owes me money. I drove this wagon for her for a week while she nagged and ordered me around, and I expect to get paid for it!"

"She told you where the money is. She told you to take what you had coming to you."

"I heard her."

"Do it, then!"

Johanna caught her breath when the pressure of the knife at her waist eased and Riggs moved away from her. He reached for the tin can and she ordered, "Give that can to me. I'll give you what you earned."

Riggs turned toward her with a menacing scowl, and the hammer of Wade's gun clicked warningly. Stiffening, Riggs handed her the can. Johanna saw the heat of hatred in his eyes as she counted out the coins, slapped them down into his hand, and said, "That's what I calculate I owe you. Are you satisfied?"

Riggs looked at the sum in his hand. He nodded.

"Then get out of this wagon, and don't come back."

When Riggs did not move, Wade said softly, "You heard the lady."

Holding her breath, Johanna watched as Riggs turned and jumped down from the wagon. She moved to the wagon opening and watched as Riggs mounted up and then rode off into the shadows. She was still crouched there when Wade said, "He won't come back."

"He'd better not, because this time I'm going to keep my shotgun loaded and ready."

Wade's lips twisted, and he said, "You're welcome, *ma'am*."

Johanna raised her chin. He had played that trick on her before. She wouldn't fall for it again.

Johanna responded succinctly. "I'm going to sleep. I'll see you in the morning."

Refusing to reply, Johanna dropped the flap in Wade's face for the second time that night. He wouldn't get any thanks from her. As he had said to her, he had gotten exactly what he deserved.

CHAPTER THREE

Life goes on.

Letty stood in the middle of her salon with a stiff smile on her face. A lighthearted crowd surrounded her, and it occurred to her in a moment of silent introspection that the old adage had never proved truer. Her eldest daughter had been located and appeared to be safe, but it also appeared that she had no intention of returning. The whereabouts of Johanna and Justine were still unknown. She couldn't even be certain if her younger daughters were alive or dead, and her ignorance of that fact was a shaft that pierced her heart. She was alone in a strange limbo, at a complete loss as to how to make up for the years of neglect that had caused her daughters to leave her.

Yet despite it all, the frivolity of her salon continued.

Letty took a deep breath to steady her thoughts.

Although she would not have chosen to attend the lively soiree that evening, her appearance was necessary. The same old rumors had surfaced again, and she needed to squelch them. She had dressed appropriately in a simple gold gown that had been designed especially for her. With the fine row of diamonds around her neck matching the slender drops at her ears, with her dark hair upswept into brilliant curls and her eyes appearing brighter than the sparkling gems themselves, her complexion seemed to glow as flawlessly as the bodice of the gold gown that hugged her delicate frame. She had flabbergasted her guests with her beauty when she had entered the room a few minutes earlier.

Matthew Thorndyke, Peter Klein, and John Bellows had rushed to her side to welcome her. They were well-known, handsome, sought-after bachelors, but she had smiled at their attentions without feeling much true emotion. She had done nothing over the years to earn their consideration, other than to perpetuate the mystique created by her beauty. When her beauty began fading, her admirers would most likely fade away also.

Letty listened as the erstwhile bachelors around her spoke enthusiastically:

"I'm glad to see you tonight, Letty."

"You add a special touch to every celebration."

"You're unique, Letty." That softly spoken comment came from wealthy Peter Klein, who openly admired her. He added, "No one can ever replace you."

"Gentlemen, you are too kind."

Letty wanted to say more. She wanted to tell each one of them that they didn't really know her, that the woman they revered had been painstakingly manufactured through the years, and that her image had very little behind it. She wanted to say that she was a failure as a wife, as a mother, and as a person; and that aside from Mason, she was presently totally alone.

But she did not.

"Hello, Letty. How are you feeling?"

Letty looked up to see that James Ferguson had joined their group. She hadn't seen him since the last time she had heartlessly sent him packing. Tall and fit, with heavy brown hair touched with gray at the temples, and with few lines on his face to mark his maturity, he appeared not to have changed at all.

But, no, that wasn't quite true. There was something about his eyes, a coldness that she had never viewed before when he looked at her.

Chills unexpectedly coursed down her spine. "I'm fine," Letty replied with a smile. She looked at the brunette at James' side. Small, petite, with white skin, a heart-shaped face, and a broad smile, the young woman looked lovely in her demure green gown. A peculiar ache inside her expanded when the youthful brunette clutched James' arm, smiling brightly.

"I'd like you to meet Eleanor Troast." he said. "She's here as my guest. Eleanor is a newcomer to this salon, and she wanted to meet you."

Silent, Letty felt the impatience of the men around her as the young woman gushed, "You're a legend in this city, Miss Wolf. James is such a dear. He had business to tend to and he didn't think that he could bring me here tonight, but I begged him. He assented, of course, because he knew how much I wanted to meet you. He's very sweet that way."

"Please call me Letty . . . and yes, James is a dear." Letty glanced up at James, remembering warm nights and a gentle touch that inspired long hours of passion. She also remembered the pain in his stunned expression at her abrupt dismissal of him, and her own deliberately harsh words calculated to send him away as she had sent so many others before him.

A nameless discomfort inside her twisted tightly as Eleanor said, "You really are beautiful!" Eleanor flushed becomingly as she confessed, "I came here believing it wasn't possible that all the raving I had heard about your beauty could be true—female envy, I suppose—but you are everything everyone claimed you to be."

"There should be no female envy involved where you are concerned," Letty responded generously.

"That's what James says, that I'm beautiful, too, but every woman wants to believe she's the most beautiful."

"Not every woman."

Unaware of Letty's discomfiture, Eleanor gushed, "Despite your modesty, Letty, I honestly believe no other woman can match your splendor."

James reminded her gently, "We can't consume all of Letty's time, dear. She's just arrived and she needs to greet her guests."

"Of course. I should have realized." Eleanor addressed Letty again as she continued enthusiastically, "I am sorry for the distraction, but I'm so pleased to have met you. You may rest assured that I'll tell my friends all the rumors about you are true."

"Not all of them, I hope," Letty responded lightly.

"All the important ones." Not allowing Letty time to respond, Eleanor bid her a quick adieu and looked up at James lovingly as they moved across the crowded floor.

"A sweet young thing, but not much between her ears, I'm afraid."

"A child, really."

"James is robbing the cradle."

"Gentlemen!" Letty turned toward her admirers with a gentle reprimand. "Eleanor has obviously not yet come to full fruition, but any man would surely be fortunate to find her favor."

"I suppose."

"That's one way of looking at it."

"You are always too generous, Letty."

"Am I?" Letty's small smile did not come from the heart. Unable to bear the direction of their conversation a moment longer, she said lightly, "My glass is empty, gentlemen, and I'm very thirsty."

A filled glass almost immediately slipped into

her hand, and Letty started across the floor with her entourage beside her. Her eyes briefly followed the youthful Eleanor as she walked confidently at James' side, and the sadness inside her deepened.

"I hope we can find some time to spend alone together, Letty." Seizing his opportunity when the two of them were briefly separated from the others, Peter whispered into her ear, "Perhaps you'll spare me a few moments when your duties here are finished for the evening."

"Peter, dear." Letty looked up at his sober expression and floundered uncharacteristically, "I . . . I can't make any promises with the evening still ahead of me. I hope you understand."

He pressed, "I've made it my business to find out that you've untangled yourself from your former intimate liaison and that you are presently unencumbered by an arrangement of that type." At Letty's startled expression, Peter added with an understanding smile, "No, please . . . don't say anything. I, of all people, understand. Wealth and fame are not particularly pleasant bedfellows when a person is mature enough to realize that they are fleeting. I have that maturity. I'm old enough to have learned a little wisdom, Letty. I think you have, too. I think we'd be particularly fine together at this point in time, and I'd like a chance to prove that to you."

"Peter . . ." Letty studied his earnest face silently. His features were unremarkable except for brown eyes that appeared to scrutinize her more closely than she wished, and a mustached mouth through which all the right words emerged with a fluidity that suggested they had been spoken before. He was a mystery to her. She knew he was wealthy, mature, and a sought-after bachelor who had not yet seen fit to settle on one woman. She responded frankly, "If you really understand my situation, you'll also understand that I'm not presently looking for someone to fill my bed."

"Perhaps not at present. Friendship—true friendship—is all I'm offering you right now. I want a chance to make you see that everything I've just said is true."

"Peter . . ."

Her response was interrupted by the timely reappearance of her entourage. "I don't know how you managed a few moments alone with our Letty, Peter, but I promise you that it won't happen again," Matthew said.

"You're sure of that?" Peter's question was accompanied by a belated smile. He added, "I guess you'll have to watch me closely, then."

"I'll do that."

Aware that the exchange between the two men had turned suddenly tense, Letty interrupted, "We're here tonight to spend a few pleasant hours, gentlemen. I hope that's what you all had in mind."

"Of course, Letty."

"It's always a pleasant few hours when you're here."

The only one of the three who did not immediately respond, Peter said reluctantly, "I surrender to your wishes, Letty." Leaning toward her, he added for her ears alone, "Temporarily."

Sweeping her unexpectedly toward the dance floor, he said over the protests of his companions, "I claim the first dance."

Letty warned as they moved gracefully over the dance floor, "You'd do well to surrender to my wishes, Peter, because that would be the only way to gain my favor."

Peter did not respond as he glanced down at her soberly, and Letty silently added, *if gaining the favor you seek is possible.*

The morning sun had not yet fully risen over the semidarkness of the vast Texas terrain when Wade examined his mare with an assessing eye. Nellie's hooves were still sore. Another few days of rest would assure that she would be fit to travel. He consoled himself that the flat landscape would reveal the approach of a pursuing posse before it became an immediate threat, told himself he was temporarily safe where he was. He could only hope that the posse had lost his trail and had become frustrated enough to give up—but he doubted it.

The same sadness he felt every time he thought of Mary Malone enveloped him. Mary had not only been a favorite of most people in Millborn; she had been special to him, too. She was the last person anyone would have expected to be found murdered. Unfortunately, he was not the last person anyone would expect to kill her.

He remembered the first time he saw Mary. She had been walking home from church with a crowd of admiring young men. He recalled thinking that her beauty, although not outstanding, was refreshing in a way that was difficult to describe . . . like dew on a new bloom. Her shiny brown hair and eyes were direct and innocent, and her broad smile flashed without a touch of guile. A stranger in town, he had looked at her curiously, and she had smiled back at him. Things had gone on from there, and his affection for her became true and strong.

He had known from the beginning that he wasn't the type of man Mary was meant to settle down with. He had told her in the kindest of ways that he wasn't the marrying kind. He had too many harsh memories behind him for that kind of a life. Theirs had been a friendly relationship, but Mary had been too sweet and honest for him to take their friendship any further. He had gone to meet her so he could explain all that before he left. The only trouble was that when he got there, she was dead.

Wade remembered his shock and grief when he was unable to revive Mary. What he still did not truly understand was how anyone could believe he had killed her.

Wade recalled with a shudder the night that a lynch mob began forming outside the jail where he was being held. The look in Sheriff Carter's eyes had said it all when he unlocked the cell door and said, "You're a stranger in this town, and everybody knew that Mary and you were close. People here are making up their own stories about her death, but that don't mean I believe any of it. As far as I'm concerned, none of it is proved. Since I can't protect you against them people outside, my advice to you is to run for the hills and not to look back, because there'll be a mob riding after you. Maybe you can escape. Maybe not. I'll do the best I can to help you, and to find out who killed Mary. I want to make sure the real killer pays for what he did, whoever he is."

Sheriff Carter had handed him his gun and said, "Get going."

He had been running ever since. The men in that posse wanted to catch him so they could make themselves believe they had dealt out the justice that an innocent like Mary deserved. His only hope was that another few days of rest for his horse would allow him to escape so he could eventually prove his innocence.

There was one thing he knew for sure: He'd never prove his innocence while dangling from the end of a rope.

Wade took his saddlebags in hand and walked toward the nearby stream. The wagon train had been lucky enough to camp beside running water for a second night. He noted that Johanna had not ventured toward the stream as she had the previous evening.

Remembering Johanna's stiff parting remarks after he had interrupted Riggs' second attack, he recalled wryly that the effort hadn't done him much good. But unlike Johanna, he was determined to take advantage of the running water while he could.

Wade removed a much-used bar of soap, a razor, and a cloth from his saddlebag. He hesitated, removed his precious change of clothing as well, and started toward the stream. He sighed with relief when he emerged from the area a short time later, invigorated, clean-shaven, and freshly clothed. Then he walked to the back of Johanna's wagon so he could hang up the pants and shirt that he had rinsed out in the stream, figuring that the long, hot day ahead would dry the clothing quickly as they traveled.

"Well, ain't you the dapper fella!" McMullen said, obviously resisting a smile. "Figure you might do better with the lady if you looked a little more acceptable?"

"That thought never crossed my mind." Not certain if those words were exactly true, Wade added, "I just got tired of trail dust, and I figured now was as good a time as any to wash some of it off."

"Temporarily, anyway." His expression sobering, McMullen said, "It looks like you got yourself more than you bargained for when you decided to travel a ways with us."

"More than you know." Wade added with a darkening brow, "Riggs showed up again after you left last night."

McMullen mumbled a curse.

"Don't worry about it. I took care of him. The bastard was a coward, anyway. He left with a week's pay in his pocket, but that's all he got. I don't think he'll come back."

"My bet is that you didn't get a word of thanks from Miss Johanna Higgins for helping her out, either."

Refusing to respond to that remark, Wade could not help asking, "What's a woman like her doing on this wagon train, anyway?"

"It's a mystery to me!" McMullen shook his head. "I admit to being surprised when she talked about traveling as far as Arizona with us and breaking off to take her wagon out on her own to do some prospecting."

"Prospecting?" Stunned, Wade said, "She wouldn't last a day in those gold fields! Doesn't she know what it's like with all those fellas not seeing a woman sometimes for months at a time—especially a woman who looks like her?"

"That's what I thought, but I figured that young lady ain't the kind to take any advice I offered, no matter how well-meaning. Besides, she had already bought the wagon and team, and all that equipment. There was no way I could turn her down."

Wade responded soberly, "Whatever daydreams she's been harboring, somebody's going to have to tell her what she's in for, sooner or later."

"I already know what I'm in for!" Unexpectedly appearing around the side of the wagon, Johanna said hotly, "I've read all about the gold fields. I've studied the situation there and I'm prepared for it. I know what I have to do—and I don't intend for anybody to get in my way!"

Johanna stood rigidly as she faced the two men discussing her fate in such a superior manner. Were she not so angry at having overheard them rethinking her situation for her, she knew she might have had a different reaction to the sight of a freshly washed, shaved, and tidied Wade Mitchell. Instead, Johanna continued tightly, "It isn't either of your concern, anyway. I'm doing my part on this wagon train, and that's all that counts."

"You're doing your part?" Wade commented. "That wasn't the way it looked to me last night."

"Only because I listened to poor advice about keeping my shotgun handy."

"A shotgun that you might have used to kill or maim an innocent person."

Johanna took an angry step toward Wade as she responded, "You think I don't know how to handle any kind of a gun, much less a shotgun, but I do."

Wade did not respond.

"That's right, isn't it?"

Again, no response.

Incensed, Johanna growled in a manner unfitting her ladylike demeanor, "I'll put my marksmanship up against yours any time, anywhere."

McMullen choked.

Wade responded enigmatically, "Are you talking about a contest to see who can shoot better, you or me?"

"That's right."

Wade shook his head. "No matter what you think, I don't take advantage of women."

"Afraid I'll show you up?"

McMullen choked again.

"Are you?"

Wade did not respond.

"Well?"

Wade's silence continued.

Johanna said frigidly, "Are we going to have a contest or not?"

Wade's jaw was tight and his eyes were cold as he responded, "If that's the way you want it."

Turning dramatically, Johanna stomped back to the wagon and climbed inside. She searched through her cases and found the revolver that was a match in size to the one Wade Mitchell wore. She had chosen to carry a derringer instead of the heavier weapon, but that didn't mean she wasn't well versed in handling a larger gun. She found the ammunition for that particular firearm, loaded it, and aimed it tentatively. It was difficult to balance properly, considering its weight, but she was satisfied that she was in control.

Determined, Johanna stepped down from the wagon to see that a crowd had begun gathering to watch the impromptu competition. She sniffed angrily as she glanced at Wade. He was no doubt aware he was being regarded with renewed interest by some of the female members of the wagon train since he had shaved and cleaned up. Scraping off his beard had revealed sharply chiseled cheekbones and a strong chin, and a surprisingly aristocratic nose, despite the subtle bump on its bridge. It did not miss her notice that the glance of his dark, sober-eyed gaze seemed all the more potent and unsettling in that setting.

Johanna's heart fluttered unexpectedly when he caught her looking at him. Annoyed at her reaction, she reasoned that Wade probably also knew that the snug fit of the fresh shirt and pants he was wearing made him appear somehow taller and his shoulders broader and more powerful; that his shirt hugged his flat, muscular midsection; and that except for the noticeable bulge at his crotch, his trousers lay smoothly against the narrow male hips around which his ever-present gun belt was strapped.

Johanna's heart fluttered again, forcing her to silently admit that although his appearance was still intimidating, Wade Mitchell was decidedly handsome and all man underneath his former grime. She also knew, however, that he was confident she would make a fool of herself while her detractors on the wagon train watched.

She wouldn't let that happen.

Johanna scrutinized the gathering crowd. Whittling Wade Mitchell down to size would also strike back at those in the wagon train who'd had the nerve to judge her without even knowing her.

Johanna took a resolute step forward. She asked coldly, "Well, do you want to bet on the outcome of this contest?"

"Not unless you do. I don't like to gamble with women."

"That's as good an excuse as any, I suppose." Not waiting for him to respond, Johanna pressed, "What's our target, that line of rocks you set up on the rise over there?"

Wade nodded as he approached to stand looking down at her from his superior height. The frowning solemnity of his gaze touched off that mysterious fluttering inside her again. She could feel the male heat he exuded as he looked into her eyes and added for her ears alone, "Are you sure this is what you really want? It's not too late to change your mind."

Johanna's heart began pounding as he waited for a response that momentarily stuck in her throat. She couldn't be sure if he was trying to intimidate her with that intimate look . . . with that gentle softness in his voice . . . with that unexpressed intimation that he was on her side. His purely male aura taunted her. His tone suggested more than he said. The unexpected heat in his dark-eyed gaze shook her as it dropped unexpectedly to her lips with a touch that was almost palpable.

Johanna swallowed and raised her chin. Two could play that game.

Johanna forced herself to look back directly into

his gaze as she said, "I don't need to change my mind. You shoot first."

Wade's gaze went cold. "Like I said, if that's what you want."

Turning obligingly back toward the targets, Wade drew his gun and fired so rapidly that Johanna barely had time to breathe. She stared, stifling a gasp when she saw the first of the rocks had been splintered into dust.

Snickers from within the gathered crowd raised her ire as Johanna leveled her heavy firearm at the second of the targets. She pulled the trigger, but she did not bother to smile at the gasps that sounded within the crowd when the second of the rocks was efficiently shattered.

Wade commented softly, "You may not be able to handle a wagon team, but you seem to know how to handle a gun." Turning back toward the target before she could blink an eye, he shot the third of the targets into obliteration.

Johanna fired again, and the fourth target disappeared.

The crowd went silent, and Johanna almost smirked. That would teach them.

The contest continued to an almost deafening silence until all the targets had disappeared without a miss. Sober, Johanna faced Wade as he said, "That was impressive, ma'am. I'm just wondering how you'd do with a live target."

"I can't honestly say." Johanna's response was frigid. "But if you'd like to volunteer, we'll find out."

McMullen's harsh voice broke unexpectedly into the moment as he glowered at the crowd and announced, "All right, this has gone far enough. We have to be back on the trail within the hour, so you'd all better get yourselves back to work."

Johanna turned obediently toward her wagon as Wade asked unexpectedly, "Are you satisfied, ma'am?"

Uncertain what to make of that question, Johanna responded with a question of her own.

"Don't you ever go anywhere without that gun belt on your hips?"

"No, ma'am. I don't feel really safe without it."

"That's pretty sad, don't you think?" Not allowing Wade time for a response, Johanna left him standing behind her as the crowd faded away. She said over her shoulder, "I have breakfast ready if you're still hungry enough to eat. In any case, it's now or never."

It's now or never.

Those words rang in Wade's mind as he picked up the horses' halters and approached Johanna silently. The contest was over, but the discomfort remained. It was time to ready the wagons, but the memory of the impromptu contest had left a bitter taste in Wade's mouth. He hadn't liked pitting himself against a woman—most especially Johanna. It went against the grain.

Wade watched as Johanna stored the last of the cooking apparatus that she had used to make their breakfast. Although she seemed to be able to shoot well enough, she certainly couldn't cook. He wondered where she had learned her cooking skills—if she had indeed been taught anything at all. The thought of spending an entire journey with each meal worse than the last was unpalatable. He attempted to console himself with the fact that his time on the wagon train was limited.

Prospecting.

She had to be crazy!

Wade reached the wagon truly uncertain why he cared that the arrogant young woman was so unprepared for the tasks she expected to undertake.

Standing behind Johanna until she noisily finished her task, Wade repeated the sober adage that she had spoken to him a short time earlier.

"*It's now or never*, ma'am, just like you said."

He noted that Johanna jumped slightly when he spoke. He saw a flash of vulnerability that was totally unexpected when she turned and glanced at the harnesses in his hand. Her lips twitched when she asked, "What are you talking about?"

"You heard what the wagon master said. I'm not going to stay with this wagon train long. When I go my way, you're going to find yourself in the same situation as before if you don't learn how to handle your wagon and team."

Johanna raised her chin, and Wade knew what that meant. She would respond confidently no matter what she was feeling. Admiration of her gumption flashed inside him even as he noted the subtle quiver of her lips.

"I've been watching everything you do," she

said. "I'll be able to handle things adequately in a few days."

"I may not be here in a few days."

"I'll take that chance."

"I won't."

Wade's voice deepened. "Let's understand each other. I'm telling you that I intend to leave this wagon train soon . . . very soon."

"I can't concern myself with that problem at present."

"You may not be in the mood to concern yourself, but I am, which means either you take me up on my offer right now, or you can forget it."

Johanna challenged, "On your terms only, is that it?"

When Wade did not respond, Johanna replied reluctantly, "All right, if you feel it's that urgent."

Johanna accompanied him silently toward the spot where her horses grazed, and Wade admitted to himself that it had become important to him that she was not at a total loss when he left the train. He did not like the thought that her deficiency might cause her to become dependent on another man.

Wade frowned when he saw Johanna take an unconscious backward step when they neared the horses. The truth was that someone had taken advantage of her by selling her a particularly unruly and nervous team that would be difficult for anyone to handle. He was still frowning when Johanna took a deep breath and then turned back toward him.

"Give me that harness," she ordered, her former arrogance returning.

Wade watched as Johanna approached the lead horse stiffly and raised the harness toward his head. The big animal snorted belligerently and stepped aside. Her gaze narrowing determinedly despite the visible tremor that shook her, Johanna tried again. Wade snapped into motion when the horse balked.

"All right, that's enough!"

Snatching the harness out of Johanna's hand, Wade moved her aside to stroke the nervous animal gently in an attempt to settle him down. He cooed, "Take it easy, fella. We've done this before, you and me. It's time to get back to work, so that means it's time for you to let me put this harness on you."

Eyeing him speculatively, the horse gradually quieted. Still speaking reassuringly, Wade slipped the harness over his head and buckled it securely. He turned back to Johanna when the task was completed, handed her the second harness and said, "Now that you've done everything wrong, let's see if you can do it right."

Accepting the harness with a deadly glance, Johanna attempted to put it on the second horse. She was barely able to conceal her fear when the second animal snorted and eyed her just as wildly as the first.

Taking the harness out of her hand, Wade slipped it over the animal's head without a problem, and said with a harshness he did not feel when he had finished the job, "That's how you should do it."

"That's what I did."

"No, you didn't."

"I did exactly what you did. I would have harnessed that horse if you hadn't taken the gear out of my hands."

"After it had trampled you, you mean?"

"I'm not responsible for the way these horses act. They won't stay still. They don't like me."

"They sense your fear."

"Fear!" Johanna's light eyes widened. "I am *not* afraid of them."

"Yes, you are."

"No, I'm not!"

"Then prove it." Loosening the horses' tethers, he motioned at the lead horse and said, "Get up on that big fella's back and show him who's boss."

"W . . . what?"

"You heard me."

Johanna raised her chin revealingly. "I can't. He's too tall."

Swinging himself onto the horse's bare back in a flash, Wade reached down and pulled Johanna up astride in front of him. She was still gasping and tugging at her skirt when he ordered, "Now . . . show him who's boss."

Wade could feel Johanna's heart pounding as he slid his arm around her waist to hold her securely. He was unprepared when she asked unexpectedly, "How am I supposed to do that?"

"Take these reins, dig your heels into his sides,

and get him moving. Talk to him like you mean what you're saying."

Wade felt the deep, steadying breath Johanna inhaled before using the heels of her boots and saying gruffly, "Get moving."

Nothing.

Wade drew Johanna closer. He didn't like this. He didn't like forcing Johanna past her fear when he could so easily accomplish the task he had set her to. It went against everything he believed in—but he could not allow her to remain helpless.

He ordered, "Nudge him harder, and sound like you mean it when you tell him to get moving."

Johanna jammed her heels into the horse's sides and said in a voice deepened to the point that it sounded unlike her own, "Get moving, damn it . . . and get moving now!"

The horse started forward. Johanna's relief was apparent when Wade said, "Don't worry about the other horse. I've got the reins and he'll follow."

Allowing Johanna to slip down to the ground when they reached the wagon, Wade dismounted beside her. Her relief did not last long, however. "Now get the horses hooked up to that wagon," he ordered.

Johanna looked at him, eyes wide. Wade's gaze dropped to her lips. They were trembling despite her attempt to hold them steady.

Damn . . .

He took a breath and forced himself to say, "You heard me."

*   *   *

Exhausted as the sun slipped toward the horizon, signaling the end of another day, Johanna glanced at Wade where he sat on the driver's seat beside her. He had taken over the reins after she had laboriously hooked up the team to the wagon that morning. He had guided the wagon into line silently. He had instructed her carefully as she had fed and watered the horses during the day, but afterward had driven the wagon without comment while a comfortable silence settled between them.

Johanna glanced at Wade out of the corner of her eye. His thigh was tight against hers on the narrow seat, and the purely male scent of him filled her nostrils. His body heat provided a sense of security that she could no longer deny, and the scent of him was surprisingly enticing. The fact that he had forced her to face fears that she had denied to both herself and him had not been lost on her. She had not fully overcome those fears, but despite the protests she had voiced so vociferously, she was glad to have taken that first step.

Johanna stared at Wade's hands as they held the reins easily. They were the broad, capable hands of a rancher. They had inspired confidence in the same massive horses that had balked at her treatment, but they had been surprisingly gentle when stroking away the nervousness of those agitated animals.

They were the hands of a gunman, evincing lightning-fast, death-dealing speed when flashing to his holster to fire in a blur of movement that defied the eye.

They were the hands of a protector when they dealt brutal punishment to the man who'd attacked her. They had provided a wall of safety when they drew her back firmly against him while she sat anxiously on the nervous horse's bare back.

Johanna recalled the sensation of Wade's sweet breath against her hair while he held her tight against him. She felt again the strong beating of his heart against her spine. She remembered the way those capable hands had stroked away fear, and she wondered how those hands would feel against her skin . . . caressing with a gentleness meant to calm while still raising—

Suddenly stunned at the direction of her thoughts, Johanna drew herself up. She was tired. She was fantasizing dangerously. She needed to bring herself back to reality and remember that Wade Mitchell was a virtual stranger. She needed to keep in mind that although he had cleaned himself up and seemed determined to teach her the abilities essential to completing her plans, *he* did not fit into her plans in any way.

Suddenly visited with the memory of the previous night, Johanna recalled the rancid smell of Riggs' breath when he'd appeared unexpectedly in her wagon. She recalled the fear that had choked her throat when he pressed that knife against her side, and her boundless relief at the sound of Wade's voice behind him. She had somehow known in that moment that Wade would protect her at any cost.

Johanna frowned in confusion. Wade had protected her. He had also forced her to face down her fear. He could have done those things for no other reason than for her own good. She probably should thank him, but somehow the words would not come.

"Are you ready?"

Johanna turned toward Wade, squinting as the sun's fading light shone in her eyes. Her confused thoughts were erased from her mind as she responded warily, "Ready for what?"

"To take over driving this wagon for a while."

"It's been a long day. I'll start driving tomorrow."

"No."

Her ire rising at his autocratic tone, Johanna heard herself reply, "I'm the boss here, remember?"

"Take the reins."

"No."

"There's something I have to do in back before we stop for supper."

"It can wait."

Wade turned toward her, his dark eyes discerning as he searched her gaze silently for a few moments. "Is there a reason you don't want to drive?"

Johanna raised her chin. "I hired you to do that, didn't I?"

Wade pressed, "You've driven a buggy before, haven't you?"

"Of course I have."

"It's the same idea."

"I know that."

Wade stared at her a moment longer and then dropped the reins into her hands. She was holding the lines stiffly, her mouth hanging open with surprise, when he said from within the wagon behind her, "We'll be stopping in about an hour. I'll take the reins before we do."

An hour?

Johanna silently groaned.

Baptism by fire . . .

Wade moved in an attempt to make himself comfortable in the wagon as it bumped and rocked from side to side, but the effort was useless. He stared at Johanna's back. He could tell by the rigidity of her shoulders that she was uncomfortable at the reins. He didn't like what he had put her through that day, but he knew it was necessary. It was important to him that she conquer her fear of the team. He needed to be able to ride off knowing that she could handle the wagon the same way she had handled a gun that morning. He needed to make sure that no man would get the upper hand with her simply because she did not have the necessary skills for independence. The thought of her relying again on a bastard like Riggs, a fellow who would try to take advantage of her simply because she was vulnerable, made his stomach twist.

Wade paused as a disturbing question flashed before his mind. But . . . even if she made it to the gold fields safely, what would happen to her there without a man to protect her? The sight of her was enough to stir the heat in any red-blooded man, much less the woman-starved lot who prospected for gold with disappointment facing them every day. Would her self-assurance be shattered at the hands of a frustrated miner ... or two ... or maybe more?

He was sick at the thought.

Granted, she was a good shot, but would she be able to pull the trigger on someone looking her straight in the eye?

He knew he could, but he was uncertain about her.

He was also uncertain why he cared.

Wade's eyes rested on Johanna's shoulders, the slender, soft line that led to womanly curves beneath. Johanna was beautiful and desirable, but he'd met beautiful, desirable women before. Admittedly, he had never seen a woman who could match her in total, natural beauty—pale hair that glittered with a glow of its own; light, confident eyes that flashed too often with a hidden vulnerability she sought to conceal; a fragile slenderness that concealed surprising strength. No, he had never met a woman like her. Johanna's scent struck a chord deep inside him every time she was near, but her beauty was only part of her allure. Her sharp mind challenged him. Her independence stirred his admiration. Her determination in the face of seemingly insurmountable odds continued to amaze him. None were qualities normally expected of a woman, but they in no way negated the innate femininity that drew him to her. Yet despite occasional softer moments, Johanna was haughty, arrogant, and demanding.

His eyes still trained on Johanna's shoulders, Wade unconsciously shook his head. And she didn't even like him.

The team broke into a run unexpectedly, interrupting Wade's thoughts. He noted that Johanna was drawing back on the reins in an unsuccessful effort to slow down the team, but the horses sensed something. They were panicking and Johanna was unable to control them.

Wade started toward the driver's seat as the wagon rattled and rocked more fiercely with the team's accelerating speed. Finally managing to seat himself despite the rough, seesawing jolting, he saw that the horses had pulled out of line and were headed toward a heavily wooded wilderness terrain. He snatched the reins from Johanna's cold hands as she exclaimed, "The horses are acting crazy! I don't know what's wrong with them."

Taking a firm grip, Wade pulled back on the reins in an effort to halt the runaway team, only to hear a distinctive wolf's howl.

So that was what had spooked them!

He gritted his teeth as the horses responded to the sound by increasing their pace to breakneck speed.

Wade glimpsed the wagon train as it slipped rapidly into the distance in the opposite direction. He was momentarily stunned to see that the other horses were maintaining a steady pace, appearing not to have heard the howls, and that the other wagons seemed unaware that the last wagon in line was heading wildly in the opposite direction.

At a loss to explain any of it, Wade struggled to regain control of a situation that was heading rapidly toward disaster.

Johanna held on to the narrow seat tenuously, her knuckles white as Wade drew back strongly on the reins of the panicked team. She gulped, her eyes widening as the team entered a heavily wooded copse where branches slapped at the canvas sides of the wagon. She held her breath as the vehicle rocked dangerously from side to side, barely remaining upright as the horses plunged deeper and deeper into the wilderness.

Johanna glanced at Wade, noting his concentration as he struggled to gain control of the horses. She heard again the howling that had stiffened her spine and had evidently set the team running. She recognized the sound. It was too familiar to deny its warning.

Danger . . . danger . . .

An image of her childhood dream flashed before her as the horses continued their frenzied pace. She remembered the ancient, gray-haired Indian who had spoken words of reassurance she had never forgotten.

Do not fear. I will protect you.

She wanted to see him again. She needed to see him.

As if in response to that thought, Johanna heard

a loud crack and felt the wagon shake. It listed abruptly to one side, slowing the team. Finally the wagon shuddered to a halt. Shaken, she looked at Wade as he sought to catch his breath, the reins hanging limply in his hands.

Replying in response to her unvoiced question, Wade said, "The rear wheel broke. This wagon wasn't meant to travel at top speed through virgin wilderness. Something was bound to happen."

Wade glanced back to see that his mare was still tied to the back of the wagon, then looked at the heavily lathered team as they stood twitching nervously. He withdrew his revolver from his holster.

Johanna asked hoarsely, "What are you going to do?"

"There's no use trying to get the attention of the wagon train by firing a shot. The foliage around here is too thick. It'll muffle the sound, and the wagon train is probably too far away from us now to hear it. We're going to be stuck here for a while, and we're a perfect target for that wolf and the pack he's probably traveling with." He checked his gun, his gaze tight. "We need to be ready."

Johanna took a startled breath. "That wolf . . . so you heard those howls, too?"

Wade looked at her strangely. "I heard it, and so did the horses."

"Why didn't the other horses in the wagon train hear it?"

"I don't know." Wade slid his gun back into his holster. "You need to get your shotgun ready.

We're going to have to protect ourselves and the horses, too."

Johanna replied instinctively, "I don't think we'll need guns against that wolf."

"You don't think we'll need—"

"No."

Wade went momentarily silent at her reply. He asked simply, "Why?"

"I've heard those howls before." Aware that her response sounded peculiar, she added, "I . . . I don't think that wolf is a danger to us. I think the howls were just a warning that something bad is going to happen."

"Something bad did happen. We had a runaway and we broke a wheel."

"I don't mean that."

"What *do* you mean?"

"Something else . . . something threatening . . ."

"If this isn't a threatening situation, then I don't know what is."

Johanna shook her head, aware that her explanation didn't make much sense. She said abruptly, "Never mind. Let's replace the broken wheel with the one that's attached to the back of the wagon."

"We can't do it ourselves. We'll need help, but I can't chase after the wagon train and leave you and the horses here if there are wolves around. We'll have to wait until morning. We should be missed by then, and somebody will probably come back to look for us. In the meantime, I have the feeling that we're going to need as much firepower as we can muster."

Johanna shook her head.

"Johanna . . ."

Relenting, Johanna said, "All right."

Wade looked at her strangely, and then said, "You'd better get out the canteens and some jerky, too. We're going to get hungry, and it looks like we have a long night ahead of us."

Twilight was quickly fading into night as Mc-Mullen scanned the shadowed terrain. He had extended the traveling time of the train longer than usual while he scouted ahead, and he could imagine the mumblings that must have begun in the wagons.

I'm hungry . . .

I'm tired . . .

My legs hurt . . .

When are we going to stop, Mama?

Riding back toward the long line of wagons, McMullen signaled them to halt for the night. He went still when he saw a mounted group approaching in the distance.

The tense lines on his face deepening, McMullen whistled several times, a warning signal to the wagons along the line to prepare for trouble. He checked his gun. His brow furrowed, he watched as the wagons began circling behind him, telling himself that he was merely being cautious, that marauders would not make such a direct approach. His jaw tightened when one of the mounted men rode deliberately over a dog that had dashed out from the train. He heard the dog yelp, and saw little Tommy Grisham run out toward the animal. Still, he did not protest when the men neared and drew their exhausted horses to a halt.

The star on the chest of a gray-haired, mustached leader glinted in the fading light as McMullen questioned cautiously, "Are you men hunting down somebody out here?"

The leader responded, "My name's Sheriff Hiram Carter, from down Millborn way. We're looking for a big fella named Bartlett who escaped from jail and was headed in this direction. We're wondering if you saw him."

The man mounted beside the sheriff added, "This Bartlett is a killer, and we ain't going to quit until we find him and hang him from the nearest tree."

Turning toward the man, the sheriff reprimanded, "You ain't got no call to talk like that, Pierce." He looked back at McMullen. "Don't listen to him. Pierce knew the victim since she was a little girl. Her pa was grieving too bad to come with us, so Pierce promised to make the person who killed her pay the price—but we ain't hunting Bartlett because he's been convicted of killing her. We're hunting him because he escaped from jail before he could be brought to trial."

His face reddening, Pierce retorted, "Maybe that's the reason *you're* hunting that killer down, Sheriff, but that ain't the reason *I* joined this posse. Paul Malone was still too broken up to leave Mary's graveside, but I didn't ride all this way just to *find* Bartlett and bring him back so he can escape again. I made Paul a promise, and I intend to keep it. I don't need nobody to tell me Bartlett is guilty when he was found with Mary's blood on his hands. He deserves the rope we've got ready for him. I ain't speaking only for myself, neither, when I say I'm sick and tired of hearing you stand up for Bartlett."

Turning to the mounted men behind him for confirmation, Pierce shouted, "Ain't that right, fellas?"

The nods of agreement from the weary posse were revealing.

Making a snap decision, McMullen responded, "I ain't seen nobody riding this way, but I'll keep an eye out. What does this man look like?"

Responding again in the sheriff's stead, Pierce said, "He's a big fella, like the sheriff said . . . young . . . not yet thirty years old, with dark hair and eyes. He's riding a roan . . . a mare. There's some women who think he's good-looking. I suppose there's no accounting for taste, but he's a real ladies' man, all right. I figure that's how he made a sweet, young thing like Mary Malone trust him in the first place."

The sheriff interjected determinedly, "It ain't been proved that Bartlett killed Mary. Whether you want to believe it or not, that's a fact, Pierce. And I ain't going to let nobody—including you— use a rope on that fella unless I'm sure."

"Is that so?" Pierce's heavy features darkened threateningly. "Too bad the rest of us don't feel that way."

McMullen frowned at the heat of the exchange, barely resisting a glance toward the rear of the train as the wagons continued circling behind him. He repeated, "Like I said, I ain't seen nobody riding this way, much less anybody who fits that description."

"I seen him, Mr. McMullen."

McMullen looked down at Tommy Grisham as the boy's high-pitched voice carried clearly in the stillness. Frowning in the brief silence that ensued, he did not have a chance to respond before the sheriff asked, "You seen him, little fella?"

"I sure did. He came riding up to the train when Mr. McMullen was scouting ahead. He asked for some grub. When he got it, he rode off real fast."

McMullen remained silent as the sheriff asked, "Where did he say he was going?"

"He didn't. He just took off riding that way . . . east." Pointing into the distance with his stubby finger, Tommy said, "He was in a real hurry, too."

A new fire in his eye, Pierce ordered, "Let's go!"

"Wait a minute!" Turning toward him, the sheriff said, "It's too dark to travel. We can't see nothing and we might miss his trail. We might as well stay here until morning so we can get a fresh start."

"I ain't waiting so Bartlett can get farther away!"

"You ain't using your head, neither! We can't accomplish nothing in the dark." Turning toward the men behind him, the sheriff said, "Does that make sense to you fellas?"

Weary nods signaled agreement. Obviously feeling the need for a vocal response, Sheriff Carter said emphatically, "I don't hear you."

Reluctant replies came from the posse behind him:

"We hear you."

"There's no use riding in the dark."

"Our horses need rest anyway."

McMullen saw frustration flash in Pierce's eyes when the sheriff turned toward him and said, "We'll rest here tonight and share your campfires, if it's all right with you."

"If that's what you fellas want."

McMullen turned away from the posse as the men dismounted and approached the circled wagons. He slid his arm around Tommy's shoulder and drew the boy along with him. Stopping when they were concealed by a wagon's shadow, he asked, "Why did you lie to them fellas, boy?"

"I didn't do nothing that you didn't do."

McMullen's lips curved up as he replied, "I know why I lied. I was just wondering why you did."

"I paid them back, that's what I did." Moisture suddenly bright in the boy's eyes, he said hotly, "They hurt my dog. Everybody saw them ride over him, and nobody said nothing." He shrugged. "That fella they said they were looking for ain't with the train no more anyway."

McMullen looked up and scrutinized the circled wagons. The boy was right. Johanna Higgins' wagon was missing.

He questioned tightly, "Did you see when that wagon pulled out of line?"

"No. They were gone before anybody noticed it."

"You can tell me the truth."

"I am telling the truth."

Dismissing the boy with a nod, McMullen frowned. He wasn't sure how, when, or why the wagon had left the train. He didn't know if it had anything to do with the posse, either, but he knew one thing for sure: Johanna Higgins was his responsibility, and he was going to search for her and her wagon after the posse left. He'd find out exactly what was going on, too—one way or another.

CHAPTER FOUR

It was dark . . . too dark for comfort.

Night had descended rapidly on the damaged covered wagon. Silently cursing his inability to see more than a few yards into the thick foliage surrounding them, Wade noted that Johanna had become strangely silent, as if her initial confidence had faded with the light. He wished he could reassure her, but the shifting shadows outside the wagon made him uneasy, too.

It was going to be a long night.

Wade glanced at Johanna, who was sitting on the mattress beside him, holding her shotgun on her lap. They had lit a lamp and had placed it between them. It amazed him to see that even in the meager light, with their current stress drawing her expression into a frown, Johanna was beautiful.

Beautiful, but mystifying.

Still puzzled, Wade went over Johanna's surprising statement again in his mind.

I don't think we'll need guns against that wolf.

They wouldn't need guns to ward off a wolf's attack? He had been as puzzled by those words as he had been to see that the howling in itself did not seem to frighten her.

I've heard those howls before. They mean danger.

He knew what danger meant—yet he somehow doubted that Johanna did.

A long, lingering howl sounded again, interrupting Wade's mental meanderings when the horses reacted with unexpected panic. Having ignored the intermittent howling of the past hour, they suddenly began rearing wildly, jerking and pulling at their traces in an effort to break free. The unsteady wagon shook violently as their terrified whinnies reverberated in the wooded glade.

Johanna cried, "What's happening? The horses are—"

"Shhh!" Wade stood up. He waved his hand to halt Johanna's protest when she stood unsteadily beside him in the violently swaying wagon. He heard a snarl over the clamor of shrieking horses, straining bridles, and clattering hooves. It was unmistakable . . . and it wasn't a wolf.

"Wade . . ."

Wade silenced her again. His fears were confirmed when the growl became an unmistakable bellow. He exchanged Johanna's shotgun for his gun and said tightly, "We have to get rid of that bear, and my gun might not be able to handle it. I need your shotgun."

"A bear?"

There was no mistaking the fear in Johanna's eyes when he responded, "If this shotgun doesn't scare him off, use my gun to defend yourself. Whatever you do, don't let that animal get near you."

"What about you?"

With no time to reply, Wade stepped out boldly into the wagon opening, the shotgun primed. The sight of a huge brown bear standing on his hind legs at his full, massive height momentarily stunned him.

He raised the shotgun instinctively to fire when Johanna called out, "No, don't shoot!"

His shot went wild when Johanna knocked the shotgun aside. Wade did not have time to react before a huge, furry shadow leapt out of the shadows to knock down the bear violently onto all fours.

"Get back!" Wade pushed Johanna behind him as a vicious battle ensued between a large gray wolf and the enraged bear. Dodging the bear's blows, the wolf warded off the full weight of the bear's crushing swipes with unyielding persistence. Bloodstained saliva dripped from his jaws as he lunged time and again at the powerful animal. His yellow eyes glowing, his furry hide becoming stained with blood as the battle ensued, the wolf suddenly leapt onto the bear's back and clamped down his teeth. Reacting with an echoing shriek, the bear shook off the wolf, but then halted his attack when the wolf landed on his feet and stood ready to lunge again.

Raising his snout toward the sky, the bear roared loudly, and then turned unexpectedly to beat a hasty retreat into the darkness.

But the wolf remained.

His jaw tight, Wade thrust the shotgun into Johanna's hands and grasped his own gun. He was about to fire when Johanna again knocked his gun aside. Stunned, he turned to see her staring motionlessly at the crouching wolf. He looked back at the slavering animal to see that the wolf's glittering gaze held Johanna's in a moment of silent, unspoken communication before he slipped off into the shadows.

Uncertain, Wade lowered his gun.

Johanna was trembling, her eyes bright with moisture when he turned back toward her. She did not resist when he took her comfortingly into his arms. He held her quietly, her womanly softness tight against him for long moments before he asked, "How did you know what that wolf was going to do?"

Looking up at him, Johanna said tentatively, "I don't know. I just did."

"You said he tried to warn you . . ."

"You don't understand." Johanna swallowed hard. "Those howls . . . I told you, I've heard them before. They were a warning of danger."

"Danger . . . but we wouldn't have been in danger from that bear if the wolf hadn't panicked the team into bolting."

"I can't explain what happened because I don't really understand it myself. I just . . ."

Johanna trembled more violently as her voice trailed away, and Wade clutched her closer. He had seen it, but he didn't believe it. All he knew for certain was that they were both alive, Johanna was in his arms, and he was glad.

Breathless and shaken, Letty stood at her bedroom window overlooking Park Avenue. She stared blindly into the darkness. The wild howling that had echoed for hours, resounding against the walls and cathedral ceiling of her elegant bedroom suite, had suddenly stopped.

She had been alarmed when the cries had awakened her from a deep sleep earlier. When they escalated abruptly to a furor, she had jumped out of bed in panic. She had known something was wrong . . . terribly wrong. She had known instinctively that one of her daughters was in danger, and an icy terror had gripped her.

Tears had trailed down her cheeks as the howling continued, as she had paced the floor, raging at her impotency. Yet she had been unprepared when the howling ceased abruptly.

The sudden silence of her room seemed deafening in the aftermath. Letty pushed a lock of heavy, dark hair back from her ashen face. Her breathing clipped, her stylish nightwear clinging to her slenderness with perspiration, she raised her chin and walked unsteadily back to her bed with the dazed realization that it was over. Whatever had

prompted the persistent, piercing cries had ceased
to exist.

A sob choked her throat as Letty lay back
down and pulled the coverlet up to her chin in
defense against a thought that was almost too
horrible to bear.

Did that mean that one of her daughters had
ceased to exist, too?

Johanna had finally stopped trembling, but she
was unwilling to surrender to the security of
Wade's arms.

It had all happened so fast—the sudden chaos
with the horses, the growling bear, the wolf's appearance. She had faltered in confusion, but instinct had overcome common sense when she had
twice prevented Wade from shooting. Yet Wade
had not reacted with anger. From the wolf's first
howl, he had remained focused and decisive. He
had protected her without showing a moment's
fear. If his reaction had not instilled the confidence in her to obey her instincts, she was uncertain what she would have done.

But . . . what had really happened? What did it
all mean? She did not understand why the wolf
had risked its life to protect her, just as she did not
know why Wade had done the same.

The memory of the wizened old man of her
dreams returned, and Johanna went momentarily
still. The wolf . . . Wade . . . had the old man fulfilled his promise by providing them *both* for her
safety?

Looking up at Wade, Johanna asked with a bluntness untouched by her former hauteur, "Why didn't you walk away from me and this whole debacle when you first came to the wagon train, Wade?"

Wade did not respond.

"Tell me."

"I can't really answer that question."

"Why?"

Wade had no response. He noted Johanna's intensity as she stared at him. Silent for a few moments, he finally replied just as bluntly, "Despite everything that happened here, nothing has really changed. I won't be staying with the wagon train for more than a day or so. There are . . . other things I need to do."

Johanna did not respond.

"I might have to leave without notice . . . without time for good-byes."

She still did not speak.

"Do you understand what I'm saying, Johanna?"

"No, not really. I don't understand any of the things that happened here tonight."

"Johanna . . ."

"Wait. Just . . . listen."

Immediately alert, Wade listened intently. He heard only common night sounds emanating from the dense foliage around them, and he replied, "I don't hear anything to be wary of."

Johanna surprised him by replying, "Neither do I. It's quiet. Even the wolf's howls have stopped." Her expression sober, Johanna whispered, "I never thought I'd hear myself say this, but . . . thank you."

Thank you.

Wade looked down at Johanna as she stood in the comforting circle of his arms. The night was dark. Night sounds hummed comfortingly from the surrounding foliage. The interior of the wagon was small and intimate, and Johanna was looking up at him as if truly seeing him for the first time.

And he had never wanted her more.

Yet his reality had not changed. Although Johanna was not aware of it, he was still a wanted man. He wanted her, but whatever she thought about him at that moment, desire was not enough. Not for her. She deserved more.

Wade drew away from her with true strength of will. He whispered, "You're exhausted. Everything happened so quickly that you're all mixed up. You need sleep. Lie down. I'll keep watch."

"I can't rest while you're awake."

"Yes, you can. That's the only thing that makes sense, and you know it." Wade continued purposefully, "I'll ride up to find the wagon train as soon as it's light and I'm sure that you and the horses are reasonably safe here."

"That isn't fair to you. You need your rest, too."

"Fairness has nothing to do with it. That's the way it's going to be." His voice dropping a note softer, Wade added, "Go to sleep . . . please."

Wade noted Johanna's hesitation before she lay down on the mattress and pulled up the coverlet.

Although she struggled to remain awake, she fell asleep minutes afterward.

Johanna was silent and breathing heavily in sleep. The thick fans of her lashes fluttered occasionally against her cheeks, and her lips were lightly parted. They moved wordlessly in the course of a dream, and Wade stared at them, suddenly hungry to cover them with his own. He wished he had not been fool enough to have turned his back on something that could have been, and he—

Refusing to finish that thought, Wade looked out resolutely into the darkness.

Nothing had changed.

Johanna deserved more than a single night of passion.

Well, it was about time.

Larry Worth's broad mustache twitched with annoyance as he walked down the narrow Texas street toward the livery stable located midway along it. A case that he had expected to finish up quickly had turned into a nightmare for him. He had not expected that Johanna Higgins would become a flitting shadow that disappeared at will. It had been difficult enough following her to Texas after her circuitous, baffling route, but ascertaining her next destination had been practically impossible.

Who would have guessed that a young woman whose beauty turned heads wherever she went could disappear into thin air? Part of the problem was his own. He had judged Johanna Higgins by the standards of behavior expected of a young society woman. He had learned the hard way that she did nothing that was expected of a young woman of her social stature. She was apparently strong-willed, with a mind of her own.

His second mistake had been believing that a young beauty accustomed to being pampered and adored would not place herself in situations where neither was likely to happen.

Wrong again.

After days of intense investigating and following up the most minuscule of leads, he had finally ascertained that Johanna Higgins had—of all things—joined a wagon train heading west! She had apparently spent what must have been her last penny to buy the wagon and team necessary to take "a historic journey across the country," ostensibly with the ultimate goal of settling on land awaiting the wagon train in Oregon territory!

Incredulous, Larry shook his head. Johanna Higgins . . . a farmer?

Reaching the livery stable at last, he paid the wiry-haired proprietor for readying a horse, absentmindedly checked his supplies, and prepared to catch up with the wagon train. He mounted and started off at a modest pace. It mattered very little that the wagon train had a head start on him. He knew the route and was aware of the slow pace the wagons would be forced to travel. He would catch up with them easily.

Larry sighed and turned his mount toward the edge of town. He had wired Robert Pinkerton that he was on his way and would soon be able to bring the case to a conclusion. And he'd be glad. As far as he was concerned, Johanna Higgins was a troubled and troublesome young woman who caused more problems than she was worth.

Well, it was about time!

As far as he was concerned, Larry Worth was not the detective he was cracked up to be, and following him had been more trouble than it was worth. He probably could've done better himself.

Percy Smart made that assessment coldly as he watched the mustached Pinkerton mount up to leave town. He grunted and spurred his own horse into motion. He was uncomfortable on horseback. He considered it a primitive means of transportation that had seen its day. He was accustomed to the city, where he was able to walk to any destination without a problem, or where he could hail a passing carriage to get him there. He was also uncomfortable in the attire he was forced to wear in order to blend in with the locals. He congratulated himself on his tried-and-true method of appearing authentic in any environment. He had simply located a fellow on the street who appeared to be his size, waited until the man entered a dark area, and struck him unconscious and taken his clothing. It hadn't been difficult; and when on the street again, no one had given him a second look.

Still, the job that Humphrey Dobbs had hired him for was not what it was cracked up to be.

It will be the easiest job you've ever handled for me. All you need to do is to follow Larry Worth, the Pinkerton assigned to Johanna Higgins' case. When he locates her, make sure she doesn't return to New York City with him. If that involves the unnatural demise of Johanna and/or her Pinkerton . . . well, that'll be your choice.

Smart remembered that Dobbs had added with a smile, *You'll be adequately compensated for your work, whatever it involves.*

Smart could not help thinking that no payment could compensate him for having endured an extended stay in a backward Texas town where impatience had become his greatest enemy. Unfortunately, however, he had the feeling that his discomfort had just begun.

Larry picked up his pace, and Smart grimaced as he spurred his mount again. It wouldn't do to lose the detective after all the time he had spent waiting for him to locate Letty Wolf's daughter. His only consolation was that it couldn't be much longer before the Pinkerton delivered him directly to Johanna Higgins. Concluding his assignment would be up to him then, and he was good at his job. He'd take care of things just like Dobbs wanted, and he'd go back to the city where he belonged.

Yes, it wouldn't be much longer.

The birds were chirping loudly in the trees overhead, celebrating the warmth of the New York

City day. A pleasant breeze lifted dark, shining tendrils from Letty's forehead as the carriage moved briskly along the cobbled roadway that wound through the vast green acres of Central Park. She turned toward the man seated beside her and looked at him silently. Peter Klein smiled as he gazed back at her, and Letty wondered suddenly why she had consented to this particular outing with this particular man—and why he was so persistent in his attentions to her.

Most women in the city's social set considered Peter an exceedingly eligible bachelor. Not only was he wealthy and mature, he had never been married, and was considered good-looking by women who favored blond-haired men with small brown mustaches. It was too bad she wasn't included in that number. Even if she were, however, she was not inclined toward another romantic liaison while her life was in turmoil.

She had tried to say that as politely as possible to Peter. She had said it with no attempt at being polite, but the result was the same. Still smiling, Peter had refused to take no for an answer, and his pleasant persistence had finally won out.

Besides, she had been cooped up in her apartment for too long while howling haunted her both day and night. Her doctor had told her that she needed to vary her routine, and to get some fresh air. She had decided to take his advice. The varied terrain of the park, with the sweeping pastoral style of the southern section, the rocky and wooded western and northern sections, and the meandering pathways that gave visitors a succession of views as they walked or rode, was appealing to her. As far as she was concerned, if Peter chose to believe she had agreed to their present outing because of feelings for him . . . well, that was his problem.

Peter asked unexpectedly, "What's wrong, Letty?"

"What makes you think something is wrong?"

"Perhaps because you're frowning. Whether you realize it or not, your emotions are very visible on your face." He paused, then continued, "But it is a very beautiful face."

Letty's smile held little warmth as she replied, "My beauty is renowned. It's too bad I can't take credit for it."

"Oh, I think you can. If you weren't the kind of person you are, your beauty would be jealously guarded under the strict hand of a tyrant husband—but you'd never stand for that."

"You're correct in that assumption."

"You've never met a man you would be willing to submit to. Even your romantic liaisons are legend. They begin when you give the nod, and end in the same way."

Letty raised her brow.

"I give you fair warning, Letty . . ." Leaning closer, Peter said, "I intend to be the exception to that rule."

"Really?"

"I'm already halfway there. You had no desire to accept my invitation today, yet you finally consented."

"I have my own reasons for consenting to be here today."

"I know." Peter smiled more broadly, his small brown mustache twitching as he added, "But you are here, seated at my side in an open carriage where all the world can see us."

"Is that what you wanted . . . to declare to the world that you've finally won out? Do you expect to beat me to ending our 'liaison' so you can say you're the first fellow to walk away from me?"

Suddenly sober, Peter responded, "No, that isn't my intention. You see, I'm going to be the man who will eventually win you over. You'll marry me, and we will live happily ever after."

"Pooh!" Letty's reaction was instantaneous. "You've allowed your daydreams to invade reality. I'm telling you now that I have no intention of taking you or any man seriously. I'm enjoying myself too immensely for that."

"You haven't been looking like you're enjoying yourself."

"Haven't I?"

"Not to a discerning eye."

"And you have a discerning eye?"

"Where you're concerned, I do, and I—"

But Letty was no longer listening. Her expression stiffened as another carriage moved briskly past and she caught the eye of the man seated beside a smiling young woman.

James.

Eleanor sat beside him. Eleanor saw her and smiled more brightly as she waved enthusiastically. Letty returned Eleanor's wave and then turned back silently to face Peter.

His smile frozen, Peter said, "It bothers you that James Ferguson has taken up with that young woman, doesn't it?"

Her response just as frozen, Letty responded, "Whether it bothers me or not is none of your business; but you're wrong."

"I am? Ferguson is one of your former lovers, isn't he?"

"I have many former lovers."

"He is your most recent former lover."

"That, too, is none of your business."

"I've already told you that I intend to make it my business."

"I thought I had made myself clear on that point, but let me state my position more directly so there will be no misunderstanding—I have no intention of allowing *my* business to become *your* business."

"I thought I had made myself clear, also, Letty. If not, I'll say it again: James Ferguson may be your former lover, but he will be your *last* former lover, because there will be no one after me in your life."

Letty was momentarily silent before she replied, "I can see you've already reached the point where daydreams have become reality for you. That's a dangerous situation."

"For you."

"No, for you!" Letty said with true heat, "I have not reached my position in life by allowing men to dictate to me, and you will not be the first! I live my life *my* way. I love the men *I* choose to love, *when* I choose to love them—and you have just eliminated yourself from consideration. Now, if you don't mind, please tell your driver to turn this carriage around and take me home."

"But I do mind."

"Do you?" Letty stared boldly into Peter's stiff expression before she turned to call out sharply, "Driver, stop this carriage!"

"That won't be necessary."

Ignoring Peter's response, Letty ordered, "Stop this carriage now, driver."

Overriding her command, Peter ordered, "Keep driving, Pierson."

When Letty turned furiously toward him, Peter said more softly, "I'm sorry, Letty. I apologize for what I said. You were right and I was wrong. I should not have questioned you about the men in your past. It was none of my business. Please forgive me."

"Tell your driver to stop the carriage."

"You don't expect me to abandon you here in the park, do you?"

"Tell your driver to let me out of this carriage."

"Letty, please. I'm sorry. I overstepped myself."

"Yes, you did, but you did something else, also." Her dark eyes sparking fire, Letty said, "You revealed yourself to me, and I will not have a man like you in my life."

"I was jealous, Letty. I sincerely apologize."

"You don't have the right to be jealous—but that

circumstance aside, I don't believe your apology. You are just saying the words, believing I'll allow you to insinuate yourself into my life until a time in the future when you think you'll have more right to repeat that statement."

"That isn't true."

"Isn't it?" Letty's stare remained cold. "Maybe not, but I don't intend to give you that chance. Now, let me out of this carriage."

Peter went still. His face turning pale, he said stiffly, "That won't be necessary. I'll order my driver to take you home as you requested." Addressing his driver, he said, "Turn around, Pierson. The lady would like to go home." He waited a few minutes before looking back at her to add, "Please believe me when I say I'm sorry."

No response.

"Letty . . ."

"I've had enough of this!"

"I've already ordered my driver to take you home as you asked. Doesn't that prove anything to you?"

Silence.

"Answer me, Letty."

Finally facing him, Letty replied, "It would be kinder if I didn't answer you right now."

"As long as you'll say you forgive me."

Maintaining her silence until they arrived at her apartment building, Letty said simply, "Good-bye."

Livid with barely controlled anger, Peter watched Letty's slender figure move out of sight through the entrance to her building. Turning to his driver, he ordered sharply, "Take me home, Pierson."

Inwardly furious at Letty's rejection of his apology, Peter maintained appearances with a forced smile as his carriage moved smoothly toward his elaborate residence. He was wealthy, good-looking, successful in business, and sought after by women respected at every level of society. He had recently built himself a palatial summer estate on the ocean in addition to the sophisticated apartment he maintained in the city. He had achieved every goal he had ever aspired to . . . save one. He was well aware that at his point of maturity, he needed a special woman—one who was beautiful, intelligent, and a match for him in every way. Letty Wolf was that woman. He had made up his mind the first moment he saw her that she would be his. Yet he had started off poorly by revealing the jealousy that had eaten at his innards throughout her affair with James Ferguson. He had proceeded wisely until that point by forcing himself to bide his time after her breakup with Ferguson. He had planned carefully for the moment when he would make his move. Noting that she had appeared particularly restless and uncomfortable of late, he had decided the time was ripe, and he would not be cheated of his reward any longer.

Wrong.

The mistake he had made that morning was unlike him, but it was a bad one. However, it would not be his undoing.

Taking a deep, determined breath, Peter decided that he would humble himself if necessary to get back into Letty's good graces. He would make that sacrifice with the knowledge that when he finally won her, he would see that she received the proper payback.

But that wasn't his present problem. James Ferguson was. It was generally known that Letty had ended her liaison with James over his objections, but she obviously still had feelings for him. It had taken only one look at that insipid young woman whom James had taken in Letty's place to realize that she would never be an adequate replacement for Letty. It had taken only one look to see that Letty's interest had been piqued by Eleanor. Unfortunately, it had also taken only one look to see that Letty could have James back with just a simple word.

Flushing angrily, Peter resolved that Letty would never speak that simple word. He would do whatever he must to make sure of that.

Letty was shaken. She now regretted accepting Peter's invitation. Riding with him that morning, however, had proved that her first assessment of him was correct. He was arrogant and controlling, a man who wanted things his way. She had avoided that type of man all her life, and she wanted no part of him.

Feeling restless, she was about to pay Alexander Pittman a visit in the hope of obtaining news about her daughters when Millie appeared to inform her that she had a visitor.

The reception room of her apartment was silent when she entered to find James waiting. Pausing to catch her breath, her heart thudding in her breast, Letty allowed herself to assess her former lover silently. A few more silver strands peppered his thick crop of brown hair, his frown lines seemed a bit deeper, and joy appeared to have left his sober brown-eyed gaze; but his stance was still erect, his appearance powerful, and when he spoke, his words were unyielding as he said abruptly, "Peter Klein isn't the man for you, Letty."

Suddenly angry, Letty responded with equal adamance, "You seem to have forgotten that you don't have the right to make that decision for me, James."

"I haven't forgotten." James' brows drew into an angry line. "I haven't forgotten anything you ever said to me, but that's beside the point right now. Klein looked too sure of himself as you sat beside him in that carriage this morning. I don't know if he had the right to feel as pleased with himself as he seemed, but I'm here to warn you . . . he's a dangerous man, as many of the women he's known before you could testify if they felt safe in doing so."

Stunned, Letty unconsciously shook her head. "It's not like you to make implications of that sort, James."

"I'm not implying anything. I'm stating the truth," James continued resolutely. "Klein has *connections*—relationships with unsavory characters that are a holdover from earlier days before he obtained his questionable wealth. He doesn't accept rejection, and he won't make an exception for you when you're through with him."

Letty raised her chin. "I would have heard rumors about Peter's past if any of this were true. Instead, Peter is highly regarded by everyone he deals with. He is considered an eligible bachelor, and he is—"

"Is that what you're looking for, Letty, an eligible bachelor?" James took an angry step forward. "I didn't think you were the type."

"What type would that be?" Letty replied stiffly.

"A woman looking for a man to take care of her . . . an *eligible* man."

"You're correct, then. I'm not *that type*. Peter understands that."

"Does he?"

Letty did not reply.

"Listen to me, Letty." Closing the distance between them in a few broad steps, James grasped her shoulders and said tightly, "It was difficult, but I've accepted that you no longer want me to be a part of your life. I've gone on from there."

"Yes, I've noticed. Eleanor Troast is a lovely *young* woman."

A smile briefly touched James' lips. "Yes, she's lovely and she's young, but she's also the opposite of everything you are. She's exactly what I need right now and I cherish her for it."

The deep commitment in James' tone struck Letty with surprising pain as she said with a sincerity that came from the heart, "I . . . I'm glad for you, James. It's important to me to know that you're happy."

"It's taken me a while to understand that you mean what you're saying right now, considering the past relationship between us, but I feel the same way about you. That's why I can't stand by while you get involved with a man like Peter Klein."

"We're back to that again."

"That's right!" James' grip tightened as he asked, "Haven't you been listening to me at all? Do you think I would have come here after you made it so clear that you never wanted to see me again if I didn't have something important to say? Peter Klein was deeply involved with the underworld when he was young. He became wealthy through activities that were illegal at best. He has since invested his money wisely and has multiplied his fortune, which is the reason he's become accepted by society—but he maintains covert connections with underworld figures to this day. His past activities never made any difference to me before this, but it's different now. Klein's not like me, Letty. He won't take no for an answer when you're through with him."

Wincing as his grip tightened, Letty said, "You're hurting me, James."

James' hands dropped back to his sides abruptly. Still standing close, he asked, "Have you heard anything that I've said, Letty?"

"I've been listening, but I don't necessarily believe you."

"Why?"

"Because . . ." Flustered as his voice dropped to an intimate note, Letty replied, "Because everything you've been saying is unlikely."

"Isn't it more than unlikely that I'd come here with a pack of lies about your newest lover, Letty?"

"Peter is not my newest lover!"

"If he isn't your lover yet, he surely intends to be."

"I have something to say about that."

James' gaze dropped briefly toward Letty's lips. "I know. I never believed you were easy."

Beginning to feel herself inwardly trembling . . . beginning to feel a desire for James' warm, reassuring embrace, Letty took a resolute step backward. "That's because I'm *not* easy, James. I will allow no one into my life whom I don't accept completely. That's the only response I'll make to you today, and I hope it reassures you . . . because I believe your concern is real."

"You know it is." James' gaze darkened. "I've gone on with my life, Letty . . . but I'll always love you."

"James . . ."

James frowned as he said, "I hope you'll remember what I came here to tell you. Peter Klein is a dangerous man."

"I heard you."

"Don't get involved with him."

"James . . ."

"He's trouble, and that isn't what I want for you, Letty."

Letty paused. She wanted to ask what James really did want for her. As for herself, she wanted . . . she needed . . .

A wolf's howl sounded abruptly in Letty's ears, and she turned pale.

"What's wrong, Letty?"

She looked up at James. She did not need to ask if he had heard the sound because he had not. And she knew what the howling meant.

Danger.

"Letty . . ."

The howl sounded again, and Letty took another backward step. She couldn't be certain what the warning meant, but neither could she take the risk of endangering James for any reason. She couldn't do that to a man who sincerely loved her . . . not again.

Letty responded flatly, "If you have nothing else to say, I think you should go, James."

"I won't go until—"

"I heard what you said, James, so please go."

"Letty . . ."

"Please."

James went still. Then he said, "I guess you're right. I've said everything I came here to say. All that's left to say is . . . good-bye."

Turning abruptly, James strode toward the door.

Letty stood unmoving as the echo of the closing door resounded in the apartment. Then she started back toward her bedroom, attempting to ignore the howling that had begun again.

The afternoon sun was high in the sky when Johanna's repaired wagon pulled into its place in line in the wagon train. The morning had passed in earnest activity that had not halted until her wagon was able to resume its slow pace forward with the rest of the train.

Wade had ridden out to catch up with the wagon train as soon as it was light. He had returned a half hour later with a party of men who had worked diligently to replace the broken wheel. Yet it was almost noon before the wagon was finally extricated from the thick foliage where it had come to a crashing halt the previous day.

Speaking his sincere thanks for their help, Wade had not bothered to watch the men as they rode back to catch up with their wagons. Instead, he had taken the reins of Johanna's team without a word.

"What's bothering you, Wade?"

He looked up at Johanna, frowning. He supposed many things were bothering him—his confusion about the unexpected appearance of the gray wolf the previous evening; the howlings that Johanna had said predicted danger; Johanna's unexpected reactions to both of those phenomena; and the reality that although he knew a relationship between them had no future, his desire for Johanna would not relent. He had also noticed that the men who had come out that morning to repair Johanna's wagon had treated him strangely.

He replied vaguely, "What makes you think something is bothering me?"

"The look on your face . . . and the fact that you haven't spoken a word to me in the past half hour."

Wade stared into Johanna's concerned gaze. She was so damned beautiful, and so damned unconscious of the way she was responding to him. The events of the previous evening had obviously affected her, too. She was looking at him openly. There was no trace of defensiveness in her incredible eyes. Instead it was almost as if she was seeing him for the first time . . . as if she totally accepted him.

He responded gruffly, "Something was wrong with the men McMullen brought with him this morning. They were too quiet."

"They were intent on getting the job done."

"No, it was more than that. Something happened. They avoided looking at me, and when they did, it was as if they didn't dare say what they were thinking."

Wade considered that thought silently a moment longer as Johanna moved restlessly beside him. The heat of her thigh against his on the narrow seat sent a fresh surge of desire coursing through him, and Wade silently groaned. Needing to distance himself from her, he handed her the reins and said, "Drive the wagon. I want to talk to McMullen. I'll be back soon."

"But—"

"I'll only be gone a little while. You won't have any trouble keeping up until I get back."

"But—"

Wade saw the hesitation in Johanna's expression and knew what she was thinking. He said softly, "I know what I said yesterday about leaving without saying good-bye. I promise, I won't leave without telling you first."

Tears sprang to Johanna's eyes.

Wade jumped down from the wagon, mounted his horse, and within minutes was galloping toward the head of the train.

A few minutes later, he caught up to McMullen, who was riding ahead of the wagons. Drawing abreast of the wagon master, he said bluntly, "Something happened here yesterday while Johanna and I were gone. The attitude of the men has changed toward me."

"It's that obvious, huh?"

"To me it is."

Wade waited with limited patience as McMullen took his time in replying. "We had a visit last night from a sheriff and his posse after your wagon disappeared. They was hunting a fella who had escaped from jail . . . a suspected murderer named Bartlett."

Wade turned pale.

"The sheriff was a man named Hiram Carter. He explained that the posse had followed Bartlett all the way from down Millborn way, but they finally lost his trail. He described Bartlett to me and asked if I had seen anybody who looked like him passing by." McMullen added, "The name wasn't the same, but the description fit you just fine."

"What did you tell him?"

McMullen shrugged. "That posse was a pretty tired lot, but there was a big fella named Pierce who had a lot to say about a noose he had ready for the man they was looking for. The sheriff tried to reason with him, but it was no use. The rest of the posse seemed to go along with what Pierce was saying."

Wade repeated, "What did you tell him?"

"I made a decision . . . and I told that sheriff I hadn't seen any stranger come this way since we started out. He seemed satisfied with my answer until little Tommy Grisham piped up, saying that he had seen the stranger they described."

Wade went still.

"I figure Tommy didn't really know you, so I didn't rightly understand why the little fella went to so much trouble to start those fellas off on a wild-goose chase."

"A wild-goose chase . . ."

"Tommy told them he had seen that fella riding east . . . in the opposite direction from where we're heading. Tommy was real convincing and they thanked him, but they decided to wait until first light before starting out to pick up the trail. They left just before daybreak—and you showed up here a little while later."

"They're trying to follow a trail that doesn't exist."

"Except in Tommy's imagination. I asked

Tommy why he sent them fellas off like he did. Tommy said that posse rode over his dog and never looked back. He said they were bad men, and he wasn't going to let them hang anybody." McMullen shrugged, adding, "There's no figuring out an eight-year-old's way of thinking, I guess."

Wade did not respond.

"But it ain't done with, as you probably realize. Everybody in the train kept quiet about you being here. I'm thinking they was just following me and Tommy's lead, but that don't mean they weren't talking in private. I have the feeling they don't like the idea that a fella who might be running away from a posse—a possible killer—is on our wagon train."

Wade confirmed flatly, "I'm the man that posse was looking for, all right, but I didn't kill anybody. I ran because I figured that rope the posse had ready for me would end any chance I might have of proving I wasn't responsible for Mary's death."

"There's truth in that, for sure. Anyways, I don't expect that posse to head back here—but like I said, that ain't the end of it. You're going to have to make a decision soon, or the men of this wagon train are going to make it for you."

"It's just my word against the posse's, if that's what you're saying."

"Right."

"They'll want me to leave?"

"That's about the size of it."

"Even if I'm not guilty . . ."

"Like I said, they don't like the idea of a wanted

man—especially a man wanted for murder— being a part of this wagon train."

Wade maintained his silence.

"Let me know what you decide to do."

Wade nodded and turned his mount toward the rear of the line. He had ridden halfway when he heard the youthful summons, "Mr. Mitchell! Wait!"

Wade drew his mount to an abrupt halt. He turned to see a boy running toward him. Small and tousle-haired, the child halted breathlessly a few feet away and said, "You don't know me, Mr. Bartlett, but I just wanted to tell you that you don't need to worry about nothing. I ain't going to let that posse get their hands on you. I heard what you did about saving Miss Higgins from that nasty fella who was driving her wagon. You stuck by her when her wagon broke down, too. You ain't no killer. You're a hero, and you showed that you ain't the kind who would ride over a poor little dog who was only trying to tell everybody that somebody was coming."

Wade frowned at the boy, who was obviously Tommy Grisham. He asked, "How is your dog?"

"He's all right . . . or he will be by the time we reach Oregon."

"That's good." Wade paused. "Thanks for your help."

Tommy shrugged. "I didn't like the looks of that posse, anyways."

Wade almost smiled as he tipped his hat. He turned back toward the rear of the train, his tendency to smile quickly fading.

* * *

Attempting to dismiss the howling that had begun echoing in her ears at almost the same moment Wade left her earlier that afternoon, Johanna was about to step out of the rapidly darkening shadows between wagons when she halted abruptly. Wade and she had returned to the wagon train with her repaired wagon just after noon. They had spent the rest of the day traveling. Wade had returned from his talk with McMullen a few hours earlier. He had taken back the reins of her wagon and had driven on in silence. He had avoided her questions about his talk with McMullen, turning quiet and thoughtful. He had remained that way when they stopped for the evening and she had cooked another mediocre meal. He had continued to avoid her questions while they had eaten . . . and her concern had grown.

That same concern was still on her mind when she spotted two women conversing conspiratorially a little distance away. Something about their manner caught her attention as she stood unseen by them and paused to listen.

The older woman leaned forward, obviously upset as she exclaimed, "But he's a wanted man! There's no way to tell whether he's guilty or innocent. I just don't want to put my family at risk by being in the company of a man who might have killed somebody."

"I hear he's only going to stay with the wagon train for a few more days."

"That may be so, but I don't feel safe no more." The older woman's voice dropped a tone lower.

"None of us are safe. He's wanted for murdering a young woman, you know."

"No!"

"They found that poor young thing dead, and her blood was all over him. My Asa says he heard one of the men in the posse say that Bartlett had—"

The conversation between the two women stopped abruptly when their husbands rounded the wagon with annoyed expressions. Their conversation died after a few sharp words from the older man, and they walked briskly back toward their wagons—but Johanna could not seem to make herself move.

He's wanted for murdering a young woman, you know. Her blood was all over him.

Johanna took a halting breath. Wade suspected of being a murderer? How could anyone believe that? He had saved her from Riggs' vicious attacks twice. He had risked his life for her when the bear attacked; and after all the strange things that had happened, he had listened patiently to her halting explanations when she was truly uncertain if she was making any sense at all. Through it all, his steady gaze had comforted her in a way she had never experienced before. It had said wordlessly that he *believed* her. It had said wordlessly everything . . . *everything* she had ever wanted to hear.

She needed to tell him that. She needed to tell him about the renewed howling, too. She had originally been baffled by the sound, but she knew what it meant now. The danger to her was real—because Wade was threatened.

Suddenly off at a run, her mind racing, Johanna headed back to her wagon. Breathless and near panic, she spotted Wade saddling his mare at the rear of the bulky conveyance. He frowned when she reached his side and said simply, "I'm leaving, Johanna."

"No!"

Noting her breathlessness, he asked tightly, "What's wrong?"

"I need to talk to you."

He raised his chin with sudden insight. "So you heard about the posse."

Confirming his statement, she said, "I don't care what the men in that posse said. I know you're innocent."

"How do you know that?" His lips a hard line, Wade replied, "What makes you so sure, Johanna? You only met me a few days ago, and you disliked me then. You hardly know me."

"I know you."

"No, you don't."

"I know that you respect women because you've always respected me. You proved to me that you always do what you think is right, no matter the risk to yourself . . . that you're honest and truthful, even if it means saying things a person doesn't want to hear. I know you would never hurt anyone who didn't threaten you. I know that because . . . because . . ."

A sudden catch in her voice halted her litany, and Johanna closed her eyes. She felt Wade's arms slip around her as he clutched her close. She opened her eyes again when he whispered against her hair, "Johanna, please, don't say anything else. You've only seen the best of me."

"If I've only seen the best of you, it's because that's what we bring out in each other," Johanna began earnestly. "I won't let you—"

Interrupted by the sound of running footsteps, Johanna stepped back from Wade's arms to see Tommy appear breathlessly around the side of the wagon. His eyes wide, the boy gulped, "They're here. The posse came back! They couldn't find a trail, and that Pierce fella says he wants to search the wagon train."

Wade's arms dropped back to his sides as he whispered, "I can't let the posse know I was here."

"I'm going with you," Johanna exclaimed.

"No."

"I won't let you leave here without me!" she insisted. "Whatever I originally joined this train to do, I know now that you're somehow a part of it—just as I know that danger for you somehow means danger for me, too."

"I don't want you to get involved in my problems."

"I'm already involved."

"I can't take a chance on the posse finding us together."

The sound of footsteps beside the wagon interrupted their exchange. Hardly aware that his hand had reached for his gun, Wade turned as Mc-Mullen appeared around the side of the wagon, a saddled horse in tow. Handing him the reins, the wagon master said in a rasping whisper, "You'd better leave right now. The posse has already started searching the train against everyone's protests, but you can slip off into the shadows without being seen back here if you act fast."

"I'm going with you!"

Wade turned toward Johanna with a frown.

"You don't have time to argue, Wade," McMullen said urgently.

Looking back at him, Wade replied, "Johanna's wagon . . . they'll know she's missing if it's abandoned."

"Tommy and I will take care of that. You can come back when you feel it's safe. You can decide what to do then."

Wade glanced down at Johanna as she repeated, "I won't let you leave without me."

Finally nodding, Wade boosted her up onto McMullen's horse without a word, and then mounted his mare. Glancing at her with a look that Johanna was certain she would never forget, he signaled her to follow him. Then he tipped his hat at the two figures standing silently behind them before they slipped off into the darkness.

The shadows closed in around them as Johanna and Wade lay silently on their bedrolls in the wooded copse. After leaving the wagon train a few hours earlier, they had ridden quietly for an inestimable time. They had put a good distance between themselves and the wagon train before they had stopped to conceal themselves in an elevated grove where they were able to view anyone approaching. Exhausted, they had stretched out in their bedrolls and tried to sleep.

The night was cold, and in the absence of a fire, Johanna shivered. Wade drew her closer to share his warmth. He hadn't wanted to take her with him. He didn't want her to risk becoming involved in the situation that threatened him. He didn't want her to see the inevitable result if the posse happened to catch up with them; but, most of all, he had no desire to test the constraints of his desire for her when they were isolated and alone. Yet, there they were, lying side-by-side in the semidarkness . . . and she was in his arms.

The warmth of her . . . the scent of her. Wade drew her closer. The steady drone of night sounds filled the silence between them. "You shouldn't be here," Wade murmured.

"Yes, I should." Her beautiful face lit by a shaft of moonlight, Johanna looked up at him as she said, "It took me a while to realize it, but I'm where I should be right now."

His heart began a slow pounding, and Wade struggled to retain an emotional distance as he replied, "You reacted to the excitement of the moment without thinking. I didn't have time to reason with you, but that doesn't mean I agree with you. I'm not the right man for you. I'm just a drifter. I'm the man that posse believes murdered a woman, and it's dangerous for you to be with me right now."

"It would've been more dangerous if I wasn't here."

"For me or for you?"

Johanna paused. "I can't honestly answer that question. All I know is that I feel safe . . . warm . . . comfortable for both our sakes now that I'm here with you . . . and the howling has finally stopped."

"The howling."

Uncertain whether she should mention the howling only she could hear, Johanna whispered, "It . . . it started again intermittently when you went to talk to McMullen. The howls grew more constant until they became a din by the time Tommy showed up to warn you that the posse had returned. I don't claim to understand it all, or to know why it's happening. I just know it tells me that I need to be here now . . . with you, for both our sakes."

"For both our sakes . . ." Wade swallowed against the thick lump in his throat.

"But I don't want you to misunderstand." Johanna continued with pain tinging her tone, "I don't want you to think that I . . . that we . . . that my being here with you means a commitment to anything. I mean . . ."

Johanna was struggling desperately for words when Wade interrupted softly to say, "You mean that you don't want me to think you're taking anything for granted."

Johanna nodded.

"You're trying to say that I can ignore the fact that you're here if I want to, that I can just go to sleep." Hesitating briefly, Wade continued more softly than before, "But what if I don't want to, Johanna? What then? What if I want to hold you in my arms and make love to you? What if I want to make sure that you belong to me in the most intimate of ways? What if I told you that I've been fighting those feelings for you from the first second I saw you bathing in the stream?"

"You were watching me, too?"

"I couldn't take my eyes off you."

"But when Riggs—"

"I'm not Riggs, Johanna," Wade interrupted harshly. Noting that Johanna swallowed tightly at his response, he continued more softly, "That's why I'm telling you that I'm taking nothing for granted, either. But I need to warn you, I can't make any guarantees."

"I've never believed in guarantees."

"I need to be sure."

"To be sure that I want you to love me?" Suddenly more certain of her response than she had ever realized she could be, Johanna whispered in return, "The answer is yes, if that's what you're waiting for. I want you to love me because I know it's right. I want—"

Her response was cut short as Wade's mouth closed hungrily over hers. He clutched her tight against him and the beauty of the moment stole her breath. She felt his lips separate hers and she exhulted in the kiss. She slid her arms around his neck as he groaned softly with the same wonder that tingled through her.

His kisses covered her eyelids, her cheeks, the line of her jaw, returning to her mouth over and over again as his passion mounted. His searching lips slipped lower with a driving hunger, and Johanna welcomed their touch. Uncertain how or when her warm, full breasts were bared to the night air, she felt his mouth against the roseate crests, and she clasped him closer to deepen his loving attention.

The caresses grew wilder. Her emotion soared. She held her breath as his lips followed a steady, downward course against her pale skin toward the virginal delta he sought. She felt his tongue enter the delicate slit, and she gasped. The sound spurred him on, and she felt his strokes surge more urgently, more deeply, sending her into a realm of unimagined bliss.

She lost herself in the wonder rapidly overtaking her. It transported her higher, lifting her on omnipotent wings to a realm where she was suddenly abandoned to the throbbing rapture that shuddered through her with an abrupt, overwhelming thrill. A captive of the pulsing ecstasy, Johanna's slender body spilled sweet homage to the emotion that Wade had evoked.

Unable to speak when she was still at last, Johanna looked at Wade to see the same wonder reflected in his gaze. Bringing the full length of his powerful, naked form flush against hers, he whispered, "There's more, Johanna . . . so much more."

Hard and firm, he paused only briefly before entering her swiftly. He filled her, then grew still, his breathing clipped. Looking down at her, appearing suddenly uncertain, he said hoarsely, "I need to tell you . . . it's not too late to stop now, if that's what you want."

"If that's what I want . . ."

"I need to hear you say the words now, Johanna."

"The words?" Johanna gasped, her fluttering gaze scrutinizing his passion-filled countenance. "The words, I want you?" Pausing to swallow against the thickness in her throat, she said, "My answer is . . . yes, I want you, Wade. I need—"

Further response was halted by her gasp as Wade plunged deep inside her. Johanna clung to him. She clasped him closer. The rhythm of love brought them swiftly to a brink of passion where they paused again briefly, before toppling together to the ultimate reward.

Long moments later, Johanna felt Wade move. She opened her eyes to see him looking down at her soberly before his mouth again covered hers.

The beauty began once more.

It lasted long into the night.

Awakening later, Johanna moved in the warm cocoon of Wade's sleeping embrace. She heard the sound of his steady breathing and it comforted her. She looked up at the stars visible through the canopy of trees overhead, then down at the bedroll cover he had pulled up over them to seal out the chill of the night. She had never felt safer . . . warmer . . .

A sound in the shadowed foliage nearby turned her abruptly toward it. She strained her gaze into the darkness, a jolt shaking her when she distinguished the unexpected outline of a furry form crouched a few yards away. She gasped when it turned to look directly at her, its yellow eyes glinting through the darkness for a long moment before it turned and slunk away into obscurity.

Johanna went still as Wade clutched her closer in his sleep. Then she closed her eyes and pressed herself into his warmth . . . content with the feeling that all was as it should be.

Chapter Five

"He must have made a mistake!"

The news that Alexander Pittman had presented to her with such pride had not been what Letty had expected. The youthful lawyer whom she had charged with conducting the search for her daughters had notified her that Johanna had been located and the Pinkerton agent assigned to her expected to accomplish his mission before the week was out.

Letty had been jubilant. She had immediately invited Alexander to her apartment so he might give her further information. She had waited with bated breath for his arrival and had welcomed him warmly—perhaps a little too warmly, considering Alexander's flush and consequent attentiveness.

Letty asked stiffly, "You're telling me that Larry Worth reported that my daughter had joined a *wagon train* heading for the Oregon territory?"

She repeated, "He must have made a mistake. My daughter would not employ such a primitive means of travel. Nor would she have any interest in farmland—much less in a place as distant as the Oregon territory."

"I assure you that it's true." Concern creasing his youthful countenance, Alexander continued, "Agent Worth found the information hard to believe, too, but he checked his facts. The truth is" Alexander leaned toward her. He covered her clasped hands with his as he said huskily, "Not unlike her mother, Johanna is a beautiful young woman. There aren't many who have seen her who could possibly forget her."

"Alexander . . ." Her exasperation barely concealed, Letty managed, "There are many beautiful women in this country."

"Not as beautiful as you are—or your daughter."

Letty slid her hands out from under Alexander's. She drew back to say, "I'm sorry, I can't believe that Mr. Worth is following the right young woman. My daughter is educated. She left New York City with the intention of taking her place in the world. Her interests are vast. An isolated farm in the wilderness would not be her idea of a promising future. She wouldn't know how to handle that situation in any way."

"Letty, let me assure you that Larry Worth is one of Robert Pinkerton's best detectives. He wouldn't have wired information he wasn't sure of."

Frustrated, Letty stood up. Alexander stood beside her as she insisted, "Let *me* assure *you*, Alexander, he is wrong. My daughter cannot be heading for Oregon. She wouldn't . . . she couldn't . . . she would become ill with so little to stimulate her mind. She would deteriorate—"

Tears suddenly choking off further comment, Letty turned away from Alexander in distress, only to feel him surround her in a comforting embrace. Almost as distressed as she, he whispered, "Please don't cry, Letty. I can understand your consternation, but giving in to your emotions isn't the answer." Anxious perspiration dotted Alexander's brow and upper lip as he tilted up her face to say earnestly, "You know how important it is to me to see that your every wish is granted, most especially in a matter so close to your heart. I'll do anything you suggest to clarify the situation for you. If you want me to wire Mr. Worth to check his facts again, I will, but please don't cry."

Suddenly aware that Alexander's lips were close to hers, and that his consolation was quickly turning into more, Letty took a determined step backward. She liked Alexander. She respected his intelligence, and she knew his empathy was sincere. He would make some woman a good husband someday, but he was a child . . . no older than her daughters. He was presently smitten with her, but she had no illusions. When gray began sprinkling her glorious black hair, when wrinkles began marking her creamy complexion, and when her slender figure began rounding, he would realize that the years separating them meant far more than he had understood. She had enjoyed a mild flirtation with him, and she had taken pleasure in the fact that he dropped everything to please her, but she wanted nothing more from him.

Her determination to make that fact known was cut off by a male voice questioning harshly, "Am I interrupting?"

Alexander dropped his arms and stepped back, allowing Letty full view of Peter Klein's stiff expression. Flustered, Millie appeared behind Peter to say apologetically, "I'm sorry, Miss Letty. Mr. Klein pushed right past me."

Dismissing her maid's explanation with a wave of her hand, Letty turned toward Peter. Her expression was as stiff as his when she said, "As you can see, you *have* interrupted us, Peter. I thought I had made it clear that I couldn't see you. Did you not understand?"

Peter responded, "I understand, perhaps far better than you realize."

"I don't think you do." Alexander's voice was cold. "So I'll express Miss Wolf's sentiments more clearly for you. She's busy. She wants you to leave."

"I don't believe I addressed you, Mr. Pittman," Peter returned frigidly.

"Miss Wolf is my client. I represent her in all matters. She wants you to leave."

"I can speak for myself right now, Alexander," Letty put in, reprimanding the younger man softly. Then she turned back toward Peter. "Please leave. I have business to conduct with my attorney."

"I've seen the business you're conducting and I—"

"That's enough!" Turning toward the foyer, Letty called out, "Millie, come in here, please. I would like you to show Mr. Klein out."

Appearing in the doorway almost as if she had awaited Letty's call, Millie said flatly, "This way, Mr. Klein."

"I'm not leaving yet."

"Yes, you are." Letty's response was unrelenting.

Peter took a breath, his expression suddenly changing to one of regret as he said, "Not until you've given me a chance to apologize. I've overstepped myself again, a habit that has become embarrassingly frequent of late. I'm sorry. I hope you won't hold these few moments of indiscretion against me."

"Please leave, Peter."

"Letty . . ."

"You heard Miss Wolf, Mr. Klein." Alexander's face was flushed, his temper barely controlled as he said again, "She wants you to leave . . . now. If you don't accommodate her, I'll be happy to help you."

"Mr. Klein will leave of his own accord, won't you, Peter?"

"Of course." Barely maintaining his smile, Peter repeated, "Please forgive the intrusion."

Turning on his heel, Peter did not wait for a response as he walked out of the room. Pausing only for the sound of the door closing behind him, Letty turned back to Alexander and said, "I appreciate your efforts on my part, Alexander, but I'm quite capable of handling these matters myself."

"The man was incorrigible! He acted as if he had the right to be jealous, and I know that isn't true."

"That's right, it isn't."

His stance rigid, Alexander added, "If you like, I'll have a man stationed at your door so you won't be bothered by the attentions of *gentlemen* like Mr. Klein anymore."

"As I said, I can handle these matters myself." Her expression softening, Letty said more gently, "But I would appreciate it if you would have Mr. Worth reconfirm his claim that he has found my daughter."

"Of course, Letty."

Dismissing Peter's unexpected arrival as if it had never happened, she added, "I hope you understand, Alexander. I just need to be sure that my daughter hasn't . . . strayed too far from her goals because of me."

"Of course, but whatever Mr. Worth replies to your inquiry, you mustn't blame yourself. Any young woman would be glad to have a mother like you."

Letty did not reply.

"Letty . . ."

"If you would contact Mr. Worth again, I would appreciate it, Alexander."

"Of course."

Extending her hand, Letty said softly, "Good-bye for now. Thank you for your help."

"Letty . . ."

"You will let me know what Mr. Worth replies to your inquiry as soon as you are able, won't you?"

"Of course."

Raising her voice in summons again, Letty called out, "Millie, Mr. Pittman is leaving now if you will escort him to the door."

Alexander took a step backward as Millie entered the room. He said, "You may depend on me, Letty."

"I know I can, Alexander."

Letty did not move when Alexander took her hand unexpectedly and raised it to his lips. She turned away as soon as his stalwart figure had cleared the doorway, her expression going cold.

Damn that Peter Klein! The scene he had made was the final straw. He had dug his own grave.

Johanna's face flashed before Letty's mind at that moment, and her expression twisted into sorrow. Dear Johanna . . . what had she done to her daughter . . . and where was Johanna now?

Johanna adjusted the bodice of her dress. She smiled as Wade's arms slid around her from behind. She leaned back against him, breathing deeply of the fresh scents of the wooded glade as the sun ascended into the clear morning sky. She turned toward him, her smile slowly fading as she asked, "Do you think we should go back to the wagon train now?"

"We don't have any choice as far as I'm concerned. You need to claim your wagon if you expect to accomplish what you came out here to do."

"But what if the posse is waiting for you?" Johanna inched closer. "I don't want to go back if it's dangerous for you."

"You don't?" Wade traced the shape of her lips with his tongue and then kissed her lingeringly. She felt the heavy pounding of his heart echoing her own as he whispered, "Why? Because you can't bear to be without me?"

Johanna nodded as emotion began taking hold of her senses.

"Or is it because you feel safe with me?"

"A little of both, I suppose."

Wade went unexpectedly still. "I suppose I'll always be able to rely on your honesty."

"Is that wrong, Wade . . . feeling safe with you, I mean?" Her expression concerned, Johanna continued, "I started out from New York City on a journey into the wilderness that I had planned over a period of years. I knew what I wanted to do."

"Prospecting . . ."

"Prospecting . . . yes . . . but that wasn't the most important part of what I intended. I wanted to discover more about my father while I finished what he had started out to do before his life was ended so abruptly. I wanted to share a part of his life, even if I was years late in doing it. I wanted to know what he was thinking . . . what he was feeling. I wanted to feel closer to him."

Wade frowned. "I'm sorry. I know what it's like to lose your parents."

"You don't understand. I never knew my father.

He died before I was born. I only saw his picture once, and my mother would never speak of him."

"She wouldn't talk about him?"

"She was too busy with her own life to pay any real attention to my sisters and me. That's why we set out on our own as soon as we were able." Johanna unconsciously shrugged. "My mother settled whatever problems we caused her by putting us in separate schools. She took care of us financially and educated us well, and we had each other, in a way, but with three different fathers that we knew so little about, we each had different questions about the past."

"Three different fathers . . ."

"And three different mysteries. I started out on this trek to solve mine. I was determined that there wasn't any problem I couldn't handle. I still feel that way—to an extent—but somewhere along the line things got complicated, and I made a few mistakes."

"*You* made mistakes?"

"I admit it. I wasn't as worldly wise as I thought I was, but by the time I met you and was saddled with a covered wagon that I didn't know how to handle, a team of horses that frightened me, and a driver who wanted to molest me, I was determined not to make any more mistakes."

"That's where I came in."

"I thought you were another Riggs, but I was wrong again," Johanna said huskily. "You're everything that Riggs wasn't—but the howling began again."

"The howling . . ."

Johanna paused. "I know you don't always hear the warnings, but they seem to begin before each crisis. I didn't understand it when I was a child, and I don't understand it now. All I'm sure of is that the warnings tie us together somehow."

"Just what you needed, to be tied to a man being hunted by a posse for murder."

"No one has to tell me that you're innocent, Wade! I believe in you, just like you believe in me."

Wade paused before asking gruffly, "Is that the reason you let me make love to you, because you've started feeling safe with me and because that howling seems to tie us together? I need to tell you now, Johanna, none of that has anything to do with my reasons for wanting to make love to you."

"What were your reasons?"

"That's easy enough to answer. I wanted you, and now that you've been in my arms, I can't seem to get enough of you."

Flushing, Johanna whispered, "You make me feel safe, Wade. That's definitely a part of how I feel, but . . . I wanted you, too. I never knew what it was to really *want* a man until you; and right now all I can think about is how you make me feel."

"Me, too." Wade searched her face before adding in a voice deep with emotion, "The wagon train travels slowly, you know. We'll have no problem catching up with it, no matter when we start out. It might even be better if we wait a little longer before we leave, so there's less chance that the posse will still be in the vicinity."

Johanna's emotions soared as Wade's arms tightened around her. She whispered in return, "I suppose you're right."

"I know I am."

His mouth found hers for a lingering kiss and then Wade scooped Johanna up into his arms. Mutual longing took hold as he carried her toward the leafy bower behind them. Their hearts thudded in unison as he lay down beside her. Without another word, the loving began again.

Alexander Pittman looked at himself in his bedroom mirror. He scrutinized the tailoring of his dark, formal suit, the cut of his heavy blond hair, and his well-proportioned physique. Then he stared at his face. Admittedly, he wasn't exactly handsome, but his features were strong and intelligent, and his smile was genuine. He was younger than Letty by several years, but he had much to recommend him, including a brilliant future and a passion for her that knew no bounds.

The sun outside the window had already begun its descent toward the horizon, and Alexander was well aware that when darkness came, Letty's salon would be a beehive of activity. He could understand why that salon had maintained its popularity over the past several years. In a word, the reason was Letty. Not only was she beautiful— more beautiful than any woman he had ever known—she was also intelligent, successful, a woman of the world, and sensuous to a degree that left him panting.

Admittedly, he was in love with her.

Admittedly, he knew that his youth was a strike against him.

Admittedly, he realized he would have to work hard to win her over, but he had already decided that he would not give up. Letty had demonstrated that she was at least *attracted* to him. It was up to him to take that attraction a step further—and he had already decided that tonight would be the night. Letty had been attending all the soirees at her salon of late, due to the talk that often circulated about her. He would make this evening memorable for both of them.

With that thought in mind, Alexander checked his appearance again. Satisfied, he reached for his hat, walked into the hallway, and locked his apartment door behind him. The thought of Peter Klein brought a frown to his lips as he walked toward the stairs. He could understand the man's fascination with Letty, but he would not allow Letty to suffer the fellow's boorishness.

Alexander stepped out onto the street and took a deep breath. He had not been born into wealth and had overcome steep odds to become a partner at Wallace, Pittman and O'Brien at such a young age. He fully intended to overcome the odds again by becoming the man who would finally wed Letty Wolf. He would put no restrictions on her, except that she remain only his, and he would settle all differences with her daughters so Letty would be truly happy at last. They would live together blissfully. With a woman like Letty, he could expect no less.

The evening was bright and clear as Alexander began walking down the rapidly darkening street, and he breathed deeply again. He had a feeling that tonight would mean—

"Do you have a match, Mr. Pittman?"

Alexander turned with surprise toward the fellow who stepped out of a shadowed alleyway. He was small, wiry, and unclean, and Alexander asked, "Do I know you, sir?"

"No, and I don't expect you ever will."

Alexander gasped when the fellow struck his chest with a knife. Unable to speak, he looked down at the man's hand, bloody with proof of the unexpected attack. He glanced up into his attacker's face, a litany of questions flashing across his mind as the knife plunged again and again.

Alexander fell heavily to the ground, and the questions faded. Semiconscious, he did not hear his attacker's grunt of satisfaction or see him escape down the alleyway. His breathing increasingly labored, he was not certain when the meager light began fading. Only one question remained before the darkness closed in around him and his breathing finally ceased.

Why?

A knock sounded at Peter Klein's library door. Glancing up from the ledger where he was calculating figures impatiently, he frowned and muttered, "Enter."

His ancient servant stood nervously in the doorway. "Excuse me, Mr. Klein. A fellow came to the back door a few minutes ago. He insisted that I give you a message from him."

"A fellow? What did he want?"

"He was a rather small and untidy-looking individual. He was not a very desirable type and I would have dismissed him immediately, but he insisted I tell you that he had just delivered the flowers you ordered for your friend. I told him I didn't want to interrupt you, but he said you'd want to know that he had taken care of it."

"Oh." A smile flickered across Peter's lips. Standing, he adjusted the collar of his velvet smoking jacket before responding, "He's the man my florist uses to deliver orders. He doesn't look the type, but he's very dependable in some matters, and he obviously delivered the flowers I ordered for Miss Wolf earlier than expected. I'm glad he took care of it so quickly."

"He said you would be pleased."

"I am."

Waiting until his servant had pulled the library door closed behind him, Peter smiled more broadly. He walked to the window and stood staring out into the gaslit street. Alexander Pittman was dead. He had always known he could depend on anyone Mr. Charles recommended. Now that Pittman had been *handled*, he would no longer be an impediment to the future he had planned for Letty and himself.

His aristocratic features growing suddenly dark, Peter mumbled, "And that'll teach the arrogant bastard not to talk to me as he did, and not to aspire to a woman so far above him, either!"

Peter halted at that thought. A smile returned as he corrected it mentally. Actually, the point was moot. It was too late to teach Alexander Pittman anything.

"I want you to know that despite Alexander's unexpected demise, your affairs will be handled expeditiously and with the greatest care, Letty. We apologize for any inconvenience this dastardly affair has caused you."

Samuel Wallace's lined face drew into an attempted smile, but the unruly appearance of his thin, white hair, and the wrinkled condition of his normally impeccable attire was silent testimony to the long night that he had passed. He continued, "I will personally handle the legal papers and the activity that Alexander was overseeing regarding your daughters. You may rest assured that I will give the matter all the attention it deserves."

Seated across from Samuel Wallace in his darkly paneled office, Letty was stunned and silent. She had arrived a few minutes earlier, still unable to believe that she had been laughing and exchanging small talk at her salon the previous evening while Alexander lay alone and dying, struck by a madman's blade in the darkness.

A tear trailed out the corner of her eye, and Letty brushed it away. She had been informed of the attack on Alexander shortly after breakfast. She had quickly dressed and had come directly to Alexander's office, hoping desperately that it was all a mistake, that Alexander would meet her at the door, flushed with delight at seeing her, as was his usual custom.

Instead, the truth had been confirmed. Alexander was dead.

Letty replied thickly, "To be honest, Samuel, my legal affairs are not the first thing on my mind at this moment. Surely the madman who . . . who did this terrible thing is being actively hunted. Surely he will be made to pay for what he did."

The weary gentleman rounded his desk and took Letty's hand. Deep lines of sorrow marked his face. "Alexander was like a son to me. You may rest assured that I will do all in my power to see that his killer pays for the crime he committed. Other than that, I have nothing to tell you. Except I thank you. Alexander thought so highly of you. It is good to know that the sentiment was returned."

Letty was unable to reply for the tears that choked her throat. Her personal loss at Alexander's death was greater than she had imagined it could be, but it was just another in a long line of losses she had suffered. Suddenly desperate not to lose her daughters, too, she said, "Locating my daughters is extremely important to me. I need to find them . . . to be able to talk to them again.

Alexander understood that. I hope you understand my urgency, too."

"Of course, I do, Letty."

"I'll leave the matter in your hands then." About to leave, Letty turned back to add, "Alexander's death grieves me deeply, Samuel. He was a truly special young man. I will miss him terribly."

"My dear . . ."

Brushing away her tears again, aware that there was nothing left to say, Letty walked out of the office.

The sun was shining when she stepped up into her carriage. The sky was cloudless and the wind was mild. Brilliant shafts of sunlight glinted on small puddles of water from a nighttime shower as birds chattered noisily, fluttering in and out to bathe. Carriages moved briskly through the busy streets and pedestrians sauntered casually on their way to their destinations, chatting and totally unaffected by the tragedy of the night before.

A sob escaped Letty's lips as her carriage jolted into motion.

Yes, it was just another day.

The sun was past the meridian in a cloudless sky when Johanna and Wade rode cautiously into view of the wagon train. Strung out in a line that snaked across the grassland, the wagon train progressed slowly, without any sign of the posse that had descended upon it the previous evening.

"I don't see any sign of the posse, Wade."

Wade looked back at Johanna where she sat

astride McMullen's horse a few feet behind him. Her gaze was direct and intent as she awaited his reply . . . and she was breathtakingly beautiful. He remembered the scent, the taste, the silkiness of her smooth, white flesh under his lips, and his throat choked tight. He had kissed her with heartfelt longing. He had caressed her in the most intimate of ways. He had claimed her for his own over and again throughout the night and long morning past, but he could not seem to get his fill. She had returned kiss for kiss, caress for caress. She had gasped with need that matched his own. She had stirred in him a passion unbounded, and she had sighed with wonder when he sated it with his ardent ministrations. He wanted her. She had become a necessary part of him; and in a flash of insight, he knew she would always remain a part of him.

He loved her.

"Wade . . ."

He loved her, but she *needed* him.

Wade frowned at that thought. She was sincere in her reactions to him at present, but when the danger and the inexplicable howling ended, would she still want him?

"Wade?"

Frowning, Wade looked down at the wagon train again. From their vantage point, he was able to see for miles on the desolate plains. There was nothing threatening in sight.

"Wade . . ."

He replied tersely, "It's safe. Let's go."

When they rejoined the train, Johanna and Wade rode up to talk to McMullen. They listened as McMullen said flatly, "The men on the train aren't happy, Wade. They didn't like the way those fellas in the posse ransacked their wagons."

"Ransacked . . ."

"It was that Pierce fella who kept pushing the others. The sheriff didn't have much control. Pierce kept saying things like, he had promised the young woman's father that his daughter's killer would get what was coming to him. He said he wouldn't go home to Millborn unless it was taken care of."

"I know how he feels, but he's after the wrong man."

"That's what that sheriff tried to tell him, that he might be making a mistake, but Pierce wouldn't listen. He got all the others so riled up that they near to tore the wagon train apart trying to find some sign of you. When some of the men on the train tried to stop them, they pulled their guns."

Wade glanced back at the wagons behind him, frowning as he said, "I didn't mean for that to happen. I expect everybody will be wanting me to leave."

"That ain't necessary no more. The men in the train had an informal meeting after the posse left. They agreed that they didn't like the way the posse acted. They said it looked like those men were just looking for somebody to hang. They said they wasn't going to hand anybody over to a bunch like that."

Momentarily silent, Wade glanced at Johanna, and then back at McMullen. He asked, "And the outcome was . . . ?"

"They all agreed that you and Johanna could travel with us just as long as you like."

"What about Johanna's wagon? Were the men in the posse suspicious when they saw it had been abandoned?"

"Tommy's older brother was driving it, with Tommy pretending to sleep in back. Nobody from the posse asked any questions, and no one volunteered any answers."

Wade did not respond.

"But they'll be happy to turn the wagon over to you any time you want."

Johanna interjected unexpectedly, "How long until we reach the turnoff to Arizona?"

McMullen shrugged. "That depends."

Johanna did not reply, and Wade extended his hand as he said, "I can't offer you anything more than my thanks, McMullen, but I appreciate all you've done."

The older man's lip ticked as he said unexpectedly, "Well, like Tommy said, I didn't like the looks of that posse neither."

Johanna and Wade had only ridden a few yards back toward their wagon when Johanna said, "It looks like the posse was finally satisfied that you weren't here, and never had been."

"Maybe." Wade's reply was clipped. "Maybe not."

"What do you mean?"

Wade glanced at Johanna's concerned expression and said, "I never would've figured that posse would have followed me as long as it did, and now I can't figure that it'll give up that easy."

"It doesn't make much difference, anyway. We're going to be turning off soon. The posse won't even realize that one wagon is missing from the train. They won't follow us."

Us.

Choosing not to reply, Wade spurred his mount to a gallop.

"That's far enough! Put up your hands!"

Percy Smart grew still at the harsh command from the bushes to his left. He squinted against the setting sun in an attempt to make out the silhouette that stepped out.

"You heard me. Put up your hands!"

Cursing under his breath, Smart raised his hands. He didn't like this. He didn't like riding horseback in the wilderness. He didn't like the heat, the insects that gave him no relief, the fact that there was no shade on the grasslands they were traveling through, or the knowledge that when this miserable day and night was past, several more miserable days and nights remained before he could head back to the city where he belonged.

"Higher! I'm going to count to three. If you don't raise your hands higher than that—"

"All right, I heard you!"

Smart raised his hands higher as he strained to see the man who walked out into plain view. It didn't make much difference, though. He knew who the fellow was. It seemed Larry Worth was smarter than he looked.

"Why are you following me?"

Smart responded spontaneously, "What makes you think I was following you? This is a big country."

"Right, and it's too big for you to just happen to be going my way all the way from the city, especially since you made sure to stay just far enough behind me to stay out of view."

"I ain't following you." Thinking fast, Smart continued, "I heard about a wagon train heading for Oregon territory. I ain't had no luck where I was living, so I figured I'd see what the Oregon territory could do for me."

"You wanted to join a wagon train without a wagon. Is that what you're trying to make me believe?"

"I don't need no wagon. I figure there will be enough honest work to make me useful on that train, and I can bed down under someone's wagon. I got enough money to buy what I need when I get where the train is going."

Larry walked a few steps closer, and Smart could see him more clearly. All of a sudden, he didn't like what he saw. That barrel chest, that head of shaggy hair, and the overgrown mustache were misleading. The small eyes under those wild brown brows were sharp and intent, and it was suddenly apparent that the easygoing exterior Larry had allowed him to see was either a pose or—

"Get down from your horse."

"Why?"

"Just do what I say!"

Smart dismounted and stood silently as his mind raced.

"Take that gun out of your holster and throw it on the ground."

Smart did not hesitate to obey. He didn't like the heavy weapon he had assumed as part of his disguise. He much preferred the small gun he had hidden in his boot. He knew from experience that it was effective and accurate.

Aware that pretense would buy him more time, Smart said, "You ain't going to shoot me, are you? That wouldn't be exactly fair. I was figuring to start a new life on that wagon train."

Larry scrutinized his appearance before saying, "It don't look to me like you've had much experience with a hard day's work."

"What, because I'm skinny? I'm like a wire, tight and strong. Once I get with that wagon train, I'm going to prove to all them settlers that I'm a handy man to have around."

Larry said with a hint of menace, "You ain't convincing me, you know. Empty your pockets! I need to see what you got in there."

Smart mumbled aloud as he turned his pockets inside out, "I ain't got nothing in my pockets except a key chain my pa gave me, and a few coins."

"You said you had money to start off real good in Oregon territory."

"Yeah, well, my money's in my saddlebags." Smart widened his eyes effectively as he said, "Wait . . . you ain't going to rob me, are you?"

Smart could sense Larry's disgust mounting as he said, "Get that rope off your saddle and knot it around your ankles."

"Wait a minute!"

"I ain't been taken in by that story you handed me. You was following me and I know it."

"All right." Smart nodded. "I was following you."

"I knew it. Why?"

"You told that fella in the livery stable where you was headed when you asked him to fill your saddlebags with supplies and all. I heard you." Smart shrugged. "You're right, too, when you think I ain't got much experience out here in the Texas wilderness. I ain't afraid of hard work, like I said, but I wasn't too sure about catching up with that wagon train . . . so when you said you was heading for it, I figured I would follow."

"You could've said something to me. You could've ridden along with me."

"It was easy enough to see that you was heading out on your own and I didn't want to take a chance of being turned down. I figured it would be easier to just follow you."

Worth's eyes narrowed. "It would've been easier to be honest with me."

"I've tried doing things the easy way. It ain't never worked out for me."

"Where are you from?"

"Up north. I've been down here for a while, looking for the opportunities that a man's supposed to have in the Wild West."

"Opportunity don't come knocking, you know. You got to chase it."

Larry studied him a few minutes longer, and Smart held his breath. He released it with relief when Larry said, "Put your hands down."

Aware that his ruse was working, Smart nodded. "Thanks. My arms was getting tired." Smart rubbed his thigh and said, "I got shot in the leg a while back. I ain't never really been myself since. The pain goes from my thigh all the way down to my calf, and these boots ain't helping any. They—"

Sliding his hand down into his boot, Smart whipped his gun up and fired in a quick flash of movement that sent Larry stumbling backward onto the ground. He walked closer as Larry lay gasping for breath and said coldly, "So I guess you ain't so smart after all."

He fired again and watched as bloody circles rapidly widened on Larry's chest. About to fire a third time, he suddenly changed his mind and said, "No, I ain't going to waste any more bullets on you. You're already a dead man."

As if in confirmation of his statement, Larry's eyes slowly closed.

Smart added in afterthought, "Dobbs figured I might have to kill you if I wanted to get to that Higgins woman. I got to give him credit on that. He was right."

Taking a moment to release Larry's horse and to chase him off with a hoot and a holler, Smart mounted and tipped his hat as he said to the inert figure lying on the ground, "I guess I'm on my own now, but I'll find her. It shouldn't be too hard. There ain't many women who look like Johanna Higgins . . . or so they say."

Digging his heels into his mount's sides, Smart rode off without a backward glance.

The long day had ended, the wagons had circled, and Johanna had prepared to cook another of her mediocre offerings. She was unprepared, however, when a few of the women from the train sauntered over with portions from their evening meal to welcome her back.

It did not miss her notice that Wade said little, but ate heartily. Neither did it escape her attention that Wade began preparing his bedroll beside the fire. Uncertain, she approached him and waited for him to look up. The fine line of her brows knitting, she asked, "What are you doing?"

Slowly standing, Wade said, "I figured what happened between us might be different now that we are back at the train. I figured that maybe you—"

"Well, you figured wrong."

Wade took a step closer to say more softly, "Look, Johanna, you're not tied to anything we did. Our conversation with McMullen showed me that nothing has changed. I'm still wanted for murder, and you're still on your way to Arizona."

"I didn't think any of *that* had changed . . . but I

thought other things had changed . . . things between us." Johanna took a step closer. "I don't care that you're a wanted man, Wade. Everybody, including me, knows that you couldn't have killed that girl."

Wade replied, "Thank you for trusting me."

"About Arizona . . ."

Wade said flatly, "I can't go to Arizona. I have to go back to prove somehow that I didn't kill Mary. If I don't, my life will never be my own and the real killer will go free."

"Arizona is a different state, Wade. No one will know you there."

"The West is a smaller place than you think. Sooner or later, someone will turn me in."

"I won't let you think that way!"

"You can't change how I think, Johanna." Raising a hand to stroke back a golden wisp that clung to her cheek, he whispered, "You can't change how I feel, either, and I already told you how that is."

A slow trembling besetting her, Johanna replied, "Then . . . then why are you fixing your bedroll out here?"

Wade's gaze was intent on hers as he whispered, "I told you before and I meant what I said. I can't make any promises."

"And I told you I don't want any."

His breathing deepening, Wade whispered, "What *do* you want, then?"

"You."

"Johanna . . ."

"No promises . . . just what we feel."

"Johanna, I'm not asking—"

"You can leave the train anytime you want . . . anytime you need to. I'll stay behind, if that's what you want."

"That's not what I *want*."

Her glorious eyes suddenly brimming with tears, Johanna rasped, "What *do* you want, Wade?"

"You."

Johanna was unable to reply, and Wade continued determinedly, "But you heard what happened while we were gone. The posse tore this place up. That'll be the way it is wherever those fellas track me. I have to find a way to prove I'm not the man they're looking for."

"All right." Johanna took a shaky breath. "Whatever you need to do is all right with me."

Aware that Johanna was trembling, Wade suddenly swept her into his arms. He clutched her close and whispered with his lips against her hair, "I know what I *want* to do, and I know what I *need* to do. They're two different things."

Johanna mumbled against his chest, "I don't care about tomorrow right now. I only care about tonight."

His throat suddenly tight and his eyes burning, Wade looked down at Johanna for a few silent moments before he slid his arm around her and turned her toward her wagon. He waited only until she had climbed inside before following and taking her into his arms. He whispered as his mouth moved toward hers, "No promises, Johanna."

Johanna did not bother to reply as she raised her lips to his.

Enthusiastic conversation punctuated with laughter filled the room, lilting music rebounded to the scrape of dancing feet, and formally dressed servants circulated, making sure every glass was filled—the scene of yet another of Letty's successful soirees. Having managed to politely dismiss the entourage of the devoted who had showered her with compliments and clever repartee since her arrival, Letty made her way across the crowded floor. She barely maintained her smile. Alexander had been killed the previous night. If it had not been necessary that she attend the salon that evening, if she had not promised important clientele that she would casually introduce them to certain individuals who could further their projects, Letty would not have attended. It had taken all her energy to leave her bed, where she had spent the afternoon crying.

Dear Alexander. No one but a crazy person could have executed such a crime. Nothing but insanity could have caused such a senseless, undeserving death.

Shaking off another wave of sadness, Letty affixed a professional smile to her face. It would not do to show her pain in public. Her patrons would not understand. They worshipped her beauty and respected her intelligence. They delighted in her sensuous manner. They marveled at her seemingly endless youth, and they appreciated the salon she had established, where valuable contacts could be casually made or they would be able to wile away a pleasurable evening with those of their ilk. She knew, however, that there were some among those smiling faces that harbored resentment and silently considered her an interloper. She knew they would be only too happy to see her fall.

For that reason, she had made sure to appear at her best that evening in a gown of startling pink silk that lent elegance to her demeanor and color to her cheeks. The diamonds at her ears and throat, and the tiny fragments of precious stones that glittered haphazardly on the bodice of her gown and in the coils of her upswept hair, added a final touch of sophistication that could not be denied. She presented a beautiful and intelligent appearance and had flawlessly performed the introductions that she had promised. She had not failed to notice, however, that Peter Klein had entered the room a few minutes earlier. Having fulfilled the demands of her position for that evening, and not presently possessing the stamina to face Peter, Letty continued her hasty retreat toward the exit.

"Letty . . ."

Letty turned toward the familiar voice as James said, "Please accept my condolences at the loss of your solicitor. Alexander was a true gentleman. I know you depended on him and will miss him greatly."

Letty nodded, momentarily unable to respond.

"What's wrong, Letty?" James asked with concern.

"Nothing." Letty's thoughts ran wild as she attempted a smile. Alexander had loved her, and he was dead, like so many of the men who had loved her. Her liaisons in the past had not been particularly serious or long-lasting, but . . . but James had been different. She had no doubt that he had truly loved her. He claimed to love her still.

"Letty . . ."

James slipped his arm around her. He forced a smile that belied the urgency in his voice as he said, "You're pale. You need to sit down."

Unable to protest as James led her to a private room, she said as soon as James closed the door behind them, "You shouldn't be with me now, James. It . . . it's dangerous."

"Dangerous? What do you mean?"

"Alexander is dead, James. He loved me. You say you love me, too."

"You know I do. I always will."

"No, don't! Don't love me!" Letty took an unsteady backward step. "There's something about me . . . a curse . . . I don't know, but every man who loves me dies! I don't want to wake up one morning to learn that you were found dead on the street just like Alexander. I wouldn't be able to bear it!"

Standing opposite James, Letty heard a soft howling that seemed to confirm her fears. A tear streaked down her cheek as she added hysterically, "Danger, James . . . you're in danger when you come here."

"I'm not in danger, Letty."

"Yes, you are. Please listen to me. It happened before. I don't want it to happen again."

"What happened before?"

"I told you. Every man who ever loved me . . . truly loved me . . . died."

"You've had many men in your life, Letty."

"Casual affairs with men who treated love casually. I've preferred it that way so that when I decided it was over, it was over without regrets."

"Unlike me."

Letty pressed, "You have to leave, James. You have to forget you ever met me."

"That's foolishness, Letty. It's too late for that."

"No, it isn't. I want you to leave."

"I won't do that."

"Then you'll die! Like all the rest, you'll die!"

Letty turned her back on James, sobbing hysterically. Unable to help herself when he turned her around and took her into his embrace, she buried her face against his chest to spill her tears. She looked up when James whispered, "You need to go home, Letty. You need to rest."

"Yes, I do." Letty brushed away her tears. "Please call for my carriage."

"I'll take you home in mine."

"No."

"Letty, listen to me." Tilting her face up so that she looked directly into his eyes, James said softly, "You're hysterical. I can't send you home alone, and I can't trust you with anyone else in your present state."

"I'm fine."

"No, you're not."

Releasing her unexpectedly, James walked to the door and summoned a servant. He accepted her wrap from the fellow when he came back a few minutes later and slipped it around Letty's shoulders. He ushered her toward the door as he said, "My carriage is waiting. Let's go."

Struggling to regain her composure, Letty managed, "I won't leave here with you, James."

"No strings attached, Letty. I'll just take you home to rest."

"No, I—"

"Come on."

Suddenly too weak for further protest, Letty allowed James to usher her out the back entrance, where his carriage awaited them. Accepting his hand, she stepped up into the carriage and closed her eyes as James sat beside her and instructed the driver. She did not protest when he drew her close, deeply grateful when he said, "No strings, Letty."

Standing on the dimly lit street outside Letty's salon, Peter watched James' carriage pull away. He had seen James spirit Letty out of the salon and he had quietly followed them. He had heard James speak Letty's address to the driver. He had seen James take Letty into his arms. His stomach had clenched tight as the carriage disappeared from sight down the street.

Letty had been crying. He supposed Alexander

Pittman had meant more to her than he had realized, but he had not expected James to use the situation to his advantage.

Scowling, Peter nodded. He supposed he would have done the same if he had been in James' position. But Letty had already tired of James and had sent him away. She was upset now, but she would not remain in an emotional state long, and she would not renew her love affair with him. It was not her style to revisit old acquaintances of that nature.

Peter considered that thought a moment longer. No, Letty's alliance with James would be temporary—limited to a single night at most. He could bear that . . . but for one night only. If not—

The thought that followed in Peter's mind was automatic.

If not, he would take care of James, too.

Silence reigned in the wagon that had been filled with loving murmurs only a few minutes before. Still breathing heavily in the throes of afterglow, Johanna raised her face to the breathless kiss that Wade pressed to her lips. She heard him whisper hoarsely, "It would be so easy to go on from here . . . to forget everything but what we have between us."

"Why don't you, then, Wade?"

His strong body still pressed intimately to hers, his mouth lightly touching her lips, Wade whispered in return, "Because it wouldn't be fair to you."

"My life hasn't been exactly a model of fairness so far. At least this time I would have a say in what happens to me."

"And it wouldn't be fair to me."

"To you . . . ?"

Wade did not say that he would not be able to leave her once a commitment was made . . . that he would die before he would allow anyone to tear them apart, and that he knew in his heart she would suffer for his weakness. Instead he responded, "I'll go to Arizona with you, Johanna."

Johanna's responsive smile slowly faded as he continued solemnly, "I'll make sure you get settled there, and that you're on your way to accomplishing what you set out to do, but then I'm going to leave."

"No!"

"It can't be any other way."

"Yes, but—"

Wade swallowed her protest with his kiss. When he drew his mouth from hers, he whispered, "No other way."

Her eyes bright with unshed tears, Johanna remained momentarily silent before she slid her arms around Wade's neck and said, "That's tomorrow, Wade . . . many tomorrows away. This is tonight, and tonight is still ours."

A shaft of silver moonlight penetrated the semidarkness as Wade repeated solemnly, "Ours."

Tender murmurs followed, filling the wagon once more.

CHAPTER SIX

"Is something wrong, Aunt Letty?"

Mason sat at a table across from Letty in Adolfo's Café with an expression of feigned concern. One of the city's premier restaurants, a haunt of the rich and famous, where people came to see and be seen, Adolfo's had a reputation to uphold. That reputation was supported by Letty's patronage, and it was obvious that Adolfo's treated her accordingly. She had been given a prominent table amid New York's social elite. It did not miss his notice that she was completely at home among the crystal chandeliers, flowers, silver, and sparkling dinnerware that graced the flawless scene. Mason inwardly scowled at the thought that her access to such luxury had come at the expense of many men like his uncle, whom she had manipulated to her advantage.

The preferential seating was not really necessary,

because no one could miss seeing Miss Letty Wolf wherever she sat. She was dressed in a conservative brown silk gown that enhanced her petite frame. The faint circles under her eyes imparted to her gaze an appealing, almost haunted look, and the hollowness to her cheeks was silent testimony to difficulties she had not yet declared. Still, she was without a doubt the most beautiful woman in the room. Silently analyzing her appearance, he supposed her apparent delicacy expanded the power of her dark-eyed gaze, while the conservative color of the gown added an aura of sobriety without distracting from her femininity. It was a ploy he was certain she had employed many times with his extremely susceptible uncle before seducing him.

Gratified that her ploys had no chance of deceiving him, Mason summoned a waiter so they could order. He waited only until they were alone at the table once more before covering Letty's small hand briefly with his own. "I received your message to meet you here for lunch, but I admit that I was disturbed. I know you don't commonly venture out until later in the day."

"You're right, of course," Letty interrupted with a forced smile. "That is one of my indulgences, but I had no desire to sleep this morning. Nothing is especially wrong. I . . . I just needed to talk to you, to *family* that I know has my daughters' best interests at heart."

"I am pleased to be considered your family, Aunt Letty, but why did you want to talk to me here?" Mason glanced around him as the tables nearby rapidly filled and the sound of conversation heightened. "You know I'd be happy to come to your apartment to talk to you privately anytime you need me."

"I didn't want to make the conversation too dreary."

"You never do that, Aunt Letty."

"Oh, yes, I'm sure I do. For that reason I chose to meet you here so we may enjoy a comfortable lunch while we speak." Letty paused, and then added, "If I am to be completely honest, this outing is also for my benefit. It helps me to maintain a certain decorum that is expected of me. I do not wish to fall prey to feelings that seem to have overwhelmed me lately."

"Of course, whatever best serves your needs; but however you feel, I must say that your worries are not reflected adversely on your countenance. You are looking particularly lovely today. You actually succeed in looking more beautiful each time I see you."

"Mason, you are too kind." Letty forced a smile and then said, "There is a situation—"

Mason was momentarily alarmed as she paused. Could Letty possibly have summoned him to the posh café to tell him politely that because of circumstances beyond her control, he was out of her will permanently? He needed that money! He was planning on it! He had already taken harsh steps to see his plans implemented, and had gone as far as discussing with certain parties the necessity of his aunt's demise in order to follow through. It was too late now to change things. If she changed her mind again, the situation would become immensely complicated for him.

"First of all, I've received news about Johanna."

Mason responded with faux enthusiasm, "That's wonderful, Aunt Letty!"

"Not so wonderful, I'm afraid. Larry Worth, the Pinkerton hired to locate my daughter, has discovered that she's joined a wagon train headed for Oregon territory."

"What?"

"I know. I couldn't believe it, either. My attorney assured me that Mr. Worth is an experienced Pinkerton, that he was certain of his information, and that he intended to conclude his assignment shortly."

"I find that report hard to believe."

"As did I. I told my attorney exactly that, and he promised to check into it for me, to make certain that the Pinkerton had found the right Johanna Higgins."

"That was wise of you. I'm sure your attorney will take care of it."

"My attorney's name was Alexander Pittman. He was attacked and killed two nights ago."

"Oh, yes, I heard about that. His untimely death was the talk of the town. I'm so sorry, Aunt Letty. It slipped my mind that he was your solicitor."

"I have been informed by Samuel Wallace of Wallace, Pittman and O'Brien that he will personally take over my case and follow through. I know I can depend on him in that matter. But not only was Alexander my solicitor, he was also my . . . friend. His death was a great shock to me. I'm afraid I have not handled it well."

"I'm so sorry." Mason struggled to retain his patience as he added, "But you seem to be in control of the situation now. How can I help you?"

"It's just that . . . well . . . I'm concerned for James Ferguson."

"For James Ferguson?"

"He is a former . . . intimate friend." Letty took a shuddering breath and said, "I'm sure you're aware that I've allowed a few intimate friends into my life since dear Archibald died."

"Of course, Aunt Letty. Life goes on, and you're a beautiful young woman."

"I fear for James' life."

"What? Why?"

"Because . . . because our liaison is over and James refuses to put the past behind him as I have done."

"In other words, he still wants you."

"Yes."

"If he has been causing you a problem, I can take legal action against him."

"No! Please, no, Mason. It's just that now that Alexander has been killed, I'm afraid James will suffer the same fate."

Mason was momentarily silent before offering, "I don't understand. Why would you think that?"

"Because it has happened before. I've had warnings that it may happen again."

"Warnings? Someone has threatened you?"

"No, warnings that you wouldn't understand . . . warnings that won't quit . . . warnings that come in the middle of the night and that I'm afraid to ignore."

"Dreams?"

"No, not dreams."

Confused, Mason looked at Letty. Could it be that her mind was slipping? If so, he would need to take immediate legal action to protect his interests.

"I'm not crazy, if that's what you're thinking, Mason." Letty gave a nervous laugh. "I just wanted to tell you, or rather to ask you if you would hire someone to look after James for me, just for a while, until I feel it's safe again."

"Someone to look after James? Do you think that's necessary?"

"Yes, I do."

Hesitating, Mason replied, "I suppose I could, but are you sure? I mean, won't Ferguson object?"

"I don't want him to know about it."

"Oh."

"This would be just between you and me. A secret. I know you're good at keeping family secrets."

Mason doubted that she knew how complex his secrets were.

"You've kept silent about my inglorious past and you've accepted me despite all of it."

Stunned, Mason said, "How did you know I was cognizant of your past?"

"Your uncle kept nothing from me."

"Oh."

"Will you do it, Mason?" Letty's dark eyes implored him. "I need to have this arrangement remain a secret between you, me, and the detective agency you'll hire to take care of it."

"Of course, Aunt Letty."

"Just present a bill to me each month and I'll pay it gratefully, with no questions asked."

"Of course, if you're sure that's what you want."

"I'm sure. Thank you, Mason. I knew I could depend on you."

Letty took another breath, and then smiled. The brilliance of her expression took Mason aback momentarily. It occurred to him that her smile was probably a weapon that she had learned to use well.

Letty added, "We can eat now. It'll be a celebration for me, the alleviation of some of my fears. Thank you so much for that."

"Don't thank me, Aunt Letty. It's my pleasure to do this for you. It makes me feel warm to know that you trust me with something so close to your heart."

Mason waited until the waiter put salads in front of them. He then picked up his fork and smiled an equally practiced smile into Letty's eyes.

After bidding Letty adieu a brief time later, Mason turned to begin walking briskly toward his office. He barely restrained a grin. The woman was crazy! Warnings . . . fears . . . pleading and finally gratitude . . . well, she had come to the right man. She wanted him to find a detective who would watch out for James Ferguson? He had seen Ferguson on countless occasions. The fellow was as tall, hearty, and as strong a man as he had ever seen. No one would dare to attempt to take advantage of him. Ferguson would be the last person who would need protection . . . from anyone!

Yet James Ferguson had one weakness—his love for dear Aunt Letty. The fool! He had been taken in by the wiles of a woman whose practiced deceptions were finally beginning to hang heavily on her conscience.

Would he hire someone to "protect" James Ferguson? No, of course not; but he would willingly supply his dear Aunt Letty with a trumped-up bill and a monthly report on suitable letterhead for the service. Of course, she would pay the sizable sum directly to him without question. He would enjoy the additional income, and he would make sure that the amounts were large enough that Mr. Charles would happily accept them in partial payment of his gambling debts.

Mason's smile faded as he straightened up his well-maintained frame. As for Larry Worth's telegram that he had finally located his dear cousin Johanna, all he had to say was—really? She had joined a wagon train heading for Oregon territory? That was unlikely, but he was sure Dobbs' man would clear it all up and handle the situation appropriately.

Mason checked his pocket watch. It was time to get back to his office. He needed to sign the documents that his clerks had spent the morning working up for his clients.

His foolish clients. Well, he would be wealthy soon, and they would be a part of his past.

Johanna's thigh was pressed tightly to his as she sat beside him on the hard wagon seat, but Wade knew instinctively that she no longer resented the pressure.

Wade glanced beside him and his heart flip-flopped in his chest. Johanna was staring forward, her mind obviously a million miles from the landscape they were passing through. He wondered if she was recalling the past night when he had lain beside her in her covered wagon. As for himself, he couldn't seem to stop thinking about it.

His gaze flicking only occasionally toward the wagon in front of them, Wade continued looking at Johanna. He expected that he would never tire of looking at her. The truth was that he had never seen a more beautiful woman. Gold hair—no, it was almost platinum. It had glittered like that precious metal as it spilled over her shoulders in the semidarkness of the wagon. It occurred to him that her smile was just as bright. As were her eyes, her silver, glowing gaze ringed by long, dark eyelashes—eyes that melted him with a glance. He had touched and smoothed the sweet symmetry of her profile and her incredibly flawless skin. He had tasted every part of her. He had breathed in her scent, and had held her tight against him, never wanting to let her go.

He wanted her.

He loved her.

But as a wanted man, his possession of her could only be temporary.

Johanna's stare became a frown when she turned abruptly toward him. He saw the fear in her eyes as she whispered unexpectedly, "Did you hear that?"

"Did I hear what?"

Johanna scanned the terrain surrounding them, hoping she was wrong. She swallowed, and then looked back at Wade, her heart pounding.

"Did I hear what, Johanna?"

She responded simply, "The howling. It's started again." She gripped Wade's arm and looked up at him. "I thought . . . I was hoping that it was over."

"What was over?"

"The danger." Johanna released his arm and clasped her hands tightly in her lap. "Maybe you shouldn't take me to Arizona. Maybe you should just get away from me as fast as you can. I can handle the horses."

"Johanna . . ."

"Wade, something is wrong, and I don't want anything to happen to you."

"You don't want anything to happen to me any more than I want anything to happen to you."

"This is my problem, Wade. Whatever the howling is . . ." Johanna covered her ears briefly as the sound persisted. Turning back toward him, she said, "It won't stop. Something's wrong, and I don't know what it is."

"If we didn't have to keep up with the train, I'd prove to you right now that you don't have any reason for fear when I'm beside you." Wade frowned as he added, "But since that isn't possible, just hold on to me so you can feel confident that I'll take care of you."

"No."

"What?"

"I said no, Wade. I won't do that to you." Looking up at him with a gaze that pleaded for understanding, Johanna said, "The posse is gone. Any danger you might have suffered is gone also. It's me . . . whatever new danger this is, it's following me, and I don't want you to be a part of it."

"You're imagining things, Johanna."

"Just like I was imagining things when the horses bolted and we were stuck with a broken wheel completely hidden from view when the posse first visited the wagon train? Just like there wasn't any danger when that bear appeared?"

With no response to her questions, Wade said, "It all worked out well enough."

"The howls were a warning. The wolf's appearance is something I can't explain, but—" A tear spilled down her cheek and Johanna brushed it away. She said harshly, "I want you to go, Wade. The wagon train will reach the turnoff for Arizona in a week or so. I'll leave the train then, and find my way to where I want to go. In the meantime, you can escape."

"I don't want to escape."

"I don't want you to stay here! It's dangerous!"

"For you or for me?"

Johanna did not respond.

"Johanna . . ."

"I don't really know."

Wade said more softly, "Then we'll stay together until we figure it out."

"No."

"Yes. I'm not going anywhere."

"But—"

"I'm not going anywhere."

Swallowing tightly, Johanna reached up abruptly and drew Wade's mouth down to hers. Her kiss was long and deep. She was breathing heavily when she drew back. Wade was breathing heavily, too.

"That was my way of saying thank you." Johanna took another breath as she said, "All right, you can stay for a while, but if the howls increase—"

"I'm staying."

Johanna whispered shakily, "I love you, Wade."

There, she had said it, the words that had whirled in her mind, begging to be said as she had lain in Wade's arms.

But Wade did not respond.

Johanna's heart plummeted. She took a breath and said, "It's all right, you know. You don't have to say anything. No promises."

"There's only one promise—that I love you, too." His voice a hoarse whisper, Wade added, "But you deserve better than a man who's wanted for murder, Johanna."

"And you deserve better than a woman who's haunted by howls that forecast danger, and who experiences strange happenings she can't explain."

"I was there, too, remember?"

"I remember."

"So you don't have to worry about explaining the unexplainable."

Johanna was unable to respond.

When he spoke again, Wade whispered, "We're going to stop for the night in a little while. I'll prove to you then how much I love you, and I'll prove that I'm not going to leave you while you still feel threatened."

"Not while I still feel threatened?" The next question sprang unbidden to Johanna's lips. "What about afterward?"

Silent for a long moment, Wade responded, "You deserve more."

Weatherby Pierce had not told the men in the posse that he wasn't returning to Millborn with them. They had decided the previous night that Bartlett had eluded them and were going to give up. He had known it would be a waste of time to disagree. He had simply awakened before dawn, rolled up his bedroll, and ridden back in the direction from which they had come. He was determined to find Bartlett's trail again, one way or another. And when he did, he'd see that Bartlett paid the price.

Pierce did not note the brilliant shade of pink that began flooding the vast Texas sky as the sun rose over the horizon. Instead, he nudged his mount on, stiffening his spine with resolution. He didn't understand Sheriff Carter's defense of Bartlett. The sheriff knew what Bartlett was: a drifter, a saddle bum, a man who had accomplished only one thing in his life—a reputation for being fast with his gun. Bartlett was worthless, a ne'er-do-well who traveled the country looking for trouble. No one would care if he were punished for his faults. No one would miss him.

Pierce took a deep breath, his expression hardening. But Mary . . . Mary was different. She had been lovely in her own quiet way. Her smile had lit up the world. She had drawn people to her without any effort at all, and she had cared . . . about everyone, including an aging, childless man who had watched her grow up and thought of her as his own daughter. He had tried to warn her against Bartlett, but it hadn't done any good. It was too late now to change what had happened, but it was not too late to see that Bartlett paid for his crime.

Pierce's broad shoulders stiffened. He pulled his hat down farther on his forehead, his face falling into hard, angry lines. He despised the men who had ridden beside him and who had sworn not to return home until Mary's killer was punished. They were weak, indecisive cowards who wanted only to be done with the difficult job they had undertaken. He had had to drive them every step of the way, but lack of determination was not truly the reason for their betrayal. Sheriff

GET UP TO 4 FREE BOOKS!

You can have the best romance delivered to your door for less than what you'd pay in a bookstore or online. Sign up for one of our book clubs today, and we'll send you **FREE* BOOKS** just for trying it out...with no obligation to buy, ever!

HISTORICAL ROMANCE BOOK CLUB

Travel from the Scottish Highlands to the American West, the decadent ballrooms of Regency England to Viking ships. Your shipments will include authors such as CONNIE MASON, CASSIE EDWARDS, LYNSAY SANDS, LEIGH GREENWOOD, and many, many more.

LOVE SPELL BOOK CLUB

Bring a little magic into your life with the romances of Love Spell—fun contemporaries, paranormals, time-travels, futuristics, and more. Your shipments will include authors such as KATIE MACALISTER, SUSAN GRANT, NINA BANGS, SANDRA HILL, and more.

As a book club member you also receive the following special benefits:

- **30% OFF all orders through our website & telecenter!**
  (Plus, you still get 1 book FREE for every 5 books you buy!)
- **Exclusive access to special discounts!**
- **Convenient home delivery and 10 days to return any books you don't want to keep.**

There is no minimum number of books to buy, and you may cancel membership at any time. See back to sign up!

*Please include $2.00 for shipping and handling.

YES! ☐

Sign me up for the **Historical Romance Book Club** and send my TWO FREE BOOKS! If I choose to stay in the club, I will pay only $8.50* each month, a savings of $5.48!

YES! ☐

Sign me up for the **Love Spell Book Club** and send my TWO FREE BOOKS! If I choose to stay in the club, I will pay only $8.50* each month, a savings of $5.48!

NAME: _____

ADDRESS: _____

_____

TELEPHONE: _____

E-MAIL: _____

☐ **I WANT TO PAY BY CREDIT CARD.**

☐ VISA   ☐ MasterCard.   ☐ DISCOVER

ACCOUNT #: _____

EXPIRATION DATE: _____

SIGNATURE: _____

Send this card along with $2.00 shipping & handling for each club you wish to join, to:

Romance Book Clubs
1 Mechanic Street
Norwalk, CT 06850-3431

Or fax (must include credit card information!) to: 610.995.9274. You can also sign up online at www.dorchesterpub.com.

*Plus $2.00 for shipping. Offer open to residents of the U.S. and Canada only. Canadian residents please call 1.800.481.9191 for pricing information. If under 18, a parent or guardian must sign. Terms, prices and conditions subject to change. Subscription subject to acceptance. Dorchester Publishing reserves the right to reject any order or cancel any subscription.

JOIN NOW!

Carter's claim that they had no proof of Bartlett's guilt was the deciding factor.

His breathing growing ragged, Pierce softly growled his reaction to that thought. He didn't need any proof! He *knew* that Bartlett was guilty. He had witnessed Mary's preoccupation with the fellow and he had warned her about the gunslinger's intentions. When he had learned that Bartlett was headed to the Lazy M for some "private time" with Mary, he had not stopped to tell Paul Malone that his daughter was in danger. Instead, he had ridden directly to the ranch. But he had gotten there too late, and he knew he would never forget the sight of Bartlett covered with Mary's blood.

At the sound of hoofbeats behind him, Pierce turned and spotted a rider fast approaching him. It was John Nells, one of the men who'd joined the posse. A thin young fellow with sandy-colored hair and a pale complexion underneath his suntouched color, Nells had never impressed him much, but as he reined his horse beside Pierce, he asked boldly, "Where are you going?"

Uncertain whether Sheriff Carter had sent Nells after him, Pierce responded tightly, "I'm not giving up. I'm not a quitter like the rest of the posse. I'm going to find Bartlett if it takes my last breath."

"That makes two of us."

Surprised at the other man's response, Pierce said suspiciously, "I know the reason why I need to find Bartlett, but I don't know yours."

"Mine's the same as yours." Nells' thin face twitched. "Mary was a good person. She was the only one who ever showed an interest in me . . . ever listened to what I had to say. There ain't many like her, and I'll be damned if I'll let her killer go free."

Pierce asked gruffly, "How come you never said anything like that before?"

"Because it didn't need to be said. Now it does."

Pierce considered Nells' response for silent moments before responding gruffly, "You're right. That makes two of us."

Pierce did not take the time to waste words as he nudged his mount to a faster pace. He had loved Mary deeply. He would avenge her death.

The sounds of popping campfires punctuated a silence broken only by the rustling of night creatures in the darkness, a baby's cry, and the echoes of distant snoring from wagons circled for the night.

Johanna awoke with a start, uncertain what had roused her. She glanced at Wade, who was lying beside her, and frowned. She remembered the touch of his hands as they had smoothed her flesh with incredible gentleness. She recalled the warmth of his muscled frame lying atop hers. She felt again the thrill he evoked each time he looked at her, each time he touched her, each time he said her name. She knew she would never forget the look in Wade's eyes when he had paused breathlessly at the pinnacle of their mutual passion to say again the words that she cherished.

I love you.

She knew that whatever happened afterward, whatever Wade decided he needed to do, he loved her as much as she loved him. Yet even in that moment of complete possession, she had somehow known it was not enough. She feared for their safety when apart. She wondered if—

Johanna started at the echo of the familiar howl. Her blood ran cold when she realized that the howling had awakened her. She stared breathlessly into the darkness, chills racing up her spine as a familiar vision began forming before her eyes. It approached her, and she saw again the raw, desert terrain surrounding the mysterious figure. The setting sun was at the image's back, enabling Johanna to gradually make out the lined, weathered face, the long, unbound hair streaked with gray, and the naked, rounded shoulders. Her heart pounded when the aged, semiclad figure came close enough for her to see small, dark eyes pinning her with their intensity. He spoke at last, and his guttural language translated clearly in her mind as he instructed her slowly.

Rely on him.

I will watch over you.

She wanted to speak to the image, but she found herself unable.

Do not fear. I am with you.

She tried to speak again, but she could not. Instead, she stared at him a moment longer, holding his gaze before he turned away abruptly. He walked slowly back toward the horizon, but not before an animal's great, furry outline bounded out of the darkness directly toward him. Uncertain, she wanted to cry out and warn him, but she could not make a sound. Frozen, she observed wordlessly as the animal reached the old man's side and stopped abruptly when he touched him. She knew she would always remember the moment when the animal turned back toward her, its penetrating, golden-eyed stare holding hers briefly before it continued on into obscurity at the old man's side.

Her breathing short, Johanna was still mesmerized by the impact of the vision when she heard Wade's whisper in the darkness.

"Did you hear something? Is something wrong, Johanna?"

Swallowing, Johanna raised a hand to Wade's cheek as she turned toward him and responded unsteadily, "No, it . . . it was just a dream."

Wade scrutinized her expression for long moments before he responded, "Just a dream?"

"Yes."

"You'd tell me if it was something I needed to know?"

"Yes."

Wade drew her closer. He whispered against her hair, "Close your eyes and go back to sleep for a little while. Don't worry. I'm right beside you."

She remembered.

Rely on him.

Do not fear.

She closed her eyes. She was not afraid now.

* * *

This wasn't going to be as easy as he had thought.

Percy Smart dug his heels into his mount's sides in an effort to make the animal move faster, but the weary horse refused to obey. Smart looked at the flat grassland surrounding him, then at the golden globe of the sun that broiled all below since early morning. He cursed under his breath.

Oh, how he longed for the civilized, cobbled streets of the city, where well-dressed pedestrians with busy lives knew where they were going as they walked the crowded thoroughfares! How he wanted to experience again the convenience of carriages, restaurants, and comfortable places where a man could eat and lay his head at the end of a long day. He thought of the past night, when he had ingested a miserable supper of dried beef and beans heated over a fire that he had struggled to light, and of lying on a bedroll on the hard ground afterward, with only a thin blanket that smelled of horses and the cold stars overhead. He hated this godforsaken land! And he was beginning to fear that he was temporarily lost in it. He fully expected that he would find the wagon train's trail again, that he would finish the job he had come to accomplish, and that he would coax his reluctant mount to return him to civilization again, but he loathed every minute of the time spent accomplishing those purposes.

Smart nodded at the thought that he would never again accept an assignment outside the city. Yet he was fully aware that he needed to take care of the present before the future would be his again.

* * *

Wade drove Johanna's wagon wordlessly as she sat beside him. He glanced at her with concern, recalling the events of the past night, when she had awakened so abruptly. It was hard for him to believe when looking at the endless Texas sky overhead, or feeling the comforting heat of the brilliant sunshine, that anything could possibly threaten the peaceful wagon train. Yet he knew that feeling of safety was misleading. He had felt Johanna's trembling and known instinctively that she was hiding something from him when she denied that anything was wrong. With each day that passed, he was more attuned to her feelings and her silent fears. He realized fully that although he was reluctant to separate himself from her now, reluctance would increase to pain when it finally became necessary to leave her.

But it *would* become necessary. He knew that his problems would follow him sooner or later, and he could not allow Johanna to become involved. He wished that he—

A disturbance at the head of the wagon train caused Wade to become suddenly alert. Watching, he noted that Tommy's elder brother had mounted up and was galloping back toward Johanna's wagon as the train plodded steadily onward. Wade stiffened when the excited teenager turned his horse to walk beside the wagon and said breathlessly, "Mr. McMullen's been hurt! His horse stumbled in a gopher hole. It fell and rolled on him. Mr. Gear thinks Mr. McMullen's arm is broken."

Wade asked tightly, "What does McMullen think?"

"Mr. McMullen ain't exactly talking. He's in a lot of pain."

Johanna's hand tightened on Wade's arm as she asked, "Why did you come back here to tell us, Jeremiah?"

"Mr. McMullen asked me to. He said he needed to talk to Wade."

Johanna asked, "Does McMullen have any other injuries?"

"We ain't got no doctor on the train, but Mr. Gear says aside from a lot of bruises and that broken arm, he thinks Mr. McMullen is all right. He's taking care of his arm right now, but Mr. McMullen still wants to talk to Wade."

"About what?"

"I don't know. He just told me to hotfoot it back here and to drive the wagon so's Wade could come up front to talk to him." The young man added almost in afterthought, "If that's all right with you, ma'am."

Wade glanced at Johanna as she said, "Of course it's all right with me." Her beautiful face drawn into an expression of concern, Johanna said, "Go ahead, Wade. Don't worry about me. I can take care of myself, and Jeremiah will make sure the wagon keeps up, won't you, Jeremiah?"

"I will, ma'am."

The young man flushed, and Wade's lips twitched. It appeared no man, even a youth, was immune to the charms Johanna could exert when she made an effort.

Addressing Jeremiah gruffly, Wade ordered, "Get down off that horse and take these reins." He turned back toward Johanna as he said, "I'll be right back."

Famous last words.

Sitting beside McMullen in his wagon and noting the pain on the other man's face, Wade remembered that statement.

As soon as Randy Gear left the wagon to allow them some privacy, the older man said, "I figure that Randy is right. My arm's broken. It sure hurts bad enough, dammit!" His face red with the effort he exerted to speak, McMullen continued, "Randy just gave me a dosage of laudanum to kill the pain. I figure I ain't got much time before I stop making sense, so I gotta say this fast. You're the only man on the train who knows this country, Wade. Every other fella riding with me is either a greenhorn or a farmer, which ain't much use when it comes to scouting out what's up ahead and knowing what to do about it."

"I've never scouted before."

"Maybe you ain't never scouted before, but don't tell me you ain't never ridden this country before with the thought of finding the best and fastest way in or out of it."

"So?"

"I'm saying you've got what it takes to do the job while I'm flat on my back. I expect I'll be fine in a day or so, but right now I figure you're the best man to take my place."

Wade scrutinized McMullen with a keen-eyed gaze. He responded, "What about the man you hired to ride with you?"

"Bruce? He ain't what I'm looking for. He follows orders. He ain't the type to give them."

Wade hesitated. "What if I don't think I'm the right man for the job?"

"It don't make no difference what you think. It's what I think that counts."

"What makes you so sure I can handle this?"

McMullen gasped as a fresh wave of pain assaulted him. He growled, "Don't ask dumb questions. I ain't in the mood for them."

Wade's gaze narrowed. "How long do you figure you'll be out of commission?"

"Like I said, a couple of days should do it. I'll be able to handle my arm and my job then."

"Johanna is going to leave the train for the diggings when we reach Arizona, and I'm going with her."

"I figured that. But we won't be anywheres near the turnoff for a few days."

His dark brows knitting, Wade replied slowly, "I appreciate all you've done for me, McMullen, sending the posse off like you did, especially after they told you what they think I did, but I need to tell you that Johanna comes first with me."

"Like I said, I figured that."

Wade observed the older man closely. Then he said, "All right, I'll do it."

"Get to it, then." His concentration obviously waning, McMullen said, "This wagon train is traveling blind right now, and that ain't safe for anybody, including Johanna."

Wade's brows knotted tightly.

"Well, it's her you've got on your mind, ain't it?" When Wade left that question unanswered, McMullen ordered, "Take the horse I lent Jeremiah. That animal's my alternate mount. He's more dependable than your horse."

"My mare's as dependable as they come."

"Maybe, but she's tired. She needs her rest. She doesn't need to be out riding all day when you're going to be putting her to the test soon enough." His face twisting with pain, McMullen said, "Get out of here. Like I said, this wagon train is traveling blind."

"I need to tell Johanna first."

"Bruce will take care of that."

Bruce . . . big, brawny, blond, and with a roving eye . . . Wade frowned.

McMullen grumbled as if reading his mind, "Don't worry. Bruce will behave himself. Even if he doesn't, you can depend on Miss Johanna Higgins to put him in his place."

Wade did not reply.

"Get out of here, and send Bruce in. You'll be back in a few hours, when we stop for the night. You can talk to her then."

Aware that he had no choice, Wade turned without a word, mounted McMullen's horse, and spurred it ahead of the train.

"We ain't getting nowhere, Pierce, and I'm tired of the trail going dead."

Pierce looked at Nells darkly from under the brim of his stained Stetson. He was tired, dirty, and wanted this to be over. Making an effort to control his temper, he responded, "Nobody asked your opinion, and nobody asked you to come along with me. I don't care how many times I lose Bartlett's trail, I'm going to find him. You can ride along with me, you can try finding him on your own, or you can go back home with the posse. But don't bother me with your complaints any longer! I ain't in the mood for them."

His pale complexion flushing, Nells bit back his response, and Pierce paused to scrutinize him closely. He wasn't quite sure what to make of the fella. He had been surprised by Nells' determination when the young man had joined him that morning, but as the day had progressed, his disposition had changed. He'd become increasingly critical and impatient of Pierce's tracking skills, and Pierce had begun seeing a side of Nells that he had not realized existed. He didn't like that side, and he didn't want to be bothered with it.

Shrugging, Nells finally responded, "I was just thinking there has to be a better way to find Bartlett, that's all. He must have left a trace somewhere. He didn't just vanish into thin air."

Pierce stared at Nells. He had to admit that he had a point. Bartlett must have left tracks behind somewhere. He couldn't just disappear into thin air, as it appeared he had done. He had to be somewhere where he couldn't be tracked. Pierce paused at that thought. Where he couldn't be tracked . . . like on a wagon train.

Recalling the tight-lipped reaction that the settlers had demonstrated when the posse searched the wagon train, Pierce frowned. They hadn't agreed to allow the search until guns were drawn. But despite the opposition the posse had encountered, Pierce wouldn't have left so easily if the sheriff hadn't insisted. Something was wrong on that wagon train. He didn't like the way that boy had volunteered information about Bartlett so easily when they had first visited the train, especially since they hadn't been able to find any trace of the gunslinger when they followed his directions. Thinking back, it was equally strange that the settlers on the train had asked so few questions when the posse had slept there that first night—almost as if they wanted as little contact with the posse as possible—almost as if somebody might slip and let out a secret.

Looking up abruptly, Pierce noted the position of the sun in the cloudless sky. It was barely past noon. If he pushed his horse to the limit, he would be able to catch up with the slow-moving wagon train before nightfall. With lengthening shadows shading the horizon, it was unlikely that the wagon train would see him coming.

To arrive in secret . . . perhaps that was the answer.

Pierce turned his mount with undisguised haste. He was riding briskly when hoofbeats sounded behind him. He turned as Nells began riding alongside him.

"Where are you going in such a rush?" Nells demanded.

"No more questions! You can find your own way."

His pale face coloring, Nells said, "I was frustrated. It's been a long morning with nothing to show for it, but you did the best you could. I couldn't do any better."

Pierce did not respond.

"I'm going to ride along with you."

Pierce still did not respond.

"Pierce . . ."

Pierce said sharply, "I'm going to check out that wagon train again . . . quietly, so they don't know I'm around. I don't want nobody to see us coming or to know we're there, *comprende?*"

Nells frowned.

"I asked a question. If you're not going to answer it, you can forget about riding with me."

"I understand."

His mount's rapid pace never slackening, Pierce added, "One last word: I'll stop anybody who gets in the way of making Bartlett pay for what he done. When I say *anybody*, that includes you. Got that, partner?"

Nells replied stiffly, "How long before we catch up with the train?"

"We'll catch up with it tonight." Pierce did not bother to add, *or I'll die trying.*

* * *

The sky was beginning to darken. The wagon train would soon be halting for the night. He had traveled miles ahead of the train to scout the territory for the best place to ford a branch of the Red River, which had flooded unexpectedly. It was the worst time of the day for a problem to crop up.

Wade looked down at his limping mount. It was obvious that the horse was in pain. Uncertain, he dismounted and touched the animal's fetlock. Its sharp whinny would have been immediate notification that something was wrong even if the leg was not so obviously beginning to swell.

Wade mumbled a few words of comfort to the injured animal as he examined the leg more thoroughly. He wasn't a veterinarian, but it was obvious that the animal would not be able to bear his weight on that injured leg.

Pulling himself up to his full height, Wade scrutinized the sky overhead. He would never make it back to the wagon train before nightfall on foot. Whether he liked it or not, he was stuck there for the night.

Damn! He was certain Johanna had been hiding something from him when she had awakened the previous night. His presence had soothed fears that she had struggled bravely to resist. She needed him . . . and he needed to know that she was safe in his arms. He could not explain the phenomena that haunted her, but he knew in his heart they were real—just as his love for her and his driving desire to protect her was real.

Johanna and he were miles apart, but the memory of her intimate warmth filled him. Her scent was in his nostrils; the taste of her lingered in his mouth, and his hunger for her was a throbbing desire inside him that never ceased. He knew that this night apart from her would be more difficult than he had ever believed possible.

Wade's frustration soared as he looked at his saddlebags, knowing he would find only emergency provisions inside. He would be forced to walk on a little farther to find water; then he would make his mount and himself as comfortable as possible for the night. He would get up at first light to begin walking back to the wagon train with the limping horse behind him.

Wade shook his head. At least he had not let McMullen down. He had found the perfect spot for the wagon train to ford the river.

"Where do you suppose he is? Why hasn't he returned yet?"

A lingering howl rebounded in Johanna's mind as she posed those questions to the lanky youth silently driving her wagon. The howling had begun again an hour earlier, when the sky began to darken.

Johanna glanced belatedly at Jeremiah. Like his younger brother, he was fair-haired and freckled, and extremely conscious of his responsibilities. She noted the young fellow's uncomfortable silence, fully aware that he would never understand the true reason for her anxiety as she said,

"I'm sorry, Jeremiah. Those questions were unfair. I know you don't know any more than I do about where Wade is right now."

Jeremiah had been present when Bruce White came to her wagon just after Wade left. Bruce was McMullen's second in command. He was blond, well-built, and of medium height, but he was also a fellow who was overly convinced of his masculine appeal. There was a glint in his eye as he explained McMullen's condition and the reason for Wade's departure, and had offered her his assistance. His smile had been too broad, his gaze too knowing.

Overwhelmed by a strong sense of distaste, she had said, "Thank you, but I don't need anyone else's assistance right now. Jeremiah is providing all the help I need. I joined this wagon train alone, and I don't need any other companionship until Wade returns." Pausing briefly, she had held Bruce's gaze directly as she added, "I hope you understand."

Her amusement at his aggrieved look faded beneath her anxiety about Wade. She looked at Jeremiah to see his expression reflecting her concern.

"I sure wish I could answer your question, ma'am. I'm thinking that maybe it got dark quicker than he counted on, and he figured he might as well stay where he is rather than take the chance of running afoul of something while he was traveling in the dark. My pa's done that, you know. My pa always shows up in the morning, rested and hungry as a bear."

"You're right, of course."

"All's I know is that Bruce just signaled for the wagons to turn into a circle for the night, which means it'll be dark real soon. I guess Mr. Mc-Mullen ain't up to the job yet. But I know my mama will welcome you at our campfire. She always cooks more than she needs to, and she'll be happy for the company of another woman."

"Thank you, Jeremiah, but I think I'll fix something for myself. Who knows? Maybe Wade will come riding back tonight after all."

"Yes, ma'am."

Jeremiah did not appear convinced, but Johanna held her head high. In any case, Wade would be back by morning at the latest. She was sure of it.

A wolf's howl sounded again in Johanna's mind, and she caught her breath.

"You heard what she said. She said *Wade* would be back." Concealed in the shadows where Nells and he had crept up on the circling wagons, Pierce gave a harsh laugh. "I knew something was fishy. Them two, that woman and that *Wade* fella, weren't with the train when we came up on it the other two times."

"That means—"

"The Wade she's talking about must be Wade Bartlett, and he's up to his old tricks. There's no way I would've forgotten a woman who looks like her if she was here before, and that means the two of them was off hiding from the posse someplace. There's only one reason they'd be doing that."

"Because he's guilty."

Pierce's expression tightened. "That woman's expecting him back, and I got to say if somebody who looked like her was waiting for me, I'd come back, all right."

"What if he don't come back?"

"He will. There's something going on between Bartlett and that old fella who's leading the wagon train, too. Bartlett feels safe here."

"So?"

Pierce growled. "When Bartlett comes back, we'll get him."

"And hang him."

"From the nearest tree—once we get far enough away from the wagon train so's the others won't interfere."

"What about the woman?"

"That's up to her."

Silent for a moment, Nells replied, "What do we do now?"

"Wait."

When Nells did not reply, Pierce said simply, "I expect it's going to be a long night."

CHAPTER SEVEN

The foyer was brightly lit as Peter Klein made his entrance to Letty's soiree. He was dressed in a formal dark suit with stark white linens. He knew the superb cut of his clothes, as well as his generally meticulous appearance, lent him an elegance that could not be ignored. He had spent years perfecting that art of distinction. He had much to offer, and he had already decided upon the woman who would be the recipient of his effort.

He was pleased to see that the recent dramatic turns in Letty's life had not affected her demeanor. Actually, nothing had changed: a uniformed butler was there at the door to take his coat; artistically arranged flowers were placed tastefully around the room; crystal chandeliers and flickering candles glowed; waiters circulated with filled glasses of imported wines and liquors; expensive dinnerware graced a buffet table with the most exotic of delicacies. Fine accessories and silverware established a tone that was completed by the swelling music of a waltz. It was no wonder to him that Letty's soirees were successful.

And then there was Letty herself . . . more beautiful and alluring than any female in the room . . . a woman of the world who was not afraid to openly speak her mind and to take her lovers, but who remained a woman to be respected at all times. He knew, of course, that there were some who loathed Letty, who thought she was a greedy opportunist with no compunction about using her beauty to greatest advantage, and they were probably right. Admittedly, however, those very traits drew him to her. She was a worldly woman who had come to terms with herself, and who used whatever attributes she could muster to achieve success. He enjoyed her. He admired her. And if he did not actually *love* her, he wanted her more than he had ever wanted any woman before.

Peter's smile faltered briefly as he scanned the room filled with smiling socialites, laughter, and the inane conversation of those whose only intention was a night of pure pleasure—unlike him. His gaze stopped on a smiling group of men in the corner of the room who surrounded the grand madam herself. It did not miss his notice that Letty had never looked lovelier in a gown of a lilac hue that added a new tone to the depth of her eyes and a subtle radiance to her skin and hair. He absentmindedly wondered if there was a color that would not suit her.

Taking the time to scrutinize Letty further, Peter also noted that she had managed quite well to overcome her reaction to the recent death of her lawyer, the very dear Alexander Pittman. He had known she would, and he also knew he could easily fill the void that Pittman had left in her retinue of potential lovers.

Drawing his well-maintained figure erect, Peter advanced toward Letty's band of admirers. Turning her attention to him, he said, "You are looking particularly lovely tonight, Letty."

"Thank you, Peter. I know I can always depend on you for a kind word."

"Not kind—truthful. You are always lovely, Letty."

Interrupting with a touch of impatience, Aaron March, the married father of three and president of March Savings and Loan, said, "That's enough, Peter. I was here first—so you can just wait your turn."

"Aaron, I'm sorry." Letty looked back at him apologetically. "Is that how it appears, that you need to take turns when in my company?"

Appearing momentarily flustered at her direct question, Aaron replied, "Not really. I just resent the addition of another man to your admiring circle tonight."

"I appreciate every one of you, Aaron." Peter noted that Aaron was not unaffected by the sensual flutter of Letty's lashes as she continued, "But I hope you will excuse me while I speak privately to Peter. It is a matter of the utmost importance."

"Of course, Letty." Flushed, Aaron continued opportunely, "If you will promise me the first dance when you're through."

"I promise, Aaron, just as I promise a dance to any of you gentlemen who offer me the pleasure."

At the surfeit of smiling nods from within the circle, Letty turned toward Peter and said, "Shall we take a few private moments, Peter?"

Peter watched the envious glances turned in his direction as Letty ushered him into a quiet room nearby. He moved toward her as the door clicked closed behind them.

Stunned, he saw Letty's smile turn cold as she said, "I did not intend to mislead you, Peter, but I can see that I did. No, I did not come here for a brief, private rendezvous. I came here to make perfectly clear something that you do not seem to comprehend." Her expression becoming frigid, Letty said, "I will never forget that you barged into my rooms and spoke to Alexander and me in such a dictatorial manner. You had no right to assume that attitude. I was not your possession then, and I never will be any man's possession—most especially yours. I have tried to make that clear to you on several occasions without success, so I will say to you now that you may attend my soirees if you wish, but I will not welcome contact of any sort with you. You will stay away from me."

"Letty, you don't understand."

"I understand only too well, Peter. You are accustomed to having your own way . . . accustomed to having everyone jump when you speak. I will *never* be included in that number. My life is my own and I will conduct it as I see fit. You will never be a part of it." Letty paused as her dark eyes drilled into his. She added emphatically, "*Never!* Do you understand?"

Letty paused for a breath, and then said, "I'm going back outside now to tend to my duties as hostess. What you choose to do with the rest of the evening is your decision."

Peter stood stock-still as Letty opened the door with a practiced smile and left. He knew her smile was for appearances only, and his jaw tightened.

How dare she speak to him that way? How dare she assume that she could shrug him off so casually?

Peter approached the door, a similar smile on his face as he opened it. It would not do to allow the depth of his anger to become apparent—but he was furious. And when he was furious, someone would pay. He could not say at that moment who that person would be.

Peter watched as James Ferguson approached Letty where she stood talking. He saw the smile she turned in his direction. It was genuine—and he saw the look James returned. It appeared that James had found a way to reestablish himself in Letty's affections.

Damn her, and damn James Ferguson! No man would take the place he intended for himself!

Peter's stare was deadly as he looked at James a

moment longer. He would not wait for Letty to shrug James aside for the second time in order to take the place he had vacated. "I'll wait for no man," he murmured.

"James." Letty smiled as she turned toward him and the music swelled around her. The inner trembling she had not allowed Peter to see during their confrontation threatened to overwhelm her, and she added without thinking, "I'm glad to see you."

Letty excused herself from the conversational group around her as James responded, "Well, that's a change . . . your being glad to see me."

"I'm sorry, James. I never meant for there to be hard feelings between us. I wanted us to remain friends."

"And I wanted more. But you don't need to concern yourself about that any longer, Letty. I've accepted the fact that you've decided to end our time together. It's just that . . . well . . . I guess it's not over for me."

"James . . ."

His expression tightening as he took her arm, James said, "You're shaking, Letty. What happened?"

"Nothing, just a confrontation with a disagreeable person."

"A man?"

She nodded.

"A man who wanted you."

Letty took a breath. "Not all men want me,

James. I'm not the femme fatale you seem to think I am."

"But this man wanted you."

Letty corrected, "This man wanted to *own* me."

"Which you would never allow."

"Never."

James smiled. Letty remembered the warmth of that smile and the touch of his lips that often followed. She remembered how he had made her feel safe and loved, and she—

Letty dismissed her roving thoughts when James said unexpectedly, "Would you care to dance, Letty?"

"I can't. I promised this dance to someone else, although I don't see him at present."

"His misfortune, not mine."

James started to take her into his arms, but she said, "No, James. I couldn't do that. I promised."

"And you always keep your promises."

Noting the change in his demeanor, Letty replied, "I try."

"That's why you never made any promises to me . . . why you never said you loved me."

"That may be one of the reasons."

"Could you tell me the others?"

Her throat suddenly choking tight, Letty whispered, "No, James, I can't."

"Letty . . ."

"Here you are!" Turning toward Aaron March at the unexpected interruption, Letty smiled. "You promised me this dance," he said. "Remember, Letty?"

"So I did. And I never break my promises."
Turning back to James, she said, "If you will excuse us, James?"

"Of course. Always."

Breathless as Aaron swung her out masterfully onto the floor, Letty managed a glance over his shoulder in James' direction. The warmth in James' eyes had not exactly gone cold. It had simply . . . died.

Letty averted her gaze. No, she would not see another man lose his life because of her.

A captive of Aaron's energetic dancing, Letty did not see Peter walk past the dance floor. Nor did she see the dark glance he turned toward James the moment before he accepted his coat from the butler and left.

Standing tall, appearing relaxed, James ached inside as he watched Letty whirl across the dance floor in Aaron March's arms. For the life of him, he could not understand himself. He was well aware of his status as an eligible bachelor. He was relatively certain he could turn the head of any available woman. His brief association with Eleanor had been pleasant for both of them. She was young, and it had not been difficult for either of them to remain friends when he had made it known that he had no serious intentions toward her. But it was different with Letty. He had tried to forget her and it hadn't worked. He had tried to recapture their time together, but Letty had refused all his advances. He had tried to go on with his life as if she'd never existed, but that hadn't remedied the situation either. He had finally come to the conclusion that the only relationship she wanted with him was friendship.

Friendship . . . when he loved her more than his own life . . . when he would never stop wanting her.

Turning abruptly toward the waiter at his side, James took a glass from the tray he offered. Catching Letty's eye, he raised the champagne toward her in salute and emptied the glass. He placed his empty glass back on the tray of another waiter who appeared magically beside him and took a fresh glass. He sipped sparingly of the second glass. His gaze intent on Letty, he accepted the part in her life that she offered. He would be her friend if she wanted it that way. And as difficult as it would be, there would be no strings attached.

Dawn touched the clear Texas sky, rapidly illuminating it with startling patches of yellow and gold as Weatherby Pierce and John Nells watched the wagon train's gradual awakening. His spyglass fixed on the wagon that sheltered the beauteous blond woman awaiting Bartlett's return, Pierce mumbled, "She's looking outside. She's waiting for Bartlett. She doesn't know we're here. She obviously expects him to show up anytime now."

"Well, he'd better make it fast. I'm getting tired of doing nothing."

"Are you?" Pierce turned coldly toward the young fellow beside him. "Like I said, you can leave anytime you want."

"I ain't leaving, but I'm sure as hell going to make sure Bartlett pays for what he did."

"Then hold your horses for a while. Bartlett will show up." Tearing off a piece of dried beef from a strip that he had retrieved from his saddlebag, Pierce chewed and then lifted his canteen to his lips for a long drag of tepid water. Swallowing, he continued softly, "One thing is for sure: Bartlett wasn't no more comfortable than we was last night. He sure as hell would've preferred lying beside that woman of his. Which means he'll be back. We just have to be patient."

"I ain't sure how much patience I have left."

Pierce looked at the younger man coldly. He said with unconcealed menace, "I told you, I'm going to get Bartlett one way or another. That means with you or without you . . . and that means doing whatever I need to do."

Pierce did not wait for Nells's reaction to his words. Instead, he trained his spyglass on Johanna Higgins as she emerged from the wagon. He saw the lanky youth who had driven the wagon the previous day approach her and, after a few words, leave to retrieve the horses that were grazing nearby. The young fellow obviously intended to ready the wagon for the day's travel— which meant that neither of them had any idea when Bartlett would return.

Pierce scowled. He didn't like this. He didn't like the uncertainty involved, and truth be told, he didn't like waiting any more than Nells did.

* * *

Wade had begun walking at first light, but it wasn't as easy as he'd thought it would be. The horse was limping badly, and though he had slowed his pace, it hadn't seemed to help. He had finally stopped to tighten the makeshift binding that he had put on the horse's affected leg, but he knew the fix was only temporary.

Wade glanced at the sun as it made a rapid ascent in the morning sky. He was well aware that the wagon train must have already started traveling. He supposed his best hope was that he would meet up with it as it approached—but that could be hours away.

Wade lifted his hat from his head and ran his hand through the heavy dark hair adhering to his scalp with perspiration. The morning was growing hotter and his mount was struggling. At the present rate, he did not expect to intercept the wagon train until after noon.

Wade felt his anxiety heighten. He had a bad feeling about being separated from Johanna.

Peter Klein advanced into the familiar paneled office of his friend. He approached the broad, cluttered mahogany desk with a smile and held out his hand in greeting to the overweight, middle-aged man who stood up laboriously behind it. He did not pause to scrutinize the baggy pants, the expensive jacket that drooped on his shoulders, the visible spots on his imported linens, or the button that had not been replaced on a sleeve that had been expertly tailored. Nor did he pay attention to the fact that the man's hair was too long, that his nails were untended, and that his puffy face was perpetually sweaty. His appearance was just like his office—filled with the best furniture but slovenly; large but located in an undesirable part of town.

Instead Peter looked directly into the man's acute gaze as the fellow asked, "What are you doing here again, Klein? Weren't you satisfied with the service you got last time? Seems to me you couldn't have asked for nothing better. My man took care of things the next day. He said it was one of the easiest jobs he's ever done."

"It was money well spent. As a matter of fact, the service was so good, Charlie, that I want to have it repeated."

"Repeated? The fella's dead. There ain't no repeating it."

Peter snickered. "The target will be different, of course, but your man was so efficient that I don't feel he'll have any trouble accomplishing this job, either."

Mr. Charles responded, "My man knows his business. Did you bring a picture of the fella you want him to take care of? He might not know what the man looks like." He added sarcastically, "It's possible that they don't travel in the same circles, you know."

Peter gave an amused snort. "That's very possible, so I brought a clipping from the newspaper, which should suffice to identify the fellow. He's active in charity events in the city. I don't think your man will have any trouble recognizing him."

Unexpected curiosity sparked in Mr. Charles' voice as he asked, "What did this fella do—get the upper hand on you?"

"You might say that." Peter's lip twitched. "And you might say that I don't intend to spend any time correcting the situation, either."

"I figured." Mr. Charles smirked. "The price will be the same. My man don't give discounts."

"I've never argued price with you, have I?"

"No."

"I'll expect quick service."

"You can depend on that. My man don't like things hanging on, either."

Peter withdrew a roll of bills from his pocket.

"I'm glad to see you brought cash, as usual."

"It wouldn't do to have any paperwork that might be traced back to me. I may have started in this area of town, but I'm an important member of society now and I can't take any chances."

"Yeah . . . I seen your name in the paper lots of time."

Peter shrugged. "You chose your life and I chose mine." He added, "You'll oversee the job and make sure it gets done?"

"Before the week is out."

Peter added in afterthought, "You might have your man make it appear to be a robbery—just to allay any suspicion that could possibly point in my direction."

"My man will be happy to take care of that."

"I'll be leaving, then. It wouldn't do for me to be seen here." Peter offered Mr. Charles his hand as he added, "You know, there are times when I long for the old life. There was an odd kind of honesty about it."

"Yeah, you look like you miss coming back to this part of town."

Peter laughed out loud at the sarcastic comment. He turned toward the door and said as he pulled it open, "Still, I sometimes think you got the best of the bargain when we split up, Charlie."

Mr. Charles did not bother to respond, except to say, "Just to be clear, what's this fella's name?"

"Oh, didn't I mention it? It's noted in the newspaper article I gave you." Peter smiled. "His name is James Ferguson."

"Bartlett ain't back yet and it's almost noon. Something's wrong, and you know it."

Pierce's stubbled face drew into anxious lines as they covertly followed the long, snaking line of the wagon train. He responded to Nells' grumbling with a nod and added reluctantly, "He should've been back by now."

"Maybe he ain't coming back. Maybe he decided it would be better to get out of this country and make a clean getaway."

"That don't make sense. There's something between that wagon master and him, I tell you. Bartlett has a connection to him somehow. From what we overheard last night, he's got a real strong thing for that blond woman, too."

Had Bartlett discovered somehow that they were watching? Did he intend to outwait them? When they gave up and left, would he ride in to reclaim his place in the wagon train *and* his woman?

Pierce unconsciously shook his head. He'd never let that happen.

"Get your gun ready, Nells. We're going to catch up with that wagon train."

Nells frowned. "What are you going to do?"

"We're going to make sure that Bartlett shows his face so we can give him what's coming to him. If he don't come back, we're going to make sure he remembers that we were here."

The morning had started slowly. Echoes of the howling that had haunted her throughout the night had sounded in her ears as Johanna waited for Wade to return. When he did not, Jeremiah came to tend to her team. The young man took over the reins without a word as the wagon train resumed its steady forward pace, but Wade still did not return.

Johanna's heartbeat accelerated when she heard hoofbeats beside the wagon. The appearance of two mounted cowpokes with drawn guns startled her.

"Who are you?" she demanded. "What do you want?" She looked down at their guns, and a tremor of fear coursed down her spine as she added, "If you're looking for money, you've come to the wrong place. You won't find much here."

"It's not money we're after."

Her lips tight, Johanna looked at the older of the two men. He was mature, with graying hair showing underneath his broad-brimmed hat. He was a big man, heavily built. His clothes looked lived in, his face bore more than a week's stubble, and his expression was unyielding. The second of the men was younger, blond, and fair-skinned, but his eyes were cold. She glanced at Jeremiah as the teenager stared wordlessly at them, the reins hanging loose in his hands as the horses continued their slow forward pace.

She responded, "If you're not after money, what do you want?"

"Where's Bartlett?"

"Bartlett?"

"You know who I mean. You call him Wade Mitchell. I don't care what name he's using, I call him a killer."

"He didn't kill that young woman! She was already dead when he got there. He tried to save her."

"Where is he?"

"I don't know." Suddenly grateful that Wade had not yet returned, she said, "He rode off. He's been gone since yesterday. He knows you're after him. He may have escaped by now."

"He didn't know we were here when he left, which means he found out somehow that we were waiting for him and he's just biding his time, hoping we'll give up—but I've got the answer for that." Turning to the fellow beside him, the older man said, "Keep your gun on the boy while the woman and me go back to get her horse."

"I'm not going anywhere with you, if that's what you're thinking."

"Oh, yes, you are," the older man warned Johanna through clenched teeth. "If you value this young fella's life, you'll do what I say. If you don't, he'll be the first to pay."

Her eyes widening, Johanna looked at Jeremiah. To his credit, the teenager responded bravely, "Don't listen to him, ma'am. You can't trust a man with a gun."

"That's right, boy . . . she can't trust me not to kill you right here and now."

Panicking, Johanna said, "What do you want? I don't know where Wade is."

"He's either watching somewhere or he's on his way back, so you're coming with us. When he gets here, this young fella is going to tell him that he'd better ride due west without his guns if he expects to see you alive again."

"W . . . what?"

Turning toward Jeremiah, the older fellow said, "Did you hear what I said, boy?"

Jeremiah nodded.

Johanna glanced frantically at the wagon ahead of them.

"If you're expecting some help from up front, you're wasting your time. You're the last wagon in line. Nobody is paying any attention to what's going on here." Johanna's heart pounded as the older man added harshly, "And I expect nobody cares."

"That's not my horse back there."

The man just laughed.

The howling in Johanna's ears grew louder as she said, "Wade won't come after me. He's probably on his way to California already."

"Get going!"

Johanna looked at Jeremiah. Noting her glance, the older man said coldly, "You . . . boy . . . make sure everybody on the train understands that if anybody rides out to rescue this woman before Bartlett comes back, I'll kill her first and then them."

Jeremiah responded boldly, "What if Wade doesn't come back?"

Speaking up for the first time, the younger gunman said without a trace of emotion, "That'll be too bad for her, won't it?"

Mounted on Wade's horse minutes later, her heart pounding, her mind going in confused circles, Johanna could only look on while the older man grabbed her reins and dragged her behind him as he spurred his mount away from the train.

Mason Little struggled to control his irritation. He glanced around him at city streets filled with refuse; at ramshackle buildings where garbage cans lay uncovered to putrify the air; and where transients and drunks found convenient doorways and gutters in which to sleep off the previous night's excesses. He had never liked this section of town. He didn't feel safe here. It irritated him that he needed to come to a seedy saloon in order to contact Dobbs about their ongoing business.

Mason entered the sordid establishment in front of him, grateful that it was almost empty of customers. The stale odor of beer and liquor filled the place. The balding, overweight, and perspiring bartender looked up at him speculatively, as did a heavily made-up woman whose pendulous breasts were provocatively exposed as she sauntered past.

Ignoring them, Mason glanced around him as he entered. Then he walked toward the table where Dobbs was talking to another individual as seedy as he. The woman batted her heavily kohled eyes at him, causing Dobbs to comment, "This fella ain't here to see the likes of you, Molly. He's here to see me."

The woman shrugged as she raised her thin eyebrows and responded, "That don't say much for his taste, does it?"

Looking amused by the woman's response, Dobbs motioned for Mason to follow him. Dobbs waited until they had emerged into the alleyway beside the saloon before pushing the door closed behind them and asking, "What are you doing here?"

"That's what I'd like to know. I thought we had agreed that I wouldn't have to come here to find out if you're making any progress."

Dobbs shrugged. "I don't remember agreeing to that. I said I'd let you know when I had something to tell you."

Inwardly seething at Dobbs' casual manner,

Mason said tightly, "There seems to be a misunderstanding between us that is beginning to irritate me. I will repeat again that I need to be kept current about what's going on. The only information I've received lately has come from Letty, who told me that the Pinkerton on Johanna's trail has supposedly located her on a wagon train heading to Oregon territory."

"What? That don't sound right to me."

Mason replied coldly, "I suppose that means you don't know anything about it."

"No, I don't, but my man's on the trail of that Pinkerton, and you can be sure that he'll take care of things. Johanna Higgins won't be coming back to the city to meet her mother's conditions, and that's that."

"No, it isn't! I have a lot riding on this."

Taking an unexpected step closer, Dobbs thrust his face so close to Mason's that Mason could smell his putrid breath as he said, "Like I said, my man will take care of everything."

"That's what you said about the man you sent out after Letty's other daughter, Meredith. You know what happened to him."

"That was a mistake that won't happen again. This fellow has the greatest incentive in the world to succeed. Money . . . and the fact that he knows what will happen to him if he fails."

Mason stared at Dobbs. With his oversized clothing, his narrow, pointed face, small eyes, and intense gaze, he appeared even more rodentlike than ever.

Mason replied, "All right, we'll let that matter rest right now, but I will be expecting to hear something about Johanna Higgins from you soon." Mason took a breath and continued, "I also have a message that you can deliver for me, since you have Mr. Charles' ear. You can tell him that he'll be receiving regular payments against my gambling debts beginning at the end of this month. My dear aunt asked me to hire a detective to *protect* one of her former lovers, James Ferguson—without his knowledge, of course. It seems she has gotten it into her head that his life may be threatened because of her. Of course I agreed, but I have no intention of following through. Instead, I will make sure that the fee my dear aunt pays me is generous and forward it to Mr. Charles as payment against my debts." He added, "My dear aunt is becoming rather unbalanced, but her fears suit me well in this instance."

"Really . . ." Dobbs raised his eyebrows as he replied, "I just talked to a fella hired to kill James Ferguson as quickly and as quietly as possible."

"W . . . what? Who wants him dead?"

"I wouldn't tell you even if I knew. Mr. Charles accepted the job and passed the word to me."

"You arranged for it to happen?"

Dobbs' small smile was chilling. "That's what I do."

"Call it off! Tell your man I'll pay him double whatever he's receiving if he'll abandon the job immediately!"

"Sorry. Mr. Charles shook hands on it. He took

payment for the job, too, and there's no reversing what's done."

"This is important, Dobbs! I can't afford to lose Letty's confidence. It will bring an end to all my plans."

"That's your problem. I'd advise you to go home and figure out a way of getting out of the hole you've dug for yourself—because I'm telling you now—my man won't be wasting any time getting the job done."

"But—"

"That's all I got to say."

"But—"

Dobbs pulled open the door of the saloon and went back inside.

Standing alone in the rank alleyway, Mason was breathless with shock at the realization that he knew of no way to stop the wheels that had already been set into motion.

James took his coat from his smiling butler and walked out of his residence. He had eaten a fairly light lunch, but it lay heavily on his stomach. He had returned to his home at midday because he had needed some time to himself before going back to the office. His life had become a quagmire of indecision with a beautiful, dark-haired, enigmatic woman at its center. He needed exercise and time to ponder the next step in his life. After the death of his wife many years previously, he had believed he would never love again. The irony was that now when he had finally met a woman he loved completely, she did not love him.

James turned to glance back at the impressive residence he called home. Large, with rooms to spare, constructed of brick, it was located on one of the most prestigious streets in the city. It was considered a mansion by most who saw it. He had charged a decorator with the task of changing the décor a year after his wife's death, when he could no longer bear the many memories of her that the interior evoked. He had then put the articles he cherished most in a chest in his library, where they would always remain in deference to the brief, beautiful years Madeline and he had shared. He had gone forward by plunging himself into work that had netted him great profits and mounting respectability, and that had consumed the dark days until he came to terms with his loss.

James mused that he had been told on many occasions that any woman would feel privileged to become a part of his life and to share in the prestige and social position that he had earned in his lifetime. He had not bothered to add on those occasions that "any woman" did not include Letty.

That thought caused him bitter amusement as he crossed the street and continued on. He glanced again at the bright afternoon sun. It was a beautiful day. He remembered that a beautiful day such as this had settled into an evening that Letty and he had shared. She had lain in his arms in the privacy of his upstairs bedroom veranda. They had looked up at the blanket of stars overhead and had laughingly told stories of childhood dreams, and the wishes they had made on those stars when they were still innocent enough to believe that wishes came true and all stories had happy endings. He had not chosen to ask Letty what had caused her belief in happy endings to end; he had not wanted to speak of the demise of his own innocence when his wife died at such a young age. He had regretted that moment countless times after Letty sent him away. In retrospect, he realized that he had lost a moment when Letty might have confided in him things that she had never confided to any other man . . . things that might now help him to come to terms with her unexpected dismissal of him.

Letty had sent him away in the middle of the night only a few days later, as if sensing that they were becoming too close. She had done it coldly, without demonstrating any feeling at all, despite the depth of the mutual emotion they had shared only hours earlier.

She had been agitated when she'd sent him away, and she had been cruel. In retrospect, it seemed to him that her words had been deliberately cutting, and that she had forced him into a situation in which he had no recourse but to leave in order to salvage whatever pride he had left.

Pride.

James shook his head. He had sacrificed his pride too many times in the months since for him to recall them with any comfort at all. He had actually believed that Eleanor was the answer for a while. She was a dear girl, but it had taken only one moment seeing Eleanor and Letty side by side for him to settle in his mind the difference between deep affection and sincere love.

Recently, in a weak moment, Letty had turned to him for comfort. Unable to refuse her, he had provided the affection she sought, promising no strings attached. The only question remaining was whether he was strong enough to fulfill that promise.

Dammit, he loved her! Had he finally managed to attain a place in Letty's life? Or had he merely found his own hell? He could not presently answer those questions. He only knew that his life had begun again the moment Letty had smiled up at him with acceptance.

Another question loomed, one that had sent him out onto the street for a midday walk to clear his mind. What was he supposed to do now?

Suddenly jostled by a man walking in the opposite direction on the empty, sunlit street, James looked up with a frown. Pausing, the fellow said, "Oh, sorry. I'm in a rush."

Small, wiry, and unclean, he wasn't the type expected to be seen in that exclusive neighborhood, and James didn't reply.

"Say, ain't you Mr. Ferguson, the one connected to all them charitable projects in the city?"

Nodding, James said, "I suppose I am."

"I thought so. Nice to meet you."

The man tipped his hat and turned away. Struck

with the peculiarity of the moment, James shrugged and resumed his walk. He did not see the stranger turn back toward him, did not see him pull out a knife. He only felt the blade plunge into his back.

Stunned motionless, James could not react as the fellow struck him again and again.

His breathing short, daylight rapidly dimming, James slipped to the ground. He felt someone rifle his pockets and then heard the sound of footsteps racing away from the deadly scene.

Unable to move for the pain that stole his breath, James glanced around him. His consciousness was fading and he was bleeding profusely, but the street was deserted at that time of day. There was no one to help him.

James fought desperately against the darkness rapidly overwhelming him. Gasping when he felt consciousness slipping away, he muttered a last, whispered plea.

"Oh, God, please . . . not now."

"What do you mean, she's gone?"

The wagon train remained motionless as Wade faced McMullen in the solitude of the lead wagon. He had seen the wagon train in the distance and urged his limping mount to a faster pace. A seemingly endless period had elapsed before Bruce reached him and exchanged mounts with him so that he could ride back and talk to McMullen directly.

Bruce's manner, and the strained look on his

face, had indicated that something was wrong, but Wade had not stopped to quiz him. Instead, he had ridden toward McMullen's wagon with his stomach tight.

Flabbergasted, he repeated, "What do you mean, Johanna's gone?"

"Two men took her off. Jeremiah left her wagon where it stood and borrowed a horse from the family in front so he could ride up and tell me that two men had taken her captive. The boy was beside himself. He said the fellas had guns, and they warned that if anybody on the train tried to rescue her, they'd kill her first, and then they'd kill anybody who came after her. He said those men had a special message for you. They told him to tell you that you'd never see Johanna again if you didn't follow their instructions by riding out due west without your guns."

"That's all they said?"

"Ain't that enough?"

"When did this happen?"

"About noontime. I stopped the train when I found out and called the men together. Some of them wanted to ride out to try to get her back, but others were afraid those fellas would kill her like they said they would. I figured you were on your way back, so I told Jeremiah to stay with Johanna's wagon while I sent Bruce out to look for you."

"What did these men look like?"

"I don't know. I didn't ask. It didn't seem important at the time."

Wade nodded. He said gruffly, "I'll take care of it."

"Where are you going?"

"Back to talk to Jeremiah."

"What are you going to do?"

Wade did not bother to reply.

Obviously shaken when Wade rode up a few minutes later, Jeremiah responded, "Them two meant what they said, Wade. I could tell by the look on their faces, but I didn't know what to do."

"What did they look like?"

"One of them, the fella that did most of the talking, was tall. He was older, about my pa's age. He was ample around the middle and had gray hair hanging over the collar of his shirt, and his face had the look of spending a lot of time in the sun. He looked like a man who didn't do no unnecessary talking. The other one was smaller and younger. He was kind of thin, blond, and pale-complexioned, but his eyes were cold as ice."

Wade nodded. He didn't need more of a description than that to figure that the older man was Weatherby Pierce. Pierce had never liked him. Mary told him that Pierce had said he was a drifter and not the right kind for her to be interested in. As for the other fella, the only slight, blond young man he could think of was John Nells. Yet Nells was the last person he'd expect to come after him. It looked like those two had either broken off from the posse, or the posse had finally quit and had gone home.

Wade verified, "They said if I ever wanted to see Johanna again, I had to—"

"—to ride out due west without your guns. I figured they must be watching for you somewhere." Jeremiah hesitated, and then added, "Mr. Mc-Mullen explained why they're after you. Most of the men on this train don't believe it. That includes me, too, because I figure like Tommy said, you're a fella who done only his best since he came here—saving Miss Johanna from that man who meant to harm her and all—and that don't sound like no killer to me."

Wade was still frowning. He looked up at the position of the sun in the cloudless sky. It was long past the meridian. In a few hours it would be dark. He knew those men were watching from somewhere nearby and had probably seen him. He remembered seeing Pierce outside his jail-house window with a rope ready. Pierce wouldn't be satisfied until he was swinging high. He supposed he wouldn't blame the fella for the way he felt—if he really was the man who'd killed Mary.

But he hadn't killed her, and the truth would never come out if Pierce got his way.

Hardly aware that he was still holding the reins of the wagon, Jeremiah asked, "What are you going to do?"

Wade looked at him intently.

He did not reply.

Weatherby Pierce growled low in his throat. Concealed in a thicket far enough away from the wagon train that he could not be seen, he watched the progress of affairs at the wagon train with his spyglass. He had seen the solitary figure ride up to the head wagon and go inside. He had watched until the figure emerged a little later and rode on toward the wagon at the rear of the train.

A smile flickered across Pierce's lips when that same figure finally began riding out toward his position in a direction that was due west.

As the fellow rode closer, his face grew clearer, and Pierce felt a flush of triumph. It was Bartlett, all right. He studied Bartlett more closely and saw that he wasn't wearing his gun belt, and that his rifle scabbard was empty.

"Don't shoot him!" Johanna cried out from where she sat with her hands and feet tied a little distance away. She continued emotionally, "Don't you see that he can't be a killer if he's willing to sacrifice his life for me?"

"Shut up!" Nells ordered roughly. "I'm tired of hearing you talk."

"Why? Because you know what I'm saying makes sense? Wade didn't kill that young woman."

"Shut up, I said," Nells ordered with growing heat. "Mary was good and pure, and he's the reason she's dead. Him and him alone."

"Wade went to talk with her that day, to tell her he was leaving, that's all. When he got there, she was dead."

Taking a few steps toward her, Nells said threateningly, "Shut up now, or I'll shut you up."

"Leave her alone, Nells." Turning back to face him, Pierce ordered, "There's only one person who's going to suffer for Mary's death, and he's riding toward us right now."

Nells said tightly, "Can you make out his face yet? Are you sure it's him?"

"It's him, all right."

Nells shoved his gun back into his holster and grabbed his rifle. Pierce ordered sharply, "Drop that rifle, dammit! There's only one way that fella is going to pay for what he did, and that's with the rope I've been saving just for him."

"I ain't taking the chance that he'll get away."

Pierce ordered with his gun drawn, "Pull that trigger and I'll shoot you right here. There ain't nobody who's going to cheat me out of what I've been planning for Mary's killer, and that includes you." When Nells hesitated, Pierce snapped, "Step back and drop that rifle or you're a dead man."

Nells dropped the rifle and stepped back. Johanna released a tense breath when Pierce tossed the rifle into the bushes. Addressing Pierce, she said, "Talk to Wade first. Ask him what happened. You'll see that he couldn't have killed that young woman. You'll see that he's not a killer."

"Shut up!"

Johanna pressed, "You've got the wrong man!"

"Put a gag over her mouth."

"No!" Johanna shook her head. "I'll be quiet."

Johanna held her breath when the focus of attention shifted to Wade as he approached. She bit her lips as he drew close enough for her to see his face.

"Get down from that horse," Pierce ordered.

Johanna struggled to stand as he complied. She saw Wade look at her as he came closer. She saw his consternation at seeing her bound.

"What are you going to do with her?" he asked sharply.

Pierce shrugged. "Like you care."

"I care. I don't want anybody suffering for me, especially her. She had nothing to do with what happened."

"But you did."

"I don't know. Maybe I did somehow. All I do know is that when I got to the ranch house, Mary was lying on the floor with a bullet hole in her chest."

"You killed her."

"No, I didn't. She was already dead, I told you. I tried to revive her."

"Bastard!" Nells took a threatening step toward Wade as he interjected, "You tried to revive her, huh? You tried to save her life. You couldn't see that she was already dead? You couldn't tell that her eyes were blank . . . still open, but blank, with all the life gone out of them."

Wade turned toward him and said, "Her eyes weren't open. They were closed."

"No, they weren't! They were open, like she was still looking at me and blaming me."

"Blaming you? For what?"

Nells shook his head and darted a glance around him. He turned toward Pierce as the older man said slowly, "Yeah, Nells . . . blaming you for what?"

"For nothing. I didn't see nothing."

Pierce took an angry step toward him. "Answer me, Nells. What was Mary blaming you for? How did you see her while her eyes were still open with no life in them? Tell me, Nells!"

Nells stuttered, "It . . . it wasn't my fault that it happened! I heard Mary had invited Bartlett to the house when nobody was going to be there. I went to warn her what people would think. She said that Bartlett wanted to tell her something, and she wanted to hear it . . . privately . . . with nobody else around. I kept telling her that nobody would believe she was innocent. I told her people would talk about her!"

"What did you care what people would think about Mary, Nells?" Pierce's face was florid as he faced the man more squarely. "Why didn't you want anybody to talk about her?"

"Because I loved her, that's why!" Nells was shaking. His pale face flushed hotly as he said, "I told her that I didn't want anybody thinking she was less than she was. She said she wasn't worried about that, and I told her that I was! I told her that I'd kill Bartlett before I'd let him tarnish her name and make her out to be something she wasn't."

Shaking, Nells continued, "I took out my gun and Mary told me to put it back in my holster. I told her I wouldn't. I said if Bartlett walked through the door, he'd have a bullet waiting for him. Mary got excited. She rushed toward me and tried to take the gun out of my hand. She bumped into me when she grabbed for the gun . . . and it went off. I didn't realize she had been shot until she fell backward."

"You . . . you killed her?"

"I didn't kill her." Nells' eyes grew wild as he exclaimed, "It was Bartlett's fault! He was the reason I was there. He was the reason Mary struggled for the gun. He was the reason she got shot!"

Stunned, Pierce looked at Nells. His gun hand drooped as he said, "You knew all the while that Bartlett was innocent."

"He ain't innocent, I tell you. He's guilty! Mary's dead because of him! It's that bastard's fault!"

Turning, Nells swung his fist at Wade unexpectedly. It connected squarely with Wade's jaw, and he staggered backward. He tripped and fell, and the crack when his head hit a rock behind him reverberated in the small campsite. He did not move and Johanna cried out his name.

Momentarily distracted, Pierce glanced at Wade just long enough for Nells to knock the gun out of his hand. Retrieving it in a flash of movement, Nells said hotly, "If you ain't going to shoot this bastard for what he did, then I will."

Johanna gasped. The howling that had begun echoing in her ears grew to an overwhelming din as Nells cocked the gun. She caught her breath, unprepared for the growling wolf that leapt unexpectedly out of the bushes.

Gasping, Johanna watched as the great animal locked its jaws on Nells' arm. She saw Nells fall under the weight of the wolf's unexpected assault. Frozen with shock, she heard Nells scream as he attempted to protect himself from the bloody fangs that tore at his flesh, but his flailing punches were no match for the animal, who went straight for his throat.

Johanna heard Nells' screams turn into a gurgling sound. She saw his blood gush. She watched as his arms went limp and the blood continued flowing. She saw Pierce scramble for the gun that had been knocked from Nells' hand. She went still when he leveled it at the wolf, whose jaw was still locked on Nells' throat.

Johanna gasped again when Pierce pulled the trigger.

The gun misfired, and shock registered in Pierce's expression. Incredulous, Pierce fired again and again, but the result was the same.

The great wolf turned slowly toward him, its fangs dripping blood.

Unable to move . . . unable to make a sound, Johanna saw Pierce scramble for his rifle. She knew she would never forget the moment when the wolf turned briefly in her direction, its jaws still bloodied from the attack, before dashing off at a run.

Johanna glanced at Wade, who lay unconscious from Nells' blow a few feet away, then gasped when she saw Pierce pursuing the wolf, his rifle readied. She held her breath when she heard his running footsteps stop.

Silence.

Johanna held her breath until Pierce reappeared at the campsite. His expression stunned, he said, "The wolf . . . it got away . . . disappeared into thin air."

Pierce kneeled beside Nells. He looked back up at her to say in a tone devoid of emotion, "He's dead."

She saw Pierce glance at Wade, who was beginning to stir. Her heart pounded as he withdrew a knife from the sheath at his waist. She gasped when he walked toward her with the knife clenched in his hand, and then knelt abruptly to slice her bonds.

Looking back at Nells, his face gray, Pierce said simply, "Nells is the one who did it. He killed Mary."

Mounting his horse, he left without another word.

Johanna looked up when she felt Wade's arms slip unexpectedly around her. His head was bloodied and she reached up to cup his cheek. She saw the concern in his eyes when he looked at her.

She said simply, "It's over."

CHAPTER EIGHT

No, it couldn't be true!

Letty stood motionless opposite the pale, elderly servant who had appeared at her door a few minutes earlier. Millie had ushered the man into her sunlit morning room immediately after his arrival with the devastating news that James had been attacked on the street outside his home.

Momentarily unable to reply to the obviously grief-stricken servant, she swallowed and then responded, "Where is Mr. Ferguson now?"

"He's at home, ma'am. The doctor has been attending him throughout the night, but his wounds are severe. He has been mumbling your name." The elderly servant paused, obviously overwhelmed. He continued hoarsely, "The doctor is uncertain whether he will survive."

Shocked, Letty was unable to respond. The wolf's howls during the night had been endless.

She had finally fallen asleep out of sheer exhaustion, promising herself that she would visit Samuel Wallace again to see if any news had reached him regarding her daughters. But never in a million years had she imagined that James—

Withholding a sob, Letty called out abruptly, "Millie, bring my wrap." Turning back to the elderly servant, she questioned, "How did you get here?"

"By carriage, ma'am. It's waiting outside."

"We'll ride back together."

Millie appeared in the doorway with Letty's wrap in hand. She said with obvious distress, "You're not properly dressed, ma'am. It'll only take a moment for me to put up your hair and ready proper attire."

"No, I don't have time." Grabbing her wrap, Letty said to the elderly fellow, "Let's go."

A short time later, Letty crouched beside James' bed, trembling with fear. His eyes were closed and his breathing was faint. She glanced up at the bespectacled doctor. He shook his head, and Letty looked back at James and whispered urgently, "James, do you hear me? It's Letty. Open your eyes, James. Please open your eyes."

James did not stir.

"James . . ."

A hand on Letty's shoulder turned her toward the doctor as he whispered, "He was calling for you, but he can't hear you now. The best thing you can do for him at present is to let him sleep. His wounds are severe. He had evidently been lying on the street for some time before he was found.

He's lost a lot of blood. If he wasn't as muscular as he is, he might not be breathing right now. Hard muscle evidently protected him; but to be honest, I can't be sure if any major organs were damaged."

"What are you saying, doctor?"

"I'm saying that a man who was not as strong as he might not have survived the night."

"But he will get better. He will survive."

The doctor did not respond, and Letty sank slowly to her knees. Sobbing, she laid her head against James' bed. It couldn't be true! It couldn't have happened again . . . despite her fears . . . despite her precautions. She could not be responsible for another man's death. She could not bear it.

"Letty . . ."

Letty felt a shaky touch against her hair. She snapped her head up to see that James' eyes had opened. He was attempting to speak.

"No, don't try to talk, James. You're weak. You need to rest."

"Letty . . ."

"James, please . . ."

"Don't cry."

Letty brushed the tears from her cheeks as she responded shakily, "I won't, not any more because I know now that you'll recuperate. I'm depending on it, James."

"Depending on it . . ."

"That you'll get well. I need to see you get well. I need to believe that at least this time, it won't all end tragically."

"Don't cry. I . . . don't . . . want . . ."

James' words trailed to a halt and the doctor brushed her aside. Her heart pounded as the physician examined James and then turned back toward her, his expression relieved as he said, "He's unconscious, but his condition doesn't appear to have worsened. I suppose we should be thankful for that."

Letty's knees trembled, and she sat abruptly on the chair beside the bed.

The doctor continued, "It would be better if you left now, Miss Wolf. If he awakens and tries to talk to you again, it might be too much for him."

Letty protested, "But he called my name! He wants me to be here."

"He saw you. You told him that you want him to get well. He needs time and rest in order for that to happen."

Letty glanced at James' still form. His skin was so white. There were dark circles under his eyes, and he was lying so still. Except for the slight rise and fall of his chest, he was motionless. Swallowing against the tightness in her throat, she managed to say, "I'll leave for a few hours if you think that's best, but if James awakens, please tell him why I left. Tell him I'll be back." She added hoarsely, "If he awakens, tell him . . . tell him I . . ." She took a breath. "Tell him I'll be back."

"I will."

Letty stared at the weary doctor a moment longer and then strode toward the door, her lips tight with purpose.

* * *

Mason Little raised his head at the sound of a commotion in his outer office. Rounding his desk with annoyance, he was about to reach for the doorknob when he recognized the angry voice in the outer office. It was female. It was—

The door burst open at that moment. "What happened, Mason?" Letty asked angrily. "Why didn't you do as I asked? James was attacked and almost killed last night. The doctor says he isn't certain he'll survive. You were supposed to see that James was protected! You said you would handle that for me. I believed you!" When Mason did not immediately respond, Letty demanded, "Answer me, Mason!"

Mason looked at her without replying. Her dark hair was unbound. It streamed down over the shoulders of her yellow morning gown in riotous disarray. She wore no makeup as she clutched a flimsy wrap around herself, her knuckles white, and he realized in that moment that he could no longer deny that Letty Wolf was one of the most beautiful women he had ever seen. It was no wonder that his uncle—

"Tell me what happened, Mason! I need to know."

"Aunt Letty, please, don't get so upset!"

Mason attempted to usher Letty to a nearby chair, but she stood rigidly still as she said, "I was worried something like this might happen to James. I asked you to hire a detective to follow and protect him. You knew how important this was to me. Why didn't you follow through?"

"I'm so sorry. The truth is, I didn't realize how

urgent it was. I contacted the detective agency just as I said I would. Robert Pinkerton said he couldn't possibly have a man in place without a week's notice. I thought that would be time enough. I had no idea that an attack was imminent."

"He's severely wounded, Mason. He may die."

His expression grave, Mason repeated, "I'm so sorry, Aunt Letty. I wouldn't have disappointed you for the world, and I certainly would not have allowed this to happen." He paused, and then asked, "What made you suspicious? How did you know this was going to happen?"

Letty stepped back. She sat abruptly on the chair that Mason had indicated. She said indistinctly, "You wouldn't understand."

"I would. I'm sure I would if you would trust me."

"It's not a matter of trust, Mason." Letty looked up at him, and Mason felt the intensity of her gaze as she said, "It's something difficult to explain . . . difficult to understand . . . difficult to believe."

"The messages you receive at night."

Letty's jaw stiffened. "I would appreciate it if you would forget I ever said that. As far as how I knew this was going to happen, call it a hunch . . . a premonition . . . whatever you choose. But I want you to make sure that a detective is put on duty immediately. James needs to be protected. I will not allow anything else to happen to him."

"You said he was severely wounded in the attack, that he might not survive. If he doesn't—"

"He will survive! He has to!" Letty paused for a

shaky breath. She said softly, "I apologize, Mason. This was my fault, not yours. I failed to say that I wanted immediate protection for James—but I do want a detective to start immediately. Do you understand? I want the protection to begin today."

"Of course, Aunt Letty." Mason hovered over her solicitously as he said, "I think you should go home now and rest. This affair has obviously affected you deeply."

Letty stood up abruptly. "No, I'm going back to James."

"I wish you wouldn't. You need to regain control of your emotions."

"I'm fine."

"Aunt Letty . . ."

"Call the detective agency, Mason."

"I will."

"I will be at James' house if you need to contact me."

"Of course."

Letty said abruptly as she looked up at Mason, "I can't let it happen again. Not again."

She left without a word of farewell.

She had said, "It's over."

But was it?

Seated beside Wade on the narrow wagon seat several days later, Johanna remembered the words she had spoken while John Nells' bloody body lay lifeless a few yards away. Weatherby Pierce had brought his pursuit of Wade to a close

with Nells' confession that he had killed young
Mary Malone, but Johanna could not easily forget
the aftermath that day.

Wade had escorted her back to the wagon train
so that she would not have to witness Nells' bur-
ial. Wade had told her in the time since that he
knew his slate would be wiped clean when Pierce
returned to Millborn and told Mary's father that
Nells was the man who had killed his daughter.
He had said he hoped that Paul Malone would
find peace in knowing that Nells had paid the
price for his crime, but he wondered if the grieving father would ever recover.

Johanna looked up at Wade as he scrutinized
the surrounding terrain cautiously. Despite his
head injury, Wade had again taken up scouting for
the wagon train until McMullen could resume
that chore. He had become a hero of sorts to the
majority of the travelers on the train, including
her. It was a term he had refused to accept.

In the intimacy and silence of night, Wade had
told her that with the charges against him
dropped, he was free to accompany her to Arizona without any restrictions involved—if she
wanted it that way. If? Her heart had sung at his
solemn declaration. She loved him with a complete and lasting emotion that she had not expected ever to experience. She knew this feeling
would not end. She knew Wade loved her, too—
but in the days since, she had silently begun questioning if that was enough.

Why had she sensed a strange hesitation in

him? Why did Wade hold her so desperately close during intimate moments, as if he were uncertain what the future held? Was it because so many questions about her personal life were still unanswered? She, herself, could not help wondering about the image that visited her in her dreams, and why he had chosen to appear to her. And was he truly a dream, a figment of her need, or was he a visitation meant to protect her?

If so, *what was the image protecting her from?*

The inexplicable appearance of the wolf that had come to her aid in two dire situations had become an unmentionable phenomena that stood between Wade and her. The animal's shocking viciousness had been almost as startling as his equally strange disappearance afterward.

Could it all possibly be coincidence?

Most disturbing of all, however, was the strange howling that only she could hear . . . the howling that still had not abated. What did it mean? Did it mean she was still in danger; and if so, was Wade in danger because of her?

Or . . . was she losing her mind?

Johanna moved unconsciously closer to Wade. McMullen had insisted that her wagon change location in the train, that it travel up front, closer to his, so that Wade would be more available to him during his scouting chores. Neither Wade nor she had protested that change, but she had the feeling that Wade, as well as she, sensed McMullen had simply used scouting as an excuse to keep them closer.

Johanna had noted that some of the women on the train had begun making attempts to chat with her. Some, Jeremiah's family to be specific, had actually become friends, and that pleased her.

Yet despite all these improvements in her life, tension still twitched at her senses. She recalled awakening with a start during the previous night. The howling had been so loud that she had barely resisted the urge to cover her ears to shield herself from the sound. She remembered that Wade had awakened, too. Appearing to sense what was happening, he had merely drawn her close in an embrace that had gradually calmed her fears without a word being spoken between them.

Rely on him.

Do not fear.

And why did those words, uttered by a dream image in a tongue that was foreign to her ears, rebound in her mind whenever she felt uncertain?

Turning to look down at her at that moment, Wade did not smile. Instead, as if reading her mind, he said softly, "It's not over yet, is it, darlin'?"

Hardly able to speak the words, Johanna responded in a whisper, "No, I'm afraid it's not."

Percy Smart cursed the hot Texas terrain that appeared to go on interminably as his mount trudged forward. He muttered soft expletives against his horse's dragging pace, against the unfamiliar clothing that chafed at his neck and legs, and against the wide-brimmed hat that had begun cooking his brains under the hot sun's rays.

He had become confused, finding it difficult to follow the trail.

His inability to sleep during the night had become almost unbearable, and his stomach was beginning to revolt against the tasteless meals he prepared over an open fire. If he did not know what awaited him should he return to the city without accomplishing his assignment, he would have abandoned it without a second thought. Even pride in accomplishing the job no longer stood in the way of his desire to go back where he belonged.

Cursing again, Percy spurred his horse, hoping for more speed. He could not find the wagon train fast enough. He could not locate Johanna Higgins quickly enough. He could not bring his assignment to a conclusion rapidly enough to suit him. When it was over—and he silently vowed it would be over soon—he had determined that he would depart this uncivilized Texas soil and never leave the city again.

Yes, *never*.

With that thought providing his only consolation, Percy continued doggedly on.

"We're going to be leaving the wagon train soon."

McMullen looked up at Wade's sober declaration. The wagon train had made camp for the night, and McMullen had just finished eating his evening meal. Johanna was concluding the last of her chores in her wagon, and Wade had taken this moment to talk to McMullen privately.

Wade frowned at what he saw when he studied the wagon master. McMullen had resumed his scouting chores, but his face was gray with exhaustion as he stood beside the fire. The night was clear and bright, the temperature comfortable, but Wade could see that those facts were far from McMullen's mind as he replied, "I figured you'd be branching off when we start heading north tomorrow."

Wade nodded. "I expect I'll turn Johanna's wagon west for Mammoth or Quijotoa. There should be any number of places along the way where strikes have been made recently."

"That sounds like as good a plan as any."

Wade could hear the disapproval in McMullen's voice, and he responded, "Say it, McMullen. You don't think it's a good idea for Johanna and me to go off on our own."

McMullen said solemnly, "It's better than watching Johanna go off all alone, like she planned when she first got here. I know it sounds strange, but Johanna has become like a daughter to me somehow. I'm worried about her. I think this whole idea of hers about prospecting is the craziest thing I've ever heard."

Wade gave a short laugh. "It's crazy, all right, but it's Johanna's dream. She's been heading toward this time and place her whole life."

"And Johanna is *your* dream."

Wade sobered. He considered McMullen's response for long moments and then replied, "I figure that's about right. I've done my share of wandering, and I know what I want. I expect Johanna has the same right to try getting what she wants in life."

"You realize that with a wagon filled with the kind of equipment that Johanna was talked into buying, you and she will be a target for every undesirable looking to make some fast money. And you'll be unprotected."

"Johanna will never be unprotected with me around."

A fleeting smile cracked McMullen's countenance. "I know you mean that, but I'm wondering if your guns will be enough."

"They'll be enough. Johanna is a determined woman. She won't give up easily and neither will I. We've been through a lot together—maybe more than you know."

"I expect you have." McMullen added, "I owe you for what you did for me, too, taking over the scouting and keeping this train moving like you did. So I feel like I need to be honest with you and tell you what's on my mind before you leave."

"Go ahead. I figured you had something to say. That's why I'm here tonight, giving you the time to say it."

"I've got the feeling that it ain't all over for you yet, Wade. I can't explain what I mean by that except to say that things don't look exactly right to me."

"You mean with Johanna."

McMullen nodded. "There's more to the determination that drives her than just plain stubbornness. There's something behind it."

It was Wade's turn to nod. "I learned my lesson long ago that if there's something you want, you need to fight for it. Johanna knows that, too, which accounts for part of what you see. If it makes you feel any better, I had the same feeling, and I expect to stay at her side to help handle whatever comes her way." A smile flickered briefly across Wade's lips as he added, "Of course, if I said that to Johanna, she'd say she was capable of handling her own problems."

"Don't I know it." McMullen hesitated, and then added, "Tomorrow's the day."

"I know."

"You'll be saying good-bye to everybody here then."

"That's right, Johanna and me."

"Think it over, Wade. I don't mean you should come to Oregon territory with us, but make sure you're both making the right decision."

"I've already thought over my part of it."

"Your mind's made up?"

"I knew from the first minute I saw Johanna that she was special. Hell, she practically knocked me senseless when I first laid eyes on her. And she is . . . well, maybe more special than I bargained for, but she's what I want. I'm willing to take everything that comes with her. That's about the size of it."

"Then I wish you luck." McMullen extended his hand. "I ain't never been more sincere, neither. We'll be hitting the branch-off sometime tomorrow, so you can start pulling your wagon out of line before midday."

"I'll do that . . . and thanks for everything."

Wade accepted the hand McMullen extended and shook it warmly. He turned back to Johanna's wagon with a sober countenance, and with a dark premonition about the days to come.

"It's been four days, Dr. Fuller. James doesn't seem to be getting any better."

Letty stood outside the door to James' room, where she had been spending the major portion of each day since the attack that had left him near death. She had even spent the first nights there, unwilling to leave him until Dr. Fuller had demanded that she go home to rest. She had followed his orders to avoid argument, and had returned home to bathe and change her clothes, then had come back early the next morning. She had been present during James' few bouts of consciousness, when he had taken some broth and other liquids. He had seemed content that she was nearby before slipping back into unconsciousness.

She had walked in on Dr. Fuller the previous day when he was changing James' bandages, and the horror of the wounds had almost drained her consciousness as well. She could not imagine who had attacked him so viciously, but she believed it was not a random attack, as the police seemed to think.

She had been pleased initially to see that a

Pinkerton had arrived to assume guard duty outside James' room almost within an hour of her visit to Mason. She had not been able to strike from her mind the belated thought that Robert Pinkerton had provided protection for James almost upon request, while Mason had said Pinkerton had claimed he could not provide a man without a week's notice.

That thought was forced from her mind when James moved restlessly in bed, an expression of pain crossing his face. Letty forced herself to ask Dr. Fuller the question that she had dreaded.

"Has he gotten worse, doctor?"

"No." Tall, thin, with a serious demeanor, Dr. Fuller frowned. "But he hasn't improved to any great extent either. The fact that nothing drastic has occurred is encouraging."

"By nothing drastic, you mean that James hasn't died."

"And his wounds haven't become infected. The pain you see reflected on his face is to be expected. The stab wounds were deep."

Letty's face turned pale, and Dr. Fuller said abruptly, "Perhaps you should sit down, Miss Wolf."

"I'm fine." Letty took a deep breath and a firm hold on her senses as she said, "Please continue."

"I don't want to lie to you, Miss Wolf. Mr. Ferguson's wounds are exceedingly severe. It's been four days, but it will take more time than that for his body to overcome his loss of blood. The fact that he isn't worse leads me to believe he is recuperating."

"Oh . . ." Letty gave a short, relieved laugh. "I

thought you were going to tell me he was going to die."

"That may still happen, of course."

Letty went still.

"Miss Wolf." Appearing to regret his former statement, Dr. Fuller continued, "I don't want to mislead you."

A rasping voice from the bed interjected, "I'm fine."

Letty's head turned toward James as he continued, "Don't listen to him, Letty. I'm getting better."

Beside his bed in a moment, her eyes brimming with tears, Letty looked down at James. Momentarily unable to speak, she saw that he was still unnaturally pale and drawn. The circles under his eyes had deepened, and his normally pink lips were gray. Without thinking, she pressed her mouth lightly against them. She saw his gaze flicker as he said, "That was good. I wish . . ." His face suddenly twisted with pain, and Letty called out, "Dr. Fuller . . ."

"Please leave, Miss Wolf," Dr. Fuller said as he pushed her aside. "Talking to you has obviously been too much for him."

Unwilling to leave while she was still uncertain of James' condition, Letty trembled uncontrollably. She saw the doctor lean toward James as he struggled to speak, and her shuddering increased. She held her breath when James' lips grew still.

When Dr. Fuller turned back toward her at last, he said, "The pain in his back is sometimes excruciating. It . . . overwhelms him at times."

Letty took a hopeful step and looked at James. He was so still. She looked up at Dr. Fuller for encouragement. When he did not speak, she finally asked, "What did he say to you? Tell me, please."

Dr. Fuller hesitated. Finally, raising his chin with unexpected hauteur, the doctor reported, "Mr. Ferguson just instructed me . . . he just told me very clearly that I should 'stick to the business of curing him and mind my own business about telling you to leave.'"

"Oh."

Letty took a few backward steps and then turned away when the doctor looked back at the bed. She could not help smiling.

"He's still alive. I wanted him dead!"

Peter Klein faced Mr. Charles in his paneled office. Unlike the last time they had met, Peter was not smiling. Neither was Mr. Charles, as he replied, "My man thought he had finished the job. He stabbed Ferguson four times. That fella had to have more lives than a cat to survive."

"Cat or not, he's still alive, and the fact that he was injured instead of being killed only worsened the situation I was attempting to correct." Peter's aristocratic face flushed as he said hotly, "You owe me, Charlie. Your man didn't finish the job. I want it done and I want it done right!"

Mr. Charles' sweaty face darkened. Former partner or not, he didn't like the way Peter had barged into his office. He didn't like the tone Peter had taken with him, either. He had read about James

Ferguson's attack in the newspaper, and he had been as stunned as Peter to read that Ferguson was still alive. He had immediately summoned his man and berated him hotly for his poor performance. The fellow had been as shocked as he was that Ferguson had survived, and he had volunteered to fix the situation as soon as possible.

"You do realize that another attack on Ferguson will negate the opinion that it was merely a random robbery. You do realize that suspicion might be cast upon me."

"Why would anyone suspect you had paid to have Ferguson killed? He ain't no partner of yours that you'd want to get rid of, and he don't have no business connections with you that might had left you in a snit. I checked all that."

"Why did you 'check all that'? I hope you weren't going to send your man out to finish the job without talking to me first."

Mr. Charles' small eyes narrowed. He didn't like Peter's tone at all as he said simply, "I like to be prepared."

"Admit it! You were as angry as I am that your man failed!"

"I don't like leaving a job half done. And you didn't answer my question."

"What question?"

"Why would anybody suspect you of hiring someone to kill Ferguson?"

"That's simple: because I want the woman who's beginning to turn her favor on him."

"A woman is at the bottom of all this? Who is

she? Letty Wolf? From what I hear, Ferguson already had his turn with her and she's through with him."

"That's *Miss Wolf* to you."

"Really? From what I hear, she don't have such a perfect background, no matter what circles she's accepted in these days."

"Like me."

"Right, like you."

"And that's why I want her." Peter walked a step closer to Mr. Charles' desk to say forcefully, "And that's why I'm going to have her."

"No matter what you've got to do to get her?"

"That's right."

"Which means . . ."

"Which means I expect your man to make another try, and to succeed this time. I expect him to come up with a way for James Ferguson to be canceled out . . . terminated . . . *to be dead this time for good* without casting any suspicion on me. I expect to be informed when your man is going to act, so I can make sure I am very visible on the opposite side of town when it happens. Do you understand?"

Mr. Charles forced himself to remain seated behind his desk. He wanted to stand. He wanted to put himself face-to-face with Peter Klein. He wanted to show the pompous fool that he couldn't get away with high-handed methods with him, but he'd be damned before he'd abandon his position of power in the office. He was a small man who did not stack up against Peter

Klein's height, but behind his desk, he gave the orders. Behind his desk he had only to glare at his subordinates to make them shake. Behind his desk he was king. Behind his desk he was still *Mr. Charles*, the most influential underworld boss in this section of the city—and he'd be damned if he'd let Peter Klein forget it.

Mr. Charles said softly, "Don't take that tone with me, Peter. I don't like it."

"You don't like it be damned!"

"Don't push me too far."

"I'll push you as far as I like! I paid to have a job done, and your man botched it. I want it fixed. Ferguson's condition is shaky. Now is the time to act."

"There's a Pinkerton watching his bedroom door. There are Pinkertons there day and night. There's no way I can get a man in there without suspicion being raised."

"Take care of it."

Mr. Charles looked at him.

"Take care of it, I said."

Mr. Charles replied, "And if I choose not to take care of it?"

Peter went still. His face turning an apoplectic color, he rasped, "I warn you, you'd better do it, and do it quickly."

Pausing only to glare at Mr. Charles a moment longer, Peter turned and stomped out of the room.

The echo of the door slamming behind Peter sounded in Mr. Charles's office. Standing slowly as perspiration trailed from his temples in snaking streams, Mr. Charles did not speak.

He had warned Peter Klein.

He had warned the bastard not to push him too far.

Percy Smart smiled with satisfaction at the wagon train tracks in front of him. He could not understand how he had missed the trail earlier. He knew he was not the tracker that Larry Worth had been. He silently regretted the moment when discomfort had distracted him enough for Worth to be able to get the drop on him. He hadn't wanted to kill that Pinkerton yet.

Smart looked up into the distance. The wagon train wasn't too far ahead of him. He would finish his job within a few days, wire Dobbs that everything had been taken care of, and then start back to the city. He looked forward to that day. The thought brought a smile to his sweaty face.

Smart spurred his mount forward with a low growl. He'd get rid of the lazy animal that stable hand had given him then, too, and he'd be damned if he'd ever sit a western saddle again.

He was looking forward to it.

Twilight was quickly approaching. Wade glanced at Johanna soberly. They were alone. There was no wagon in front or behind them. They had broken off from the wagon train where McMullen had indicated, and after a few, brief good-byes, had headed west.

Wade studied Johanna's sober expression and then dismounted from the wagon. He couldn't read what she was thinking as he lifted her down as well, and that worried him.

Johanna turned toward him abruptly. Her eyes were sober as she said, "I'll get supper going if you'll make a fire."

"All right." But Wade did not release her. Instead, he drew her closer and asked abruptly, "Are you sorry that we left the wagon train, Johanna?"

"No."

"Are you worried about being alone without the security of the others?"

"No!"

"What's wrong, then?"

Johanna shook her head.

He said softly, "It's the howling. It hasn't stopped."

Johanna gasped hopefully, "Do you hear it, too?"

"No."

"Then how . . . ?"

"I just knew."

Johanna's brow furrowed as she said, "I thought it had all ended when Nells was killed, and for a while it did. Then the howling started up again. I tried to ignore it, but I couldn't. It frightens me, Wade, because nobody hears that howling but me."

"You forget that I was there when the horses bolted and we lost a wheel. I saw what happened to that bear. I saw what happened to Nells, too. I figure there's no explanation for that, either."

"But I don't know how to make the howling stop."

Wade drew her closer. He tilted her face up to

his as he whispered, "Rely on me. Don't be afraid."

Wade saw Johanna's eyes widen. He felt the trembling that beset her. Frowning, he said, "Remember that you're going forward just like you planned your whole life long. Maybe the howling has something to do with that sense of purpose. If it does, I'll make sure that it doesn't get out of hand. Just remember, whatever it all means, we'll face it together."

Her eyes moist, Johanna replied, "I didn't want it to be like this. I figured my life was my own responsibility. When I came out here, I was certain that I would be able to handle everything on my own. I didn't expect things to happen that I didn't understand. I don't want to do this to you."

"You don't want to do what? You don't want me to love you? You don't want to give me the direction that I've been searching for all my life? You don't want to make me feel the wonder of holding you in my arms and of making love to you? You don't want me to look forward to a place in the future where I've never looked before?"

"It's the same for me, Wade. I never loved any man before you. I never dreamed it was possible to feel anyone else's happiness or pain, to look forward to night when I can feel your arms around me—or to see a new direction in my future that I've never dreamed of before."

Overwhelmed by her words, Wade whispered, "Is that how I make you feel?"

Johanna said in a rush, "But I feel guilty, too,

when I see that along with the joy we share,
you're also sharing my uncertainties. I wish—"

His expression suddenly intense, Wade interrupted, "Don't wish. Just listen. I would've believed in you even if I hadn't seen what I saw in
the copse that night, or when Nells pointed that
gun at me. You're beautiful, but you don't give a
damn about beauty. You're stubborn and bossy,
but the determination that has made you what
you are fuels those traits. I love what you are, Johanna. I love *you*." Wade's voice grew hoarse.
"The truth is, you're everything I ever wanted,
and nothing and no one will ever take you from
me while there's still a breath in my body."

Raising her hand, Johanna covered his mouth
as she pleaded, "Don't say that!" She did not
protest when Wade's hand rose to press her palm
more tightly to his lips. He kissed it in wordless
repetition of his statement. He released her hand
and lowered his mouth to hers to kiss her in silent
promise. He drew her closer, his hands touching
her in intimate exploration that raised their emotions higher. He stroked her soft flesh. He
breathed in her sweet scent. He tasted her, and
felt a driving hunger for more. Scooping Johanna
up into his arms, he walked a few steps to lay her
in a leafy bower nearby. He lay beside her and
trailed his mouth over her fluttering eyelids, the
slope of her cheek, the curve of her chin. He
found the moist acceptance of her mouth and in-
tensified his kiss before trailing his caresses
downward once more.

Wade was shuddering when the impediment of clothing became suddenly more than he could bear. Reaching up under her skirt, he drew down the undergarment that shielded her warm delta from him. He tossed it aside as he loosened his own clothing. Unwilling to wait a moment longer, he thrust himself into her moist core.

Wade looked down at Johanna when he came to rest inside her. He saw the flush that had transfused her face. Knowing that she shared the rapture of the moment, he thrust more deeply. He was uncertain when Johanna began meeting the power of his movements. He felt only the supreme ecstasy that grew between them. He knew only that this was their moment to share . . . that it was meant to be this way, and that he would never let her go.

His restraint gone, Wade abandoned himself to the moment, welcoming the throbbing spasms that sent them careening into the beauty of their love.

Moments later, Wade raised his head to look down at Johanna. Breathing as heavily as he, she opened her eyes and then drew his mouth down to hers. Her kiss was lingering before she drew back to whisper, "I love you, Wade. In some ways, I think that I've already found much of what I've wanted all my life."

"But not all." His voice heavy with promise, Wade whispered, "I'll help you find the rest— whatever it is. That's a promise that's easy for me to make to you."

"When I'm lying in your arms?"

"Always."

Wade's words lingered in the quiet solitude surrounding them.

Johanna realized gradually, with growing incredulity, that all *was* silent around her, and that the strange howling that had allowed her no rest had stopped.

Uncertain how long the respite would last, Johanna only knew that this time was theirs alone. Sliding her arms around him, she drew Wade down against her once more, determined to make it last.

CHAPTER NINE

Letty went momentarily still as she attempted to open the front door of James' house with the key that his butler, Willis, had provided. The chain lock had been engaged, hindering her entry. She had been arriving early each morning since James was injured and had remained long into the night, leaving only after others in the household had retired and when she was certain that James was asleep. Giving little thought during that time to her soirees, she finally left for a few hours rest, but not before cautioning the Pinkertons to check on James periodically.

With the Pinkertons outside James' bedroom door affording the unconscious man protection, Willis had arranged to leave the chain lock on the front door disengaged at night so she might enter at will in the morning. Willis was a dear fellow who had demonstrated in so many ways that his affection for James was deep and sincere, and that he appreciated the comfort that Letty had provided his master during his fight for life.

So why was the chain lock suddenly engaged?

Letty rang the doorbell, uncertain how to react. The flustered, gray-haired woman in early morning dishabille who responded to her ring startled her.

Letty asked bluntly, "Who are you?"

Just as blunt, the woman responded, "Who are you?"

Determined to break the stalemate between them, Letty said, "My name is Letty Wolf, and I'm here to see James. As a matter of fact, I've been at his bedside most of the time since he was attacked, so I'm asking again, who are you?"

"Oh, dear . . ." The older woman's eyes filled. She looked back at the gray-haired gentleman approaching behind her and said, "This is Letty Wolf, George." She turned back to say, "Please come in. My name is Ethel Hathaway, and this is my husband, George. I'm James' aunt, his mother's only sister and his only living relative. George and I have come here from Poughkeepsie to stay with him until he recuperates. We learned of the attack on him belatedly. I can't imagine why it took so long for someone to notify us, but we came as soon as we were able. We arrived late last night."

Aunt Ethel brushed away the tear that slipped down her sagging cheek as she ushered Letty in and said, "Willis told me how much you've done for James, staying by his bedside and arranging for Pinkertons to be stationed at his door while he is helpless. That has meant so much to us, and I know it means a great deal to James as well."

Stunned by the woman's unexpected appearance, Letty was momentarily hesitant.

"Please . . . feel free to go right upstairs. James may be asleep, but he will be happy to know you were here when he wakes up."

Letty started toward the stairs to James' second-floor bedroom. James had never mentioned his Aunt Ethel or Uncle George, although there was no doubt that the woman's grief was real. She turned to look at Aunt Ethel as she climbed the stairs beside her and said, "Willis is an old friend, of course. He has been so helpful to us. He installed us in our room and outlined all the arrangements you have made for James. He told me that you and James are long-time friends, and that my dear nephew asked for you by name. He said that you've taken over his care as Dr. Fuller outlined, and that you've spent every minute of every day by his bedside. I can't thank you enough for that, and I'm sure James feels the same."

Letty nodded briefly to the Pinkerton seated outside James' room and then entered, with Aunt Ethel close behind. She walked directly to James' bed. The sight of him so pale and listless touched a vulnerable spot deep inside her and her eyes filled. She was unprepared when James' eyes fluttered open and he muttered, "Letty . . ." And then, "Don't cry."

"I'm not crying, James." Letty swallowed the

thickness in her throat as she said, "Aunt Ethel and Uncle George are here."

"Yes, I'm here, dear!"

James nodded. He rasped in a whisper, "Stay. Don't leave." His eyes drifted closed as he repeated, "Don't leave."

Letty turned when Dr. Fuller appeared at the door unexpectedly and said, "He's better, you know." He continued as he approached, "I arrived earlier. Ethel told the cook to make me some breakfast after I checked on James. I'm pleased to report that his heartbeat is stronger and more regular. He has already taken some nourishment, and I've instructed that he is to receive more in small doses, but whenever he wants it." He added, "I'm quite sure now that James will survive."

"Praise the Lord!"

Aunt Ethel turned into the arms of her husband after her exuberant exclamation and sobbed uncontrollably while Letty restrained her emotional reaction to Dr. Fuller's statement with sheer strength of will.

Composing herself at last, the older woman dried her eyes and took Letty's arm as she said, "Dear, I think it would be best if we allow James to sleep for a while. Why don't you come downstairs with me to partake of some tea? I would very much like to hear your report of all that has happened."

Letty looked back at James. She didn't want to leave him. The Pinkerton was outside his door, his aunt and uncle were there to watch over him, and

Dr. Fuller had declared for the first time that he would survive. She wanted nothing more at that moment than to allow Dr. Fuller's announcement to eliminate the anxiety that had been a constant undercurrent in her thoughts. She wanted to hold his hand and reassure herself that he was indeed improving. But the solitude and quiet of the countless hours she had spent with James was no longer possible.

"Come, dear. James needs his sleep and Dr. Fuller needs to check his wounds. You wouldn't want to be here for that."

Really . . . she wouldn't want to know that the vicious stab wounds were healing, so she could be certain that James was getting well?

Aunt Ethel led her from the room as Letty protested, "I wanted to make sure Helen takes special care when changing the bed linens on James' bed."

"I've already done that."

"I need to make certain that Dr. Fuller has everything he needs, that the dosage of James' medicine remains the same, and that everything is ready when James asks for it . . . broth, juice . . ."

"I've already done that, too. I've also arranged through Dr. Fuller for nurses to be on duty in his room at all times. The first one should arrive shortly. I've made sure that the house will function as it did before James was injured. I've told the servants to bring any problems that may occur to me. I've also checked to make sure that Pinkerton's men remain in the house for as long as James is off his feet. I appreciate those arrangements, which I understand you made. I will leave it to James to decide when they're no longer necessary."

Taking her arm again, Aunt Ethel guided her into the sitting room. She rang a bell on the table and said to the maid when she responded, "Miss Wolf and I would like some tea, Helen." She turned toward Letty as the maid scurried to comply and said, "I know James' mother would want me to be here. She loved James dearly, and George and I are the only relatives he has left. Willis told me that you and James have been friends for a long time, and that you've been very helpful during this difficulty. Now that we are here, we can relieve you of that burden."

Burden?

Letty did not reply.

"I must admit, however, despite all the positive things Willis had to say about you, he never mentioned that you were so lovely." Aunt Ethel smiled. "My dear, you are a beautiful woman." Letty remained silent as Aunt Ethel continued, "I hope you will still stop back to see James during his convalescence now that you have been relieved of your daily duties here."

Stunned, Letty realized that the well-meaning woman—who unlike her had a legitimate place at James' side—was dismissing her! Her throat tightened as she responded, "Yes, of course."

She was relieved when Helen came back into the room carrying a large silver tray and Aunt Ethel said, "Here is our tea. If you would like to look in on James again before you leave, that will be fine."

Letty waited wordlessly as Aunt Ethel prepared to pour.

The hours had dragged on endlessly for Letty after she'd left James' house earlier that morning. Her mind in a turmoil, she had been unable to accomplish even the smallest chore, and the distraction of evening had been long in coming.

Concealing the dead weight inside, Letty glanced at the unrelenting gaiety and sophistication of the people around her. She recalled her brief visit with James before she'd left. She had gone up to his room with Aunt Ethel following close behind. She had approached his bed and had sat beside it, intending a few, private moments with him. She had taken James' hand as he slept, and Aunt Ethel had advised fearfully that she might wake him. She had attempted to fix his bed, but Aunt Ethel had said she shouldn't bother because the nurse she had hired would see to his comfort. When there appeared to be no hope of solitude, she had attempted a chaste farewell kiss on James' cheek, only to have Aunt Ethel warn her not to jostle him.

The anxiety on the older woman's face had been sincere. It was also obvious to her that the woman's concern and determination to do her best for James had removed any need for her own presence. She had faced the fact that her being there would only give James hope for something that would never be.

With an ache deep inside, she had then glanced at James once more before leaving. Her farewell to Aunt Ethel and her silent husband was short and sincere. The older woman obviously loved James. He was in the best possible hands.

Her mind snapping back to the present, Letty acknowledged without joy that another successful soiree was in full motion. This was the pursuit to which she had devoted her life. In retrospect, the supreme effort she had extended—appearing to be so necessary at the time—now seemed excessive; and the accomplishments in which she had previously felt such pride seemed of little consequence. She was older, better dressed, more experienced, but nothing *real* had changed. She was still alone and uncertain what the future would hold.

She was, of course, a far cry from the destitute mother of three that she had been when Archibald died. Strangely enough, however, she seemed to have traded off the love of her three daughters for a sizable bank account, and the realization was deadening.

A soft howling echoed in her mind, and Letty grew still. Haunted by the cry and uncertain of the danger it foretold, she took an unsteady breath and started toward the nearest group. She knew she would be welcomed there, and she needed the distraction that the senseless chatter would provide. The fact that she would show interest in them appeared to please even the most difficult of men. The women, of course, often reacted differently. It was for that reason she took such care in her appearance, so that she would not give even the most difficult of females an opportunity to disparage her.

The brilliant red taffeta of Letty's gown rustled as she walked determinedly toward her animated guests. She needed a challenge that night. She needed to forget for a moment the ache deep inside that her dismissal from James' bedside had evoked. Although Aunt Ethel believed she was doing her a favor by releasing her from a demanding chore, the truth was that remaining close to James allowed her the only respite from fear available to her.

"Letty, I'm so pleased to see you."

Letty looked up, her forced smile fading at the sight of Peter Klein. She did not need to reply as Peter continued, "I wanted to express my deep concern about the attack on your friend. It was shocking. There appears to be no safety anywhere these days from thugs that walk the streets of the city."

"Thank you."

Ignoring her cold response, Peter continued, "I was hoping you could tell me that James is recuperating."

"The doctor now believes he will survive."

"Then his condition was uncertain at first?"

"Yes."

"I'm sure you were relieved to hear the doctor's report."

"Yes."

Peter hesitated at her clipped responses. He

said more softly, "I assumed when I saw you here tonight that reports of his health were favorable. I understand that you did not leave his bedside for days."

Letty did not respond, and Peter's lips twitched. He added, "I hope you will allow me to inquire about his recuperation from time to time. I have spoken only briefly to James, but I found him to be a very pleasant fellow. An attack in broad daylight in that section of the city is incomprehensible."

"Yes."

Peter hesitated again. When she said nothing further, he offered, with an attempt to conceal his annoyance, "I will leave you to your duties then, Letty. You have my best wishes for a good evening."

Letty turned her back as Peter walked away. He was angry at her treatment of him. She joined a group nearby to an enthusiastic reception and hoped Peter remembered that anger went both ways.

The noise in his outer office caused Mr. Charles to look up from his cluttered desk as morning sunlight streamed through the blinds behind him. He had begun working on his ledgers at daybreak, and his consternation had set his mood for the day. He was frowning darkly when the door burst open to admit Peter Klein.

Peter's expression was rabid as he advanced toward the desk with Mr. Charles' men in close pursuit. Dismissing the men with a nod, Mr. Charles noted that Peter did not wait until the door closed behind them to begin hotly, "All right, I want to know what you've done to fix the problem your man created with James Ferguson—and I want an answer now!"

Unwilling to reveal his own anger, Mr. Charles responded coolly, "My man is waiting for an opportunity to finish what he started."

"Opportunity be damned! James Ferguson is recuperating. If your man doesn't soon find a way to make his death look like the result of his injuries, it'll be too late." His expression tightening, Peter added, "I tell you now that I will not abide any blame for his death to fall on me."

His tone unchanged, Mr. Charles responded, "I need to remind you that a Pinkerton has been stationed outside Ferguson's door day and night for his protection. Since the arrival of Ferguson's aunt and uncle, there are also nurses on continuous duty—women who rarely leave the room—and there is interference from the old woman and her husband in the form of intermittent visits."

"Excuses!"

His temper rising, Mr. Charles said, "My man is good at his job."

"Then why did he fail?"

"He did not *fail*. Four stab wounds would have felled any other man permanently."

"But they did not fell Ferguson. Your man should have made certain that Ferguson was dead before he ran off."

"Circumstances require—"

"Circumstances be damned!" Peter walked a

step closer. Fury quaked in his tone as he said softly, "I have spoken to Miss Wolf. She tells me Ferguson will survive, and I will not abide that. Do you understand? I will not abide it! Fix it! Without delay, or I will see to it that you regret your failure."

Mr. Charles replied slowly, "Is that a threat, Peter?"

"Take it any way you please, but get the job done—and get it done without delay!"

Peter left as abruptly as he had arrived, slamming the door behind him. Mr. Charles stared at the doorway through which his former partner had disappeared. He was silent and angry, and his patience was rapidly fading.

There was more than one way to skin a cat.

That thought was prominent in Sylvester Key's mind as he skillfully scaled the rooftop of the Ferguson residence. Darkness shrouded his efforts as he dropped a rope and carefully lowered himself toward Ferguson's second-floor veranda. He smiled to himself at the ease of his covert access to a residence where Pinkerton protection was supposed to mean complete security. He knew, however, that there was no complete security against a fellow as resolute as he.

Key wiped his sleeve across his sweaty forehead, his smile disappearing when he recalled his angry conversation with Mr. Charles a few days earlier. Mr. Charles was under pressure to see that the job he had been hired to do was finished to complete satisfaction. As a result, Mr. Charles had bypassed contact with Humphrey Dobbs and had put that pressure directly on to him.

Key was determined to restore Mr. Charles' faith in him. He had returned to his place of concealment near Ferguson's home, where he had watched the comings and goings in the sickroom through his spyglass. The beauteous Letty Wolf had originally remained with Ferguson day and night. She had constructed so complete a circle of protection around Ferguson that he had been temporarily helpless to complete the job. Studying the situation more intently after his conversation with Mr. Charles, he had found a way . . . had waited until dusk, and here he was.

Key crouched in the shadows of the veranda as he peered through the French doors. He had been able to set a timetable of sorts for the sickroom since Letty Wolf had been forced to abandon the scene. He knew the nurses' schedules. The day nurse would leave the room to wash out her patient's basin after she refreshed him and administered his last dose of medicine for the day. Ferguson would then be alone for at least fifteen minutes while the household was otherwise engaged and the nurses' shifts changed.

He couldn't ask for a better opportunity.

A pillow over Ferguson's face while he was weak but appearing to recuperate would stop his breathing. It would only take a few minutes, and it would be easily accepted as an unforeseen consequence of the original attack. The idea was foolproof, and Mr. Charles would congratulate him for his resourcefulness.

Key waited. As expected, the nurse picked up the basin at Ferguson's bedside and left the room after refreshing him. He would have fifteen minutes to finish the job he had started.

A veteran of surreptitious entrances, Key worked knowledgeably at the lock on the veranda door. In no time he was pulling it open and advancing cautiously into the room, pleased to see that the nurse had turned the lamp down low and that Ferguson was asleep. He picked up the extra pillow lying on a nearby chair as he advanced toward the bed, only to be startled when Ferguson opened his eyes unexpectedly and mumbled, "It's you."

Cursing, Key forced the pillow down over Ferguson's face before he could call out. He held it there with all his might as Ferguson fought with unexpected strength. He told himself that Ferguson's weakness would betray him, that he only needed to hold out a little longer.

Perspiration dotting his brow, Key heard the sound of footsteps approaching the door. Ferguson was weakening. It would only be a little longer.

The door opened almost simultaneously with Key's leap toward the veranda. He heard a gruff male voice shout, "Stop where you are or I'll shoot!"

The first shot hit Key as he broke through the veranda doorway. The second and third shots struck him as he took a few more steps toward the rope still dangling from the roof.

Key gasped as the heat of each bullet struck him. He fell to the veranda floor under the overwhelming weight that pushed him downward.

Breathing raggedly, Key peered up at the people standing over him as he lay motionless. Their images grew hazy and their voices blurred into incomprehension. Darkness began closing in around him as their faces dipped closer and the unintelligible questioning continued.

His mind reeled with the fading light. His final realization was that he had calculated incorrectly. He hadn't had fifteen minutes after all.

Peter sat at his breakfast table, fork in hand. His dark suit was elegantly cut, his linens spotless, and his daily toilette aristocratic perfection. He stared at the meal his cook had prepared: eggs, slices of lean ham, steaming biscuits, and a bowl of freshly cut fruit to entice a weary pallet. He had no doubt that the preserves in the crystal dish nearby had been tediously prepared by the cook herself, and that the tea in the pot on the table had been steeped according to his instructions, yet the offerings failed to appeal. He was bored with it all. He needed something new . . . something different. He needed *someone* to stir appetites that had long ago become jaded. He needed to have a special woman seated beside him; a woman who was as certain of her attributes as he was of his; a woman like him, who had faced the challenges that life had to offer and who had won; a woman who was not afraid to challenge him, but who remained feminine at all times.

He knew who that woman was.

Looking up at the sound of a woman's voice in the hallway, Peter blinked. He listened a moment longer, then stood up abruptly.

Speak of the devil . . .

He was walking toward the door when Letty stepped into view, with his butler apologizing behind her. "I'm sorry, sir. The lady would not allow me to announce her."

Waving his servant's explanation aside, Peter exclaimed, "Letty! What a pleasure to see you here!"

"Is it?" Her flawless complexion flushed with emotion and her dark eyes snapping, she was more beautiful than he had ever seen her as she continued tightly, "I didn't intend that it would be. I came to ask you a question. A man sneaked into James' bedroom last night and was killed attempting to smother him."

"No! I don't believe it! Is James all right?"

Ignoring his question, Letty continued, "The second attack signifies to my mind that the attack James suffered on the street was not random. James has no enemies, but I do. I know I have made a particularly venomous enemy in you, and that you have rumored connections to underworld figures. I have ignored those rumors in the past, but I came here to warn you now—if you are responsible for the attacks on James in any way, I will see that you pay the price."

"Letty, how could you believe that to be true?" His expression pained, Peter walked closer as he continued, "I have no grudge against James."

"Except that he appeared to be reclaiming what you have said countless times you want from me."

"You told me yourself that your involvement with James is over."

"Did I? I suppose I said that before I became infuriated at the audacity of your proclaimed intentions toward me . . . before I told you that those intentions would never become reality . . . before you stormed into my rooms and became enflamed when you saw Alexander and me in a compromising posture . . . before you offered me consolation that I refused when Alexander was killed, and which I allowed James to provide . . . before James was also attacked mysteriously on the street. Tell me, Peter, is it coincidence that you confirmed I had spent all my time at James' bedside after the attack, and that afterward there was a second attempt on his life?"

"Letty, your shock and grief have obviously affected your thinking. I had nothing to do with the horrendous affairs you suspect me of."

"I hope not." Letty's expression grew frigid. "Because if you did, you may rest assured that I will see to it that you pay, even if it takes the rest of my life!"

"That would be such a waste, Letty, because I'm innocent. I don't know how you could possibly entertain the thought that I or anyone else would attempt to gain your favor in such a way."

"It doesn't make sense, does it, Peter? But many things have happened in my life that don't make sense. I am determined to do all in my power to see that those senseless incidents don't occur again."

"My dear . . ." Peter reached toward her as he said, "I am happy to see you here today, but the reason for your visit grieves me."

"Don't touch me!" Backing up, Letty said softly, "Be forewarned, Peter: If you are guilty, you will suffer for what you did. In the meantime, you are no longer welcome at my soirees. I do not wish to see you or hear from you in any way. All communication between us is over . . . done. Do you understand?"

"Letty, I assure you that these imaginings are a figment of your distress!"

"Are they?" Letty stared at him a moment longer before she responded, "If so, I've lost very little in coming here because I had no intention of ever seeing you again anyway."

Waiting a few seconds for the portent of her words to register in his expression, Letty turned and walked out of the room.

Standing where she had left him as the echo of the door closing reverberated in the silence, Peter felt a flush of rage. He knew who was to blame for the entire debacle between Letty and him, and he would answer for it.

Mr. Charles stood up at the sound of angry footsteps outside his office door. Late morning sunlight filtered through the blinds behind him as Peter stormed into the room. His expression was livid as he shouted hotly, "You're a sham, that's what you are, Charlie! You're spineless, worthless, incapable of directing or controlling your men with any vigor. Your men fear you, but you're not who they think you are. They would have found that out sooner or later, but I'm not willing to wait for later now. I told you what I'd do if you didn't fix the mistakes you made. I warned you that you would suffer if you failed me, but it didn't make any difference what I said to you, did it? You sent that fool out again to finish the job on Ferguson, and all he managed to do was get himself killed, and alert others to the fact that the attack wasn't a random robbery."

"The man I sent is dead?"

"You know damned well he is!" Mr. Charles listened without expression as Peter towered over his desk, ranting, "Do you know what just happened? Miss Wolf came to my house and declared that if I had anything to do with the attacks on Ferguson, she would see that I paid for them. Her accusation is the first blot on the reputation that I have worked so hard to attain over the past years. It is also a solid rejection from the woman I want most. I do not take either situation lightly."

"Calm down, Peter."

"I will not calm down. I will *never* calm down, and you may rest assured that if I suffer, you will suffer, too. I will see to it that if I am suspected in regard to this, you will be suspected also—and if the police come looking for me, I will lead them directly to your door. I serve you notice here and now that you will not get away with this!"

"I don't like being threatened."

"You should've thought about that earlier, when you hired a fool to handle a delicate task. You know me, too. You know I don't make promises that I do not keep."

Peter's malicious harangue continued as Mr. Charles listened emotionlessly. His only reaction was a slight tightening of his brow as he reached toward his desk drawer. Peter was still spewing his anger when Mr. Charles raised his gun into sight and fired three quick shots directly into Peter's chest.

The impact of the shots knocked Peter backward. With no time to react, he struck the floor with a loud thump, his eyes rolling back in his head as bloody circles widened on his spotless linens. His breath gurgled in his throat, then stopped abruptly.

Mr. Charles looked up as his men burst into the room. They halted when they saw Peter lying motionless on the floor. At their startled glances, Mr. Charles said flatly, "Get him out of here and dump his body far enough away so that I won't be implicated in his death." He hesitated, then added, "Dump him in the park. Yes, that will do. Peter always did like the park."

Mr. Charles watched emotionlessly as his men picked up Peter's body and carried it laboriously through the doorway. Then he sat back down, wiped away the blood splatter that marked his desk, and picked up his pen. Returning to where he'd left off in his meticulous ledger, he frowned and mumbled as if in afterthought, "I did tell him not to push me too far."

Percy Smart spurred his mount to a faster pace across the endless Texas terrain. He had spent another long night in his bedroll before finding the wagon train. He had rejoiced when it came into view as dusk of another day closed in around him. When he failed to see anyone on the train who even resembled the blond young woman who had been described to him, he had gone directly to the head wagon.

He hadn't liked the way the wagon master looked at him. He knew suspicion when he saw it, and that fella, McMullen, had been full of it. McMullen had refused to give him any information. If it hadn't been for that blond fella, Bruce, who had not had similar compunctions about speaking freely regarding Johanna Higgins and her *friend*, Wade Mitchell, he would still be wandering.

The information that Johanna Higgins and her friend had broken off from the train to head for the Arizona mining fields had been difficult to believe. First, who was this Wade Mitchell—or Bartlett—whatever his name was, aside from being a formerly wanted man? Second, did they really intend to prospect in Arizona? He found that idea as hard to believe as Larry Worth's original claim that Johanna Higgins had joined a wagon train of families intending to homestead in Oregon territory.

Determined to end the search once and for all, he had gotten up at sunrise after another night on the hard Texas ground and had retraced his steps to find the place where Johanna's wagon tracks had turned off from the train. Infuriated by his own ineptitude, he had gotten lost in the attempt.

Smart's frustration mounted. No, he'd never leave the city again, no matter how important the job Dobbs assigned him seemed to be. If he weren't aware of the danger involved in incurring Dobbs' displeasure, he'd demand more money for the completed job when he got back to the city. Maybe he would anyway.

Encouraged by that thought, Smart continued on. He'd find the trail again, and he'd find the wagon. When he did, he wouldn't ask any questions. He'd just make short work of both Johanna Higgins and her boyfriend, and then he'd go home. It was just a matter of time.

Letty shook uncontrollably as Mason stood in front of her in the silence of her sitting room.

She had made a difficult decision after her volatile discussion with Peter Klein the day before. After the heat of their discussion had passed, she realized that other than gut instinct, she'd had little proof that Peter was responsible for the attempts on James' life. She had renewed her determination to keep her distance from James, for his safety. Her continued anxiety about his state of health, however, had caused her to send a messenger to his house to ask how he was faring. The news that he was convalescing slowly and that no further attempt had been made on his life had allowed her only a moment's respite. She had discovered that her soiree had not provided the diversion she needed. The note she received from Aunt Ethel that morning, stating that James wanted to see her, had been almost more than she could bear.

She had been relieved not to have heard from Peter since her visit to him. She had told herself that even if Peter's claims of innocence were true, he could never be *completely* innocent. Just one look at his expression when he did not get his way was enough to establish that truth in her mind. She had concluded firmly that she had done all she could for James, and that she would not expose him to more danger with her presence.

But she had never—never in a million years— expected Mason to visit with the news he had just imparted.

A sudden wave of dizziness assaulted her, and Letty grasped at the chair beside her.

"Are you all right, Aunt Letty?" Mason ushered her to a seat as he said, "You'd better sit down. I didn't expect the news to affect you so deeply."

Letty responded incredulously, "You said that Peter Klein is dead?"

"Yes, I'm afraid so. A couple strolling in the park found his body lying in the bushes. His pockets were turned inside out and his valuables stolen. They think it was a robbery gone bad."

"But Peter would never have walked in the park alone. It was beneath him. He was more likely to ride through the park in his carriage so that everyone could see how grand he was."

"Aunt Letty . . ."

"It's true! Peter enjoyed exhibiting his wealth. He wanted people to envy him."

"He's dead, Aunt Letty."

"That doesn't change what he was, or the fact that he was murdered."

"A robbery gone bad."

"I don't believe it! There's more to it than that, just like there was more to the attack on James than was first apparent."

"No one knows what that Sylvester Key had against James. James is involved in many projects in the city that could have caused a backlash. Perhaps he played an instrumental part in the legalities that brought down housing in Key's part of town."

"New housing was constructed in its place. I would think the fellow would have been thankful for that, instead of making an attempt to kill James."

"We can't be sure what he was thinking."

"Mason . . ." Letty's trembling increased as she said with increasing passion, "There's more to this than meets the eye . . . so much more."

"I don't know what you mean by that," Mason replied, but his expression revealed his uncertainty.

Letty took a breath and then blurted, "Jeopardy seems to follow every man who's ever been involved with me."

"Aunt Letty . . ."

"It's true! Every man who has ever truly loved me has died prematurely."

"Uncle Archibald was an old man, if that's what you're saying, and his death was an accident."

"My first husband was young. He was killed protecting me and my unborn child. My second husband was young, too. He died in a terrible accident before Johanna was born. Archibald wasn't young, but he was killed shortly after Justine was born."

"Coincidence."

"Truly?"

"Aunt Letty," Mason began patiently, "you said yourself that you've had many liaisons since Uncle Archibald's death. None of those men have died prematurely."

"None of them truly loved me . . . except James."

"James Ferguson?"

"James loves me still. He said so, and he was nearly killed because of it."

"Coincidence, I tell you."

"Peter Klein loved me as much as it was possible for a man like him to love! He told me he wanted me. He told me that he would not be satisfied until I was his wife. He said he could picture himself living out his life with no one else but me beside him."

Mason was momentarily speechless. Letty saw him swallow before he abruptly sat on a nearby chair and said, "As strange as it seems, we're still talking about coincidence, Aunt Letty."

Letty took a breath and then said, "Then what does the howling mean?"

"The howling?"

"The wolf's howls that haunt me . . . that forewarned of danger before each tragedy struck? Those howls will now give me no rest. They echo through the night until I am beside myself."

"You hear a wolf howling?"

"I have heard it all my life. It has warned me of every terrible loss I've ever had. I had thought for a few years that the howls had come to a halt, but it all started again when my daughters left me."

Letty read the incredulity in Mason's expression, but she persisted, "It's true, Mason."

"Did you ever think that this howling might have been a reaction to your anxiety about the future when you were young, and perhaps a reaction to the part you might have played in causing your daughters to leave you?"

Letty responded resolutely, "Then who is the gray-haired figure who comes to me at night? Why has he always confirmed the danger and sometimes whispered reassurances?"

"You're saying an image comes and talks to you in your dreams?"

"He speaks a strange language that I don't comprehend, but his meaning always comes through clearly." She hesitated, and then added, "He now walks with a wolf at his side."

"A wolf again!"

"Mason, you must believe me! Every man who has ever loved me has died. Only James has escaped . . . barely, and I am determined not to expose him to further danger with my presence."

Mason stared at her blankly before asking, "Have you told any of this to your doctor?"

"You think I'm crazy, but I'm not."

"No, but perhaps you need a sedative of some sort. Perhaps your sleepless nights are causing you to hallucinate."

"I'm not hallucinating, either." Letty's voice was clipped.

"I'm not trying to make you angry, Aunt Letty. I only came here to tell you about Peter Klein because I knew he attended your soirees on a regular basis. I didn't know anything else or I wouldn't have stirred all this up."

"Mason, I'm sorry." A tear trailed down Letty's cheek, and she brushed it away. "I didn't mean to burden you with this. It's just that Peter's death is part of a pattern."

Mason stood up unexpectedly. He smiled stiffly as he said, "Did Dr. Bosworth leave you any sleeping pills . . . any sedatives that you could take when you feel overwhelmed?"

"I'm not crazy, Mason."

"No, but you need rest." Taking her arm, Mason raised her to her feet and said solicitously, "You need some undisturbed sleep. A few hours this morning will help you." He ushered her toward her bedroom determinedly.

"I don't want to sleep. I need to think. I need to find my daughters before it's too late."

Pausing at her bedroom door, Mason said, "Take a sedative and lie down, Aunt Letty. Please, do that for me. You'll feel better if you do."

"I don't want—"

"Please, Aunt Letty."

Letty paused before responding. Mason was such a dear young man. She had burdened him with her heavy thoughts, and she shouldn't have. She needed to allow him to believe he could help her . . . to believe everything she had told him was just the result of sleepless nights.

"Perhaps you're right, Mason. A sedative and some rest might be exactly what I'm looking for right now. I'll do what you suggest, I promise."

"Thank you, Aunt Letty. You'll be fine, you'll see."

"I know I will, Mason. Thank you." She kissed his cheek lightly and said, "I'll take a pill right now. Millie will show you out."

Mason remained where he was standing until she entered her room. The sound of his retreating footsteps held Letty stock-still until she heard the outside door close behind him.

Beginning to shake again, Letty approached the bed and picked up the bottle on the night table. She unscrewed the cap, took out two pills, and swallowed them in a rush. Then she lay down and resolutely closed her eyes.

Escape. She needed it, however temporary it might be. She would face it all later . . . when she felt better.

Perhaps Mason was right. She *wished* he was right, and that all the deaths were merely coincidence.

But she knew they weren't.

Mason pulled the door to Letty's apartment closed behind him. A smile moved across his lips as he walked down the hallway. So it was confirmed: Dear Aunt Letty was crazy! She had slipped over the edge! She was hearing and seeing things, and the situation could not suit him better.

Out on the street, Mason turned toward his office with a new sense of purpose. He had gone to Letty's apartment that morning as soon as he had heard about Peter Klein. He had told Letty the truth as far as that was concerned. He knew Peter was an attendee of her soirees, and he had wondered what Peter had told her during their brief, close association. He knew that Klein had underworld ties that he had never quite severed, and he had thought he might be able to use any information she could give him, since Dobbs was becoming difficult, and Dobbs reported to Peter's former partner, Mr. Charles. The confidences that Letty had shared with him that morning, however, had been unexpected.

Delusions appeared to have taken over her life! She was crazier than a loon, which might work out to his advantage in the long run. He had worried that Letty's sudden demise after he became her sole heir again might be suspect, but it now appeared that final step might not be necessary. Committing her to a mental institution would be the perfect answer. As a lawyer he understood the legalities involved, and as sole beneficiary in her will, he could find a way to manipulate matters so that he would manage her funds until she was stable again. Having the ear of several well-placed judges who owed him favors would facilitate the situation for him.

It occurred to him that Letty's faithful physician, Dr. Bosworth, would probably be his best witness to her instability. After all, dear Aunt Letty had already been prescribed sedatives and sleeping pills. After losing all three of her daughters in one way or another, hearing howls and voices warning her of danger, and seeing visions that talked to her in her dreams, she would be a perfect candidate for institutionalization.

And he, as her faithful and concerned nephew, would be so devoted to her welfare that he'd see to it she was never released.

Mason paused for traffic and then crossed the busy street without delay. He needed to reach his office as soon as possible so he could check some of his legal volumes. He would then begin writing up the papers to declare his dear aunt incompetent.

Commitment to a mental institution. Power of attorney afterward.

Mason breathed in the fresh, warm air of the city. He looked at the well-dressed pedestrians who walked the street, and at the traffic that moved along the busy thoroughfares. He loved New York, and he would soon have the money to truly enjoy all that the city had to offer.

CHAPTER TEN

He'd found it at last!

At least, he thought he had.

Smart looked again at the rutted tracks of the wagon train that marked the Texas terrain. Uncertain exactly when and where Johanna's wagon had turned off, he had followed the wagon train's trail backward—to no avail. He had then ridden out in several directions, hoping to pick up the trail of a single wagon heading west—to no avail. In the middle of nowhere after the third try, with nothing but an increasingly dry Texas landscape in sight, he realized that he was lost and would have to find the wagon train's trail again before he could start all over.

He had completely lost his bearings. His only certainty had been that the sun set in the west, which had given him a clue which way to turn. It hadn't been until he had spent another night on hard Texas soil that he had found his way and discovered the trail of the wagon train again.

He had finally found the spot where a single wagon had branched off from the train to strike out on its own, and he had been elated. He told himself that he would soon come up on Johanna and her friend, and put an end to all his misery and go home with a smile on his face.

Dobbs would be happy. He would be happy. The only people who wouldn't be happy would be Johanna Higgins and her "friend."

He could see Dobbs smiling now. He could feel the payment being counted out into his hands. He could even feel his own bed underneath his back—a simple comfort of life that he would never take for granted again.

With that thought in mind, Smart spurred his horse to a faster pace.

She saw him approaching in the semidarkness of her wagon.

Johanna sat up abruptly and glanced out at the starlit sky visible through the opening, and then at Wade, who lay sleeping beside her. There was no use waking him. He had not heard the sudden howling that had awakened her, and she knew he would not see the vision of the thin, gray-haired figure walking toward her in the shadows.

Johanna stared at the image as it drew closer. She was able to see the old man's small, dark eyes pinning her with their intensity. She viewed the concern on his weathered face as the distant howling that had awakened her went abruptly silent, and he started to speak.

Using the same guttural language that she had become accustomed to hearing, the old man spoke.

Caution.

Danger lurks.

Anxiety closed Johanna's throat. She wanted to ask the old man who he was, but she could not. She wanted to ask him why he came to her and what his warning meant, but the questions were frozen in her throat.

Apprehension trailed down her spine when he spoke again.

Speak to him.

Warn him.

Johanna looked at Wade.

Tell him what is to come.

Johanna looked back at the image. She felt the renewed intensity of his gaze as he warned again:

Beware.

Johanna panicked when she saw the image turn away. She wanted to stop him, to beg him to tell her what he meant, but she knew her effort would be useless.

She waited for her first glimpse of the slinking form lurking in the shadows as the old man continued walking. She recognized the animal that leapt out suddenly and loped to his side. She waited for the inevitable, the moment when the great gray wolf would look back at her with its brief, eerie stare before continuing on at the old man's side.

A chill ran down her spine as they disappeared into the horizon together.

The howling resumed.

What did it mean? Why would danger be lurking here? Who would want to hurt her? How could she warn Wade about something so vague?

The questions were still reverberating in her mind when she felt Wade's hands on her shoulders as he sat up.

"What's wrong, Johanna?"

She could not reply.

"It was the vision again, wasn't it?"

She nodded. She managed to croak, "He told me to warn you to be cautious."

"I'm always cautious."

Hardly believing her own words, she heard herself say, "He said to tell you that danger lurked, that you need to prepare for what was to come."

"What did he mean, what is to come?"

"I don't know, but he was worried. He said to beware."

Momentarily silent, Wade responded, "So you told me. Your job is done."

"Wade . . ."

After another moment, Wade repeated, "I'm always cautious, Johanna. That's part of my nature, but I'm even more cautious now that I have something to lose."

"Something to lose?"

The look in Wade's eyes said it all.

"Wade . . ."

"No, don't say anything else right now. There's been enough talk. Just go back to sleep."

"But—"

"Please."

Johanna saw the shadows in Wade's gaze. They were not unlike those that haunted her. She clutched him close, determined to blot out the uncertainties of the present and a warning she could not explain.

Wade's flesh was against hers. The sweet scent of his breath brushed her cheek. The caress of his mouth touched her lips. She surrendered to the heat that rose between them.

Within a few moments she had no conscious thought at all.

It wouldn't be long now.

Percy Smart stood up beside the remains of the campfire that Johanna and her friend had abandoned that morning before moving on. The embers were still hot.

Silently congratulating himself on the tracking skills he had so laboriously acquired, Smart mounted his horse and rode cautiously forward. He was only too aware of his failures in the past. He would not allow impatience to interfere with success, as had happened when he had trailed Larry Worth. He needed to make sure that neither Johanna Higgins nor her friend knew that he was behind them.

Johanna's wagon came abruptly into view, and

Smart's heart pounded with excitement. He saw the figures of Johanna and her friend perched on the wagon seat and realized the moment was finally upon him. He reached for the rifle sheath hanging from his saddle. Aware that the first shot would warn them of his presence, he knew he needed to make it count. He smiled at the thought that the second shot would be pure pleasure.

He told himself that when the job was done, he would inspect the wagon so that he could positively identify Johanna Higgins and her friend. He would take a souvenir from the wagon to prove to Dobbs that he had finished the job before leaving this desolate land behind.

Smart raised his rifle to his eye, his anticipation mounting.

Wade glanced around at the vast Texas terrain stretching out before him in the morning sun. It would be days before Johanna and he reached Arizona, but the warmth of her thigh pressed against his was a comfort that did not fade, and the realization that evening would bring her into his arms again raised his heartbeat to a thunder. Yet he could not deny the anxiety that threatened the wonder of their idyll.

Wade glanced at Johanna. She forced a smile for his benefit, but it did not hide her concern.

Caution . . . danger . . .

What . . . why . . . from whom?

He wished he could dismiss those questions, but he could not.

Wade reached subtly for the assurance of the gun holstered on his hip, knowing that the rifle lying easily accessible under his seat was added security. He looked back at Johanna. She was a feast for his eyes. He knew he had never seen a more beautiful woman. Nor had he ever believed he would be so lucky as to have a woman like her, and that he—

The report of a rifle was simultaneous with the sudden impact that slammed into Wade's shoulder. He saw the horror on Johanna's face the moment before a second shot rang out, knocking him backward into oblivion.

Johanna gasped as Wade hit the ground with a hard crack. She shouted his name and scrambled for the reins as the frightened horses took off, leaving him where he lay.

Hardly aware of the terrain flashing by as the runaway team raced forward, Johanna strained to reach the reins that had fallen from Wade's hands. She finally caught the leather straps just before they slipped out of her reach. She pulled back on the reins in an effort to halt the horses' flight, but the team did not respond.

Furious that her lack of control over the team was taking her farther away from Wade with every passing second, Johanna strained against the reins. She pulled back hard, maintaining unyielding pressure despite her waning strength.

Unaware of the tears that marked her cheeks, Johanna was conscious of the exact moment when the team began slowing its pace. Taking advantage of the first sign of victory, she gripped the reins more firmly as she shouted commands at the horses in a voice totally unlike her own. She gasped aloud when the team slowed to a gradual halt. She shuddered with relief when the horses responded to her commands, turning the wagon back in the direction from which it had come.

Percy Smart drew his mount to a halt, astounded as he watched Johanna's wagon turn back toward him. What was she doing? He had realized after his first two shots struck Johanna's friend instead of her that he would have to chase down the runaway wagon in order to finish the job. He had been enraged at the thought as he started toward it. He had not yet neared the fallen man when Johanna turned the wagon unexpectedly and headed back into his sights!

Smart drew up his horse within some nearby foliage and waited with his rifle cocked. At her present rate of speed, she would be within range in a moment, and he was determined not to miss again.

Smart squinted through his sights as Johanna Higgins drew closer. He studied her face. He saw the incredible color of the strands of hair that had come loose from her bun to stream out behind her. He noted the beauty of her features and the emotion that flushed her perfect skin. He saw the strength of her slender body, and a familiar heat rose inside him as he wondered how it would feel to have that body stretched out under his.

With his finger on the trigger, Smart hesitated. He took a breath, and then shoved the rifle back into its sheath as he reached for the gun on his belt and waited. He wanted to see Johanna Higgins up close. He needed to see if she was really everything she appeared to be. He reasoned coldly that if she were, it would be a shame to waste what she had to offer.

Johanna held the reins in tight control as her team galloped back toward the spot where Wade had fallen. Her heart pounded as he came into view, and she pulled back forcefully on the reins.

He wasn't moving.

The team drew to a halt and Johanna jumped down from the wagon. She scrambled to Wade's side. His eyes were closed and the bloody circles on his chest were widening. Uncertain what to do, she leaned over him and whispered, "Wade, can you hear me? Wade, please open your eyes."

"You're wasting your time!"

Johanna's head snapped up toward the thin, unkempt fellow who stood some distance away, his gun pointed in her direction. He walked closer as he said, "If he ain't dead yet, he soon will be."

"He needs help!"

"Maybe so, but I ain't about to give him none."

"You shot him, and now you want to finish the job!"

"I don't care about him one way or another."

"You don't care about him? What *do* you care about?"

Her eyes blazing, Johanna stood up and took a step toward him as Smart warned, "Stay back. I'm warning you."

"Why are you warning me when you didn't warn Wade?" Johanna said hotly. "What do you want from me?"

Johanna's questioning halted abruptly at Smart's leering expression, and her eyes widened. She grated emphatically a moment later, "Well, you won't get it—not now, not ever!"

Smart's eyes grew cold as he grated, "I'm warning you for the last time—"

"Drop your gun, fella, and drop it now!"

Startled, Smart turned toward the deep voice behind him. His eyes widened at the sight of Larry Worth standing unsteadily there. He gaped as the Pinkerton and said, "You heard me. Drop it!"

Smart blinked and dropped his gun. He gasped, "I thought you were dead."

"Well, I ain't."

Johanna moved back to Wade's side as Larry Worth wavered on his feet. Inadvertently moving his vest, Worth revealed that his shirt was stained with blood that was again flowing a deep red.

Seeing it, Smart laughed, "You're dead on your feet, Worth. You ain't going to last another few minutes."

"That's what you think," Worth responded weakly. "I ain't been trailing you all these days for nothing. Now step away from your gun."

"No."

"I said—"

"I heard what you said, but I'm betting you ain't going to shoot me in cold blood because you're a Pinkerton, and you ain't trained to act that way. No, you're going to see if you can take me alive. The only problem with that is, I ain't going to let you do it."

Smart stared at Larry Worth coldly. He saw Worth's eyelids flicker. He saw his gun hand tremble. He anticipated the moment when Worth's eyes flickered briefly closed and he stumbled against the tree.

In a blur of movement, Smart jumped toward his gun, where it lay on the ground near him. He was unprepared for the shot that sounded simultaneously with the impact of the bullet that knocked him to the ground. He turned, managing to grip the handle of his gun when he saw the revolver that Wade still held in his hand. He attempted to pull the trigger the moment before Wade's second shot struck him.

Johanna looked down at Wade. She snatched up his gun when it fell from his hand and his eyes closed. She gasped his name.

"Where is she?"

James' slurring voice was heavy in the silence of his bedroom. Aunt Ethel glanced up at her husband, who stood beside the door, his expression grave.

"Where is she?"

Trembling, Aunt Ethel glanced at Dr. Fuller and saw him shake his head. She responded as calmly

as she was able. "If you mean Letty Wolf, she . . .
she left to get some rest, James."

His face pale, his eyelids heavy, James replied,
"Tell . . . tell her I want to see her."

"I sent her a note, James. I'm sure she'll come as
soon as she can."

"I need to see her now."

Suddenly breathless, James gasped for air. Panicking, Aunt Ethel said reassuringly, "I'll send her
another note. She'll come. I know she will."

"Now. Please . . ."

Her throat tight, Aunt Ethel stood up beside the
bed and walked unsteadily toward the door. She
did not realize that Dr. Fuller was behind her until
the door closed behind them in the hallway and
he said, "It's important that you get Letty here
now, Ethel. James is upset. He won't allow himself to rest until he sees her. His condition has re-
versed itself and is now showing steady
deterioration because of his stress."

"I don't know what's keeping her away. I'll . . .
I'll go to her house." A sob escaped Aunt Ethel's
lips as she said more emphatically, "I'll beg her if I
have to!"

Gripping her arm in an uncharacteristically
emotional gesture, Dr. Fuller said softly, "Soon,
Ethel, or it might be too late."

Her eyes widening, Ethel raced toward the
steps, with her husband close behind.

Letty walked rapidly through James' front door.
She headed for the stairs with Aunt Ethel run-

ning breathlessly behind her. She noted as she turned that Uncle George remained at the bottom of the stairs while Aunt Ethel struggled to keep up with her.

Letty recalled the moment earlier that morning when Aunt Ethel had entered her sitting room in a rush and exclaimed emotionally, "You have to come to see James now. The doctor said if you wait, it may be too late!" Her response had frozen in her throat as Aunt Ethel continued, "I'm so sorry. I wasn't aware of the relationship between you and James. I wouldn't have come between you if I had known."

Letty had responded as breathlessly, "There is no relationship between James and me other than friendship."

"I realize that . . . that the tenor of things has changed between the two of you. You may feel only friendship for James now, but the truth is that he still loves you. You can't desert him now. He's dying!"

"No, that can't be!" Letty had walked unsteadily toward the tearful woman, insisting, "Dr. Fuller said he's convalescing."

"That's all changed, and it's my fault." Aunt Ethel had sobbed openly as she continued, "I didn't mean to chase you from his bedside. I thought I was freeing you from obligation. I had no idea that James depended on you so heavily."

"He didn't depend on me. Most of the time, he didn't even know I was there."

"He knew, just as he knew when you were gone.

He's been asking for you. He won't rest until he knows you're beside him. He is insisting on seeing you now. I think even he realizes it may be too late if you delay."

Gasping, Letty had responded, "No, he's better off without me. He'll recuperate and he—"

"He won't recuperate! He'll die!"

Letty had gone still. She had known she couldn't let that happen.

She had called out, "Millie, please get my wrap."

Letty remembered that Millie had met her at her hallway door with her wrap, but she did not recall the ride that had delivered Aunt Ethel, Uncle George, and her to James' front door.

As she stood outside James' bedroom door, the sound of howling grew suddenly louder in her ears. Letty wiped the panic from her expression with pure strength of will. She stayed Aunt Ethel with a touch on her arm before opening the bedroom door and walking inside.

Dr. Fuller left, quietly closing the bedroom door behind him when Letty took up her position beside James' bed. She held James' limp hand in hers and whispered into his pale, still face, "I'm here, James. I'm going to stay here, too, just as long as you need me. Do you hear me, James?"

Letty choked back a sob when he did not respond.

Then she took a gasping breath. Her face broke into a shaky smile—because James had gripped her hand.

CHAPTER ELEVEN

Mason worked zealously on the papers in front of him as the daylight hours waned. He smarted at the fact that this project required him to spend so much time with legal volumes. He was unaccustomed to the labor involved in legalities. He had managed to avoid most of it while in school by paying others to handle the paperwork for him. In the time since, his clerks had done most of the work—but this project was a secret that he could not trust to anyone.

Commitment papers.

Aunt Letty would be stunned when they were served on her, but by that time her instability would be firmly established. Dobbs' men would take care of the first part of his plan. Letty's daughters would not return to the city to be reestablished in her will. Then, as her sole beneficiary, he would make sure Letty confessed her secrets about hearing wolf's howlings that never ceased, and about visions that appeared to her in the middle of the night. The rest would be easy. Once in control of her money, he would make sure she "received treatment" and never emerged from the mental facility.

And then he would be rich.

Damn it, he would be rich!

Mason returned to work feverishly, congratulating himself on the efficiency of his plan.

The sun had barely risen as Letty's carriage approached. Her suitcase in hand, she looked back at James' house—the distinguished structure that had been her home during his steady recuperation.

Letty raised a hand to her smooth brow and pushed back a strand of dark hair before climbing into the carriage and closing the door behind her. She issued a soft command to the driver and remained face forward as they pulled away. She had left a note for James. She had explained that since he was presently convalescing well, it was time for her to leave. She apologized if she had raised any hopes in his mind with her constant presence at his bedside, saying that she had done what she needed to do because he was her friend.

Letty told herself that Aunt Ethel and Uncle George would watch over James for the remainder of his recovery and that he would be all right. In the meantime—

The echo of a familiar howling brought Letty abruptly upright in her seat. The houses passed by without her realization as the echoes continued, and she closed her eyes. Grandfather had chosen not to visit her of late, but the howls were a ceaseless warning of danger that she could not ignore.

She was unsure exactly what danger the howlings foretold. She only knew that when James' situation was secure, she needed to find her daughters and correct the missteps of the past.

Surrendering to impulse, Letty glanced back at James' house as it slipped from view. Another certainty emerged clearly in her mind as she did.

Sadly, she would never come back.

The great black train engine belched gritty smoke as the handsome couple climbed the stairs to the rail car. The woman entered and grabbed a nearby backrest for support as the train jerked suddenly into motion. She laughed at her awkwardness as she turned back to look at her companion. Finally finding two vacant seats, she sat and waited until her companion sat beside her before shifting closer to him. She paid little notice to the attention she garnered from the other passengers on the train, accustomed as she was to admiring glances. Plainly dressed, she did not cause others to glance her way by wearing sophisticated apparel. Instead, it was her unadorned beauty and perfection of feature that drew their eyes. Unconsciously tucking a stray wisp of platinum hair into the neat knot at the back of her neck, she smiled up at her companion. He looked down at her, his eyes filled with passion, and she caught her breath.

Weeks had passed since the peace of that sunny

day on the trail had been shattered by the unexpected, cracking report of a rifle shot.

She was still uncertain how she had managed to get Wade into the wagon in his semiconscious state—or how she had roused Larry Worth enough for him to do the same. She only remembered driving the wagon recklessly over a narrow trail, hoping that it would lead her to some sign of civilization.

She recalled the moment when the town of Ellsworth came into view and she drove the wagon down the narrow main street at full speed. The few men who jumped out of the way were the same men who ended up carrying both Wade and Larry into Dr. Pillson's office for treatment.

Her heart had skipped a beat while Doc Pillson worked on Wade and the unknown man who had drawn the killer's attention from them. She recalled thinking that in finding Wade, she had finally found true love, that he had given her more reason to look to the future than any quest she could have pursued, and that she could not bear to lose him.

She remembered kissing his pale cheek as he had lain so still after Dr. Pillson operated, and then the sensation of Wade's hand moving against her hair as he had drawn her closer. She had whispered the words, "I love you," and that spontaneous statement had never meant more—especially when Wade mumbled it in return.

The man named Larry Worth had been a mystery to them at first. They had known only that his identification as a Pinkerton was in his saddle-bags, along with a waiver and an addendum to her mother's will—and that without him, they might not have survived.

She remembered the day Larry was coherent for the first time, when he whispered hoarsely to her, "My name is Larry Worth. I'm the Pinkerton your mother hired to find you."

And she remembered her shock.

Wade had been standing beside her. Not entirely recuperated from his own wounds, he had been held steady on his feet by determination and a dark frown as the Pinkerton spoke. His only concession to his wounds was the sling he had finally consented to wear to support the injured arm and shoulder that had absorbed the two rifle shots.

Strangely, in the confusion of the moment after Larry Worth collapsed, she had not even seen Wade draw his gun. She remembered only her relief when his bullets finally felled the man later identified as Percy Smart. In retrospect, Johanna was surprised that Larry Worth had survived the wounds that had gone untreated while he followed the erratic path of the man who had shot him.

Johanna had slipped her hand into Wade's warm palm as Larry Worth spoke. The strength of Wade's grip was silent reassurance as she responded incredulously to the Pinkerton. "My mother hired you to find me? How could that be? She never gave my sisters or me a moment's thought when we were near."

"I don't know about that," Larry Worth had responded weakly. "I only know that Robert Pinkerton said she hired him to find her daughters and to let them know she would reinstate them in her will if they would return to New York City to see her before her fortieth birthday."

She remembered asking, "Why?"

When Larry Worth had no answer, she had asked, "The fellow who shot you—Percy Smart— was from New York City, too. Did you know him?"

His response was an unequivocal, "No."

She had retorted, "He tried to kill you!"

He had replied, "He tried to kill both of you, too."

She had frowned then and looked up at Wade and commented, "None of this makes any sense. Why would a man come all the way from New York City with the intention of killing me—or both of us?"

"If that was his intention." To her puzzled expression Wade had added, "You won't find out what he intended if you stay here."

"I'm not going back to the city, if that's what you're saying." In firmer control of her emotions, she had continued, "It took a long time for my sisters and me to come to the decision to leave my mother, but the emptiness of our lives finally became too much. My mother deliberately forced that emptiness on us. I told you what she did. Our different fathers were mysteries to my sisters and me because of her. She gave us little to cling to except each other, and then separated us purposely, with her only thought her own convenience. In actuality, it was my mother's choice to lead her life without us, not ours."

Wade had ventured, "Perhaps she's changed."

Looking directly into Wade's eyes, she had replied, "My sisters and I decided long ago that we would go forward and not look back."

Suddenly aware that Larry Worth's eyes were drooping weakly, Johanna had said, "We've notified the Pinkerton Agency about your injury. They're sending someone to escort you home."

Larry had nodded when she added, "I've also signed the waiver saying that I don't intend to go back to New York City."

He had nodded again. Then he'd looked at Wade and said, "Thank you."

Wade had inquired spontaneously, "For what?"

"For taking that pesky city fella down."

Larry's eyes had closed then and he fell asleep. Wade did not bother to reply.

Later, Johanna had seen Wade look out the window at her wagon, where it still remained on the street. She remembered him saying, "The horses have been stabled since we got here. They're waiting for a strong hand to drive them on."

Johanna had replied laughingly, "Well, it's not going to be mine."

Wade had said, "There are a lot of questions that still need answers, darlin'."

She had responded softly, "I know."

She had moved into Wade's arms then. The sling had been between them and she had protested when Wade dropped it onto the floor and wrapped both arms around her. She had known then that with his strength against her, she was stronger. Under the warmth of his love, she blossomed. She had felt the security of that love, and she had known she could not ask for more.

Except . . .

Brought back to the present of the rocking railway car and the steady, endless clattering of metal wheels against rails, Johanna looked up at Wade silently. He was thinner, and a little pale, but he was tall, handsome, and all male as he looked down at her. He said in quiet reminder, "Your sister may not still be in Winsome when we get there, you know."

"I know, but I need to find her. I need her input about some things, and I can't wait until the date we all arranged to meet again in a year's time. Meredith went to Winsome to discover her past. She won't leave there easily, not until she finds out all there is to know about herself. It's important for me to talk to her before any more time passes."

Wade frowned, and she said, "I used to resent it sometimes, you know, that Meredith always seemed to have all the answers."

"But now you know it just looked that way."

"Now I know that she just tried to make it appear that she was never afraid so Justine and I would have someone we could depend on. I love her even more for that."

Wade did not respond.

"I want you to meet her."

"I'd like that."

"She and Justine are even more beautiful than I am."

Wade shook his head with a smile. "That's impossible."

The echo of a wolf's howl sounded unexpectedly in Johanna's mind, and she frowned.

Danger.

Still?

What did it mean?

Johanna asked soberly, "Will you always love me, Wade?"

As sober in return, Wade whispered, "Always."

Suddenly alone in a world that included just the two of them despite the din around them, Johanna looked up at Wade. She knew his response had come from the heart.

Safety . . . security . . . a love that would last forever. She had it all in Wade's arms. That was where she wanted to stay . . . always.

Deneane Clark

Grace

The institution of marriage held no attraction for Grace Ackerly. The world, she had noticed, expected nothing more from women than that they be submissive, demure brood mares, allowed absolutely no rights or even opinions of their own. No—she was fairly comfortable declaring—she would never marry, no matter the temptation set before her.

With a flashing green gaze potently combining warmth, humor and seductive promise, Trevor Christian Caldwell was resisted by few women. But never had there been a woman he truly respected. Not until now. Here, in Pelthamshire, a spirited redhead forced a decision he had never before considered: He would marry Grace Ackerly, no matter what protestations, no matter what travails.

ISBN 10: 0-8439-5997-5
ISBN 13: 978-0-8439-5997-0

CONNIE MASON

The Black Widow

That was what the desperate prisoners incarcerated in Devil's Chateau called her. Whatever she did with them, one thing was certain: Her unfortunate victims were never seen again. But when she whisked Reed Harwood out of the cell where he'd been left to die for spying against the French, he discovered the lady was not all she seemed.

Fleur Fontaine was the most exquisitely sensual woman he'd ever met, yet there was an innocence about her that belied her sordid reputation. Only a dead man would fail to respond. Reed was not dead yet, but was he willing to pay…

The Price of Pleasure

ISBN 10: 0-8439-5745-X
ISBN 13: 978-0-8439-5745-7

JOYCE HENDERSON

Kalen Barrett could birth foals, heal wounded horses, and do the work of two ranch hands, so she was hired on the spot to work at the Savage ranch. But the instant attraction she felt to sinfully handsome Taylor Savage terrified her. Each time she glimpsed the promise of passionate fulfillment in Taylor's heated eyes, she came a little closer to losing control—but he always held back the words she longed to hear. If he would only give her his heart, she would follow him body and soul...

TO THE EDGE OF THE STARS

ISBN 10: 0-8439-5996-7
ISBN 13: 978-0-8439-5996-3

To order a book or to request a catalog call:
1-800-481-9191
This book is also available at your local bookstore, or you can check out our Web site **www.dorchesterpub.com** where you can look up your favorite authors, read excerpts, or glance at our discussion forum to see what people have to say about your favorite books.

Tempted Tigress

JADE LEE

Orphaned and stranded, Anna Marie Thompson can trust no one, especially not her dark captor, a Mandarin prince. Not when his eyes hold secrets deadlier than her own. His caress is liquid fire, but Anna is an Englishwoman and alone. She cannot trust that they can tame the dragon, as he whispers, that sadness and fear can be cleansed by soft yin rain. Safety and joy are but a breath away. And perhaps love. All is for the taking, if she will just give in to temptation....

ISBN 10: 0-8439-5690-9
ISBN 13: 978-0-8439-5690-0

DIANA GROE
SILK DREAMS

Forced into a harem in Constantinople's strange land of flashing swords and swirling silks, spicy aromas and hot breezes that feel like a lover's breath, Valdis is utterly lost. Her family cast her away for seeing portents of the future, and now her visions are turning even more ominous: they foretell the death of the one man who could help her escape, an exiled Viking who braves the wrath of a kingdom to awaken her passion one sinful pleasure at a time. To save him, Valdis must play a high-stakes game of power and seduction that will either get her killed or finally allow her and her love to live their *Silk Dreams*.

ISBN 10: 0-8439-5869-3
ISBN 13: 978-0-8439-5869-0 $6.99 US/$8.99 CAN

To order a book or to request a catalog call:
1-800-481-9191
This book is also available at your local bookstore, or you can check out our Web site **www.dorchesterpub.com** where you can look up your favorite authors, read excerpts, or glance at our discussion forum to see what people have to say about your favorite books.

The Marsh Hawk

Dawn MacTavish

Was Lady Jenna Hollingsworth's new husband the same man who had killed her father? After one night of passion, she begins to wonder. The jarring aroma of leather, tobacco and recently drunk wine drift toward her on the breeze—she remembers it so well, as well as the tall, muscular shape beneath the multi-caped greatcoat and those eyes of blue fire through the holes in his mask. Oh yes, she remembers that man with whom she shares a secret past. He is the highwayman known as the Marsh Hawk.

ISBN 10: 0-8439-5934-7
ISBN 13: 978-0-8439-5934-5 $6.99 US/$8.99 CAN

To order a book or to request a catalog call:
1-800-481-9191

This book is also available at your local bookstore, or you can check out our Web site **www.dorchesterpub.com** where you can look up your favorite authors, read excerpts, or glance at our discussion forum to see what people have to say about your favorite books.